Sister to the Wolf

Sister to the Wolf

by Maxine Trottier

Kids Can Press

Acknowledgments

The author would like to thank Andy Gallup, historian and friend, for his thoughtful reading of the manuscript.

KCP Fiction is an imprint of Kids Can Press

Kids Can Press acknowledges the financial support of the Government of Ontario, through the Ontario Media Development Corporation's Ontario Book Initiative; the Ontario Arts Council; the Canada Council for the Arts; and the Government of Canada, through the BPIDP, for our publishing activity.

Published in Canada by
Kids Can Press Ltd.
29 Birch Avenue
Toronto, ON M4V 1E2

Published in the U.S. by
Kids Can Press Ltd.
2250 Military Road
Tonawanda, NY 14150

www.kidscanpress.com

Edited by Kathryn Cole
Designed by Marie Bartholomew
Typeset by Carolyn Sebestyen

Printed and bound in Canada

CM 04 0 9 8 7 6 5 4 3 2 1
CM PA 04 0 9 8 7 6 5 4 3 2

National Library of Canada Cataloguing in Publication Data

Trottier, Maxine
        Sister to the wolf / Maxine Trottier.

ISBN 1-55337-519-X (bound).   ISBN 1-55337-520-3 (pbk.)

I. Title.

PS8589.R685S48 2004   jC813'.54   C2003-906496-4

Kids Can Press is a LORUS^{TM} Entertainment company

To the memory of young Jacques

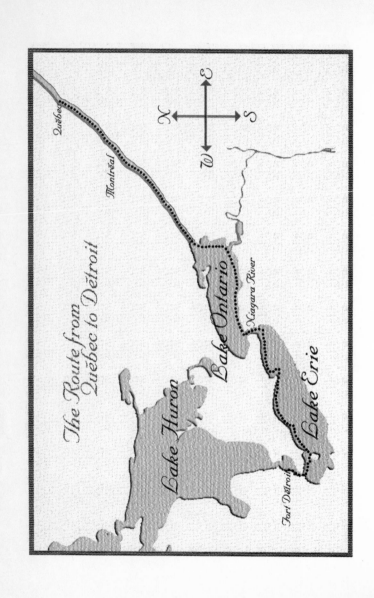

The Route from Québec to Détroit

Québec

Montréal

Lake Huron

Lake Ontario

Niagara River

Lake Erie

Fort Détroit

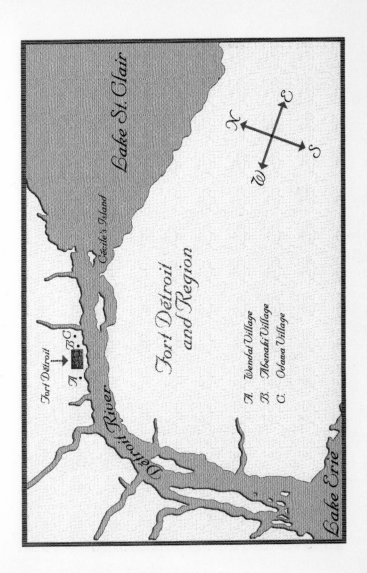

Lake St. Clair

Cécile's Island

Fort Détroit

Detroit River

Fort Détroit
and Region

A. Wendat Village
B. Abenaki Village
C. Odawa Village

Lake Erie

N
E
W
S

Chapter 1

The first time Lesharo saw the girl, she was a slash of brilliant color against the cool gray of the stone wall behind her. She was just lifting the heavy braid from her neck when his eyes were pulled to her like an arrow to its mark. It was the hair that had drawn him, of course, hair a pure, burnished red, uncovered by any cap. What would it be like to touch my fingers to that hair? he began to think. Would it be copper warmed by the sun, or would it be like the chilled wine that the servants poured into crystal glasses at the grand houses? He closed his eyes and held on to that question as the branding iron came down upon his upper arm.

. . .

It was a strangely quiet part of the lower town. No carts rumbled along the dirty streets, and if people had business to conduct, they did it elsewhere in Québec this morning. She should have felt a sense of relief, since after three years away from the city,

Cécile found the crowds and noise disturbing. Her daily errands completed, the thick silence of their home would be a melancholy refuge. Now, though, her feet rooted to the ground, she stared at the young man from whose arm a small wisp of smoke was rising. Later she would see that her fingertips had left gouges in the loaf of bread she was carrying home.

Stripped to a breechcloth and leggings, his wrists tied to an iron ring embedded in the wall of a building, he was braced against the pain. The muscles of his arms trembled, and his skin was shiny with sweat in spite of the cold air. She could smell his burned flesh.

"You will not run again, I think," said the man who held the branding iron. "Try it even once more before you are sold and it will cost you the toes of one foot." The iron came very close to the *indien's* cheek. "Missing toes or not, you are for sale." The man's eyes flicked to Cécile, and he nodded a good morning. Then he set down the still-hot iron, rubbed his hands briskly and walked out of her sight. The indien slumped then, his forehead against the stones.

Cécile stepped backwards, stumbling over a half-frozen lump of horse droppings as the heel of her moccasin sank in. She carried the rich tang of excrement with her when she walked away, revolted by what she had witnessed.

He was a *pani*, she knew, an indien slave, one of many who were here in the town of Québec. She had seen them as well in the villages she had visited with her father. Once when they were wintering among the Abenaki, a war party had returned with six Pawnee prisoners. Four of them were children whom families quickly adopted to replace warriors killed in battle. Her father had been ready to leave immediately if the other prisoners had been destined for torture and death. They had not been. The two women — pitiful creatures with dead eyes — had been kept as slaves.

Here in Québec some indien slaves lived well enough, being decently housed and clothed. Others were treated little better than animals. Brandings and other mutilations were not uncommon; owners did what they wished to quench their spirits, to put out any of the fiery independence that might smolder deep within them.

At the doorway of their house, Cécile put thoughts of the pani out of her head as well as she could. She scrubbed her moccasin in snow that remained in the house's shadow. That would have to do. Her mother would have scolded and clucked her tongue at the mess. No dirt had been permitted inside their house. Dust dared not gather anywhere. *Maman's* voice echoed softly in Cécile's mind, and she flinched at the exquisite pain it caused her.

All this time and it still hurt as much as ever.

Cécile unlatched the heavy door and pushed it open. Inside, she set the cloth-wrapped loaf down upon the bench next to it. Papa's *sabots* were there with hers. She should have worn them, she thought as she hung up her cloak and slipped off her moccasins. Horse manure! She pulled up her skirts, frowning at her right ankle. I have it on me. She untied the ribbons that held up her wool stockings, peeled them off and left them on the bench. Then she padded toward the kitchen in her bare feet, the bread in her hands. It was at that moment that she heard her father.

"It may be all you say it is, Antoine, but what is untouched forest — if there is such a thing any more — and plentiful game to me? If I wanted that we would have remained in the wilderness, out in fur-trading country with the indiens."

"What is it you do want, Robert?" asked a man in low silky tones. "Not a life such as this, I venture. You were not meant to work for a merchant. You are a *coureur de bois*, not a shopkeeper, Robert."

Cécile heard her father sigh impatiently.

"You are as persistent as you always were, are you not, Antoine? You will worry at a thing until you have it."

The man Antoine laughed softly and said, "My dear Robert, you recognize that trait in me because you see it well enough in yourself."

"What would I do there? There are no trading licenses now."

"Since when has that made a difference? Of course. I see I am correct. Do you think you are the only one who trades illegally with the indiens,

Robert? You always were willing to take a risk." There was the sound of his knowing laughter. "It will all be legal now if you are working for me, Robert. Fear not."

"The prices you are charging for goods are outrageous, Antoine. The indiens cannot be paying them willingly."

"Wrong again, Robert. There are few complaints."

Her father's face appeared around the corner of the doorway, and Cécile gave a small shriek.

"I was certain I had heard you. Snooping, is it? It has not taken you long to pick up town habits once more, Cécile, though I suspect it was only the lack of doorways in the woods that kept you from doing it there. Come inside."

The stranger rose to his feet.

"My daughter, Cécile," said her father. "Cécile, this is an old acquaintance of mine, Antoine Laumet."

The man bowed deeply, a courtly gesture that had not often been made to her. Of middle age, he had a striking face with a prominent nose; dark glossy hair curled to the shoulders of his full-skirted coat. Unlike her father, who persisted in wearing the breechcloth, *mitasses* for his legs and a coarse linen shirt suited to the woods, this man wore expensive clothing, the wool fine and spotless. Clutching the round loaf to her bosom, Cécile was suddenly conscious of the unboned corset she had made herself with the plain linen *chemise* beneath it. And her bare feet! Her skirt might be faded and there was a patch — at the back, mercifully — but at least it was clean.

"Antoine Laumet, Sieur de Lamothe Cadillac," he corrected. "Mademoiselle Chesne, it is my pleasure." His voice was polite, but his narrowed eyes drifted over her with calculation, and he cocked an eyebrow just a little at her bare toes.

"Ah, yes," said her father coolly. "My error. You have come up in the world."

"As you could, Robert. There is no need for you to remain here at Québec, not with the chance I have offered. I will pay you very well," Cadillac went on. "See here; if trading does not suit you, then hunt for me. I suspect you are still an excellent tracker and a superb shot; with all the indiens living around the fort, we tend to be short of fresh meat at times. My two sons are there; more young people such as your daughter would be welcome. But I will not push; I shall leave it to what I recall is your excellent judgment." He bowed to Cécile a second time and strode across the kitchen saying, "Do not trouble yourselves; I will see myself out. I will be at Joclaire's tavern tonight if you wish to discuss it further, my friend." At the door he paused and added, as though Cécile was not there, "She is a quiet one, Robert, but then I have always found docility to be an asset in a girl."

The front door slammed shut behind him. For a few heartbeats the only sounds in the small kitchen were the snap of logs on the hearth and the sizzle and pop of fat dripping from the joint of venison roasting on a spit.

"What was *that*, Papa?" asked Cécile faintly.

Again the silence, then her father began to laugh loudly. Caught by it, Cécile smiled and laughed too.

"*That*," explained her father when he could again speak, "is one of the most insatiable, devious schemers I have ever known in my life." Wiping the tears from his cheeks he added, "Docility. I would dare him to spend a week in the forest with you, but I have too kind a heart. Give me the bread, Cécile, before I perish. Is there still cheese? The joint will not be done for hours." He frowned down at the loaf and then shook his head. "You have been a bit hard on this poor bread, have you not?"

Cécile saw the marks her fingers had left, just as she smelled the cooking meat. A scent of burned flesh seemed caught at the back of her throat. Unbidden, the image of the young indien rose into her mind's eye. She blinked hard as her stomach did a long slow roll.

"It will taste just the same," she said, as she brought her father a wedge of cheese. "What did he want, Papa? What did he offer you?"

Robert did not answer at once. He leaned back in his chair and began to turn a cup of beer in circles upon the table. He picked it up, sipped and wiped his lips with his fingers. Cécile thought he looked tired; there were circles beneath his blue eyes. He ran a hand over his long blond hair — hair that three years ago had not been quite so streaked with silver — and he tightened the thong that bound it back.

"Antoine is here to do business with merchants of the Company of the Colony of Canada." When Cécile looked bewildered, he went on to explain: "The merchants are no longer simply merchants these days. Since we have been away, they have organized. The king himself signed an agreement with them last year, it seems. The Company now has full control of the fur trade in New France, and so Cadillac must deal with them. He will return to Détroit when his affairs are completed, and he has suggested that we accompany his party."

"Détroit?" she asked, watching her father tear a chunk from the bread.

Robert nodded. He pulled out his knife and sliced off a piece of cheese from the wedge.

"It is a place where the river narrows between two of the western lakes, Lake Erie and Lake St. Clair. He took a party of one hundred soldiers and *voyageurs* in twenty-five canoes there last year, and they built a fort." Robert shook his head in wonder. "Only Antoine would have been able to convince the tribes to resettle there and come to the fort to trade for furs. Fort Pontchartrain du Détroit, he calls it. There is work to do, he said; houses to build and such, and there will be trading — legal trading, as you must have heard."

"We have been here only three months, Papa," Cécile said softly. "What will *Grandmère* say? She and the sisters will not be happy at all."

Robert watched his daughter's face. She was much as her mother had been, thoughtful and tender, with the same red hair and green-blue eyes. There it ended, though, for beneath that tenderness was an iron will her mother had never possessed. His wife could not ever have adapted to life in the woods, but Cécile had.

"Your grandmother and the good sisters took you in when your maman died and I was away. For that I will always be grateful," he reminded her, "but it does not give any of them the right to claim you for the Church. We could remain, but what is there for us in Québec? Besides, are you so happy here?" he asked, though he already knew the answer. She was miserable and as unsuited to Québec as he was. The small house, each room filled with memories of her mother, his dear wife, Jeanne, haunted them both.

She ignored his question, understanding full well that it did not need an answer. The answer showed clearly on her face, for she was seldom able to hide her feelings. "You are considering his proposal, then."

"Perhaps," Robert said gently. "It would mean a life of hardship once more."

"Where you go, I go, Papa. You know that." There was that edge of stubbornness in her tone. "You swore that you would not leave me behind here ever again." She crumbled a bit of bread on the table and added, "It will make Grandmère quite cross, though."

Robert sighed. Cécile was growing up wild, his old mother-in-law, Soeur Adele, had fumed more than once; she went about bare headed and she could not embroider. The girl was more like one of *les sauvages* than a proper French girl. If things went on as they had she would be fit for nothing, neither marriage nor the convent, and she would live out her days as a pathetic lonely spinster.

"Leave Soeur Adele to me," said Robert. He tore a bit of bread for himself. What had the girl done to it? And why, in the name of *le bon Dieu*, was she without stockings? "Put it all from your mind, Cécile; I need more information from Antoine if I am to make a decision on this. That is for later, though. I am away. I have a day's work ahead of me."

He brushed Cécile's cheek with his lips, and then he was gone.

She was alone. Cécile added water to what was already in the kettle; there would be laundry later this morning. Many of the neighbor women did laundry only two or three times a year, but that had not been Cécile's mother's habit. Clothing lasted longer if it was soaked, washed and then hung in the sunshine every few weeks, and so Cécile did her best to carry on as her mother would have. How it had amused the indiens to see her spreading her chemises out on the grass so that it and the sun would bleach them.

If she had time when her work was finished, she would get out her journal and make an entry. She had not done so for a few days, and she did not like to leave too many gaps; it ceased to make sense then. She had not included dates when she began writing in the book when they had left Québec after her mother's death. Time had a different meaning out in the wilderness. At first she had only written because her grandmother had insisted upon it. It would keep her from forgetting what she already knew. Then she did so for enjoyment. It was a pleasure to look back in the book sometimes, to recall fine days, interesting things she had seen while traveling; to recall the life they had lived among the indiens for those years. That part of her life was over, it had seemed, until today.

She wet and wrung a cloth and began to wipe every perfectly clean surface in the kitchen as she had done yesterday — the table, the copper pots, the shelves — while softly humming. She would not have admitted it to anyone, and certainly not to herself, but all the while the same words played at the edges of her thoughts. *You are for sale.*

· · ·

Papa set out for Joclaire's tavern this evening. It came as no surprise to me that I was to be left behind. He is too protective.

Papa said that the tavern is a rough place, and the men who may be there worse. As though I have never been in the company of rough men before. I suspect that he fears more the fact that Soeur Adele would learn in an instant that I had been inside Joclaire's, and that would be the end of both of us. Soeur Adele has strange sources of information for a nun, and for a dignified grandmother.

He left his musket here in the house, but Papa was armed with knives and his tomahawk. The streets are safe enough, but one cannot be certain who might choose to drink tonight at Joclaire's establishment. As he walked down the street I could not resist leaning out the door and calling that I would not go to bed until he returned, and I wanted to hear every word.

"At least the respectable ones," Papa called back.

• • •

Cécile woke with a start, her neck stiff from having fallen asleep in a straight-backed chair. She had been dreaming of the forest and of tiny branches scratching one against the other as the wind shook the trees. The scratching came again. Mice, she thought sleepily, stretching her arms over her head. We should get a cat.

She had sat down near the fire with a basket of mending. Determined to stay awake, she had worked for a while, sewing a heavy linen shirt where its seams had separated. She patched tears in the worn fabric of several others. Cécile had made this clothing herself. At first, her father had sewed for them, doing the work that had once been her mother's. Then Cécile took on the task.

Seeing her talent — any coureur without a woman had to fend for himself when it came to clothing — the other men sought her out. Her stitches were close and tight; any shirt, waistcoat or set of mitasses Mademoiselle Chesne made would last a good long while. They were willing to pay — not much, of course. Given the shortage of coins, as often as not it was with card money, the promissory notes written on the back of playing cards. The cards were legal tender; by law, merchants had to accept them, and to her embarrassment her father insisted she keep them all for herself.

"You work hard, Cécile, and that money goes into your own pocket," he had said only once when she protested. "Your mother, may she rest in peace, would be most distressed if I did not see to it."

Cécile rubbed her aching neck and wondered how long she had been asleep. Long enough she supposed; the fire had died down to softly glowing embers. She was just setting on another log when she heard her father's footsteps outside. The door opened and her father hurried in, stamping his feet and brushing snow from his clothing.

"I miss the wilderness, but I am pleased not to be sleeping out on a night like this," said Robert. He pulled off his mittens and warmed his hands at the fire. "Snow!" he snorted. "It is only the end of September."

"You have been in Québec too long, if you think this is cold," laughed Cécile. Then she grew serious. "What did you learn, Papa?"

Robert took his white clay pipe from the mantel, dropped into a chair and regarded his daughter. He packed and lit the pipe, then drew in and blew out a stream of fragrant smoke. It was illegal to have or use tobacco here in Québec; a law passed years ago showed how much fire was feared in the town, so his pipe was only brought out at home. It was one of the few luxuries he occasionally allowed himself, and he only did it when he had something to think over. Or to celebrate.

"Antoine's — oh, pardon me; he prefers that I call him Cadillac now — Cadillac's business is finished here. The Company was deaf to him," said Robert, stretching out his long legs with pleasure. "He risked his scalp to see the fort built, and they will not give him full control of it. They sent out their own men to manage the place and its affairs. That is why he came here to reason with the Company. It was to no avail. They pay him and Tonti, who is his second in command, a wage as if they were a pair of laborers, for the love of all things holy! Cadillac wanted the trading monopoly, but that is out of the question." He frowned down at his pipe. The tobacco in its tiny bowl had gone out, and so he again began the ritual of emptying, refilling and lighting it while Cécile waited.

"He intends to return within a few days or next week at the latest. We will go with his party, if you are willing." Robert watched his daughter's composed face, her stillness. Only the widening of her eyes gave away her excitement. "There is no future for us here. I will not say I entirely trust Cadillac, but I trust my own judgment regarding what is best for us. The town? There are too many people, and the stink of it sickens me. This house? The memories of your mother, of our life as a family —" He shook himself and went on. "It may be a difficult journey, Cécile," he warned. "Cadillac wishes to push hard and return as quickly as possible."

"I can keep up."

"The weather may turn bad; it will be nearly the end of November before we arrive there."

"I will dress warmly."

"The lakes breed terrible snowstorms."

"I will have high *boites sauvages* on my feet."

"There will be no shelter. You have always had the luxury of a longhouse in the winter."

There was silence at that. A knot of sap popped and a log fell with a soft thump. Then Cécile roared with laughter.

"Longhouse?" she said, wiping her eyes with the heel of her hand. "Luxury? Oh, yes, Papa, it is warm enough, but the smoke and the people all crowded together are hardly luxury."

"And the fleas. Remember the fleas?" Cécile felt like scratching at the mere thought.

"That is because you always had to have at least two dogs sleeping with you," she reminded him loftily. She dropped down on her knees next to her father and hugged him. "Luxury is a place of our own. Together. If it means hardship at first, then I am willing to endure that."

"It is likely you will remain at the fort, Cécile, if I am to travel out," he said, watching her carefully. "The indiens with whom we lived in the past were one thing. Those people I knew well, but the western tribes are an uncertainty." She opened her mouth to protest, and he held up a silencing hand. "I would make sure that you are comfortably and safely settled, of course, so that my mind would be at rest. Both Cadillac's and Tonti's wives are there now. Perhaps you may find a friend in one of them. We shall see."

Cécile held herself very still, her face expressionless, but her mind swirled with turmoil as wild as the rapids in the river. She would not be left behind; oh no. She would find a way to make him see the reason of it in time, but for now she had no energy left for argument.

"We shall see, Papa," was all she said, and her tone was so much like her father's that laughter rumbled deep in his chest. His pipe clenched between his teeth, he hugged her hard, and his throat grew tight with the love he felt for her. "Good enough, then. It is decided. To bed with you, Cécile; I will bank the fire. There will be much to do tomorrow," said Robert, his hands now laced behind his head.

Later in her room, combing out her hair, she could hear him moving around the kitchen. Bank the fire, was it? He would be up for hours, planning, turning over one idea then another, most likely deciding things he felt she should not hear.

In her chemise, she crawled beneath the icy bedding and settled herself in a ball, pulling the wool blankets up to her chin. It did not take long for her body to grow warm. Tired, but too excited for sleep, she began to list what she must do in the morning.

Bedding to sort out, she thought. More laundry to soak so that everything is clean when we leave, and I must find all the warmest of our clothing. I will purchase heavy wool stockings. We both require new ones.

Before she fell asleep she whispered aloud, "We will not need a cat after all, I suppose."

Chapter 2

I had a strange dream last night. We slept in the open forest as we used to do when the weather was fair and no rain or snow threatened. It was always more pleasant out in the fresh night air than inside a longhouse with so many other people.

I woke suddenly. The forest was still. No owls called, nor was the wind stirring in the birches above us. The moon was there, almost round, caught in the branches of the trees, and it was when I looked away from the moon's face that I saw him.

He was large and silvery red, an enormous wolf, a creature that seemed as though he was made of moonlight. His eyes were so yellow and so wise, but filled with a fierceness that turned my blood to milk.

"The choice will be yours to make Cécile," the wolf told me. "Your brother or his life. If you choose as your heart bids you, his spirit will die. Use his medicine." Then, like smoke, he drifted away.

. . .

Cécile had left the house late that afternoon with an empty basket, the one her mother had always used for market. There were two bags of coins and card money, one in each of the pockets that swung under her skirt. In the right pocket was what her father had given her for fabric, needles, thread, thick wool stockings and whatever else she felt they needed. In the other were her earnings from the clothing she had sewed. Now, though, the purse in her right pocket was considerably lighter. Every item she had set out to buy was tucked into the basket.

Cécile was heading home, walking carefully along the street, chilled by the damp morning under a sky of flat gray. Yesterday's first snow was nothing more than dirty slush beneath the feet of the people who were out on business. She gathered her cloak about her neck. A raw wind blew up from the river where three ships lay at anchor in deep water. Whitecaps raced around their hulls, sending spray up onto the oak boards.

Cécile paused a moment, peering out at the nearest ship. She could see miniature sailors up in the rigging, like busy spiders performing their mysterious magic, an alchemy of air and water. She loved the heady beauty of any sort of boat, though she had only ever been in her father's canoe. The return to Québec had been bittersweet, but once again being able to watch the ships, launches, bateaux and canoes ply across the harbor of this city was a joy.

The wind gusted just then. Her cloak lifted and swirled; her skirt blew flat against her legs. There was a long whistle from a passerby and several men clapped their hands. Unaware that it was all meant for her, Cécile pulled her cloak tightly around herself and turned her back on the river, thinking of how the fire at home would soon warm her cold feet. Her sabots splashed through the slush; she kept her head down to be sure of her footing. Then she heard the sound of an ax striking wood — good hard wood — ash or oak that would burn well, and she looked up.

How odd. She had not meant to come this way at all. It was snowing again, and through the flakes that sped past her, she saw the indien raise the ax once more, muscles beneath his shirt bunching, and hit the log a heavy blow to split it. It was the young pani, of course.

Cécile walked past him, her eyes again on the slush. There was the soup she must begin to prepare; the laundry was soaking nicely, and she had piles of clothing set out. More lay on drying racks. It would need to be shaken and turned over. She would make up blanket rolls and sort through Maman's old skirts and chemises. Some would fit her. And which neighbors, old acquaintances recently renewed these last months, should she plan to visit and say her farewells to first?

It was no use. She stopped in the street, turned and walked slowly back to the door of the house.

Cécile pulled off her mittens and knocked.

"I will say a prayer to Mary, the Holy Mother of God," she muttered, "and if no one comes before I am finished, then it is a sign that I should leave."

She began to pray as quickly as she could and was at *"priez pour nous pauvres pécheurs,"* when the door opened. The branding man — she would always think of him as the branding man — stood in the doorway. Behind him, the young indien was carrying in an armful of the wood he had been splitting.

"Yes?" the man asked sharply.

It was the same short, balding fellow she had seen yesterday. This close, she could see the marks of food on his clothing and smell the sour reek of brandy on his breath.

"I would like to make an offer," Cécile began. "That is I want to buy your — him there behind you — I want to make an offer to buy him. The indien. The pani. The one with the wood." I sound crazy, she thought.

The man's mouth dropped open in surprise, revealing a few yellow teeth like those of a horse. What she was saying was very bold, and so it was little wonder that he stared. Then his face changed. His mouth closed and the eyes, his little pig eyes, grew calculating. In an instant Cécile could see him taking the measure of her clothing and what she carried in her basket.

"My pani?" he asked. "Who has told you about him? And what sort of girl buys a slave?"

"For my father," Cécile lied, and the words felt oily on her tongue. She had not ever lied before. "How much are you asking for him?"

The man smiled then, a rather nasty smile made worse by his teeth, as his mind turned all this over.

"One hundred *livres*."

"One hundred livres!" cried Cécile. "What nonsense! He is not worth more than thirty. He is thin, and he seems to me to be lazy and not to be trusted. He has the look of a slave who runs. Has he all his toes? One hundred livres is too much at any count."

Puzzlement swept across the man's face. Cécile was certain that behind the little pig eyes was a brain of the same species, but the blood of a merchant ran in his veins and so he asked, "How much *do* you have?"

"Thirty-one livres." She said it as loudly as she could.

"What!"

"Thirty-one livres, mostly in card money, which, I remind you, you must accept. And six *deniers*."

"Shall I give him to you?" shouted the man. He pulled at his greasy hair until it stood out in spikes like a devil's horns. "I have an idea! Why do I not simply wrap him in gold cloth, carry him to your doorstep and present him to you as a gift? Are you mad? I am a poor man, a workingman, with only this pani to help me here and in my fields. I can barely walk on my good days — a wound from the wars —

and on bad days, my life is a misery. Ask for no details. It is only this pani who makes a difference. Like a son he is to me. Like the child of my own loins! And you expect for me to part with him for thirty-one livres?"

"And six deniers," Cécile said. Would you brand your own child? she thought.

A heartbeat. Another. Two more.

"Sold."

Cécile gave him the money. He leaned back into the hallway and then bellowed out a name. She stood there in the falling snow wondering what could possibly have possessed her to do such a thing. Then it was too late, and the pani was there before her.

"If he runs it is not my affair any more. Do not even think of coming back here to redeem your money," warned the man. "The brand will help. I did it myself, and it is a nice job if I do say so. It will make him easier to identify and it was a good lesson taught, you see. You could have his toes cut; that slows them down. Gelding would be better still. Perhaps you will want to set your own mark upon him. Something decorative might be interesting; if you wish to do so, I can recommend someone. Oh. The pani's name is Lesharo." Then to the pani — *my* pani, Cécile thought with mounting horror — he said, "You are hers. Go with her."

Cécile heard the last only faintly, for she was hurrying down the street, heedless of the slush. She slipped a bit on an icy patch and then got her footing.

"*Maistresse!*" Leisharo shouted.

"Do not call me that!" she answered over her shoulder. She turned around and walked backwards a few steps. "There is no need to follow me. You are free to go."

A very large woman passed by her as Cécile turned around. They collided. The woman staggered, swore with surprising gusto and stomped off. Cécile was left on her face in the slush.

Leisharo ran to her. I dare not touch her, he thought, even to help her to her feet. He had heard of another pani losing a hand for laying his upon a white woman. He wanted to stand there, his own hands safely behind his back; instead, he crouched down and took her by an elbow.

"Your palms. They are bleeding, maistresse," he said. His voice was low and soft, the French strangely accented.

"No! Go away, I said!" Cécile, on her knees now, pulled from him and fell onto the slush.

Leisharo saw the man only for an instant before he was wrenched to his feet and the fellow's fist connected with his mouth. He fell flat on his back, blood pouring from his split lip as his head hit the ground with a crack.

I will lose my hand, he thought dazedly. Then he passed out.

• • •

Her father's rage was far greater than Cécile had expected. It was he who had delivered the blow, of course. Coming back from the merchant's shop — he had resigned from his job — filled with anticipation for this adventure on which they were soon to set out, Robert had seen Cécile fall. His daughter in the muddy snow with the indien holding onto her was a sight that had angered Robert in a way he had not thought possible. His anger had been tightly controlled as they half dragged Lesharo through the streets back to the house. He had held it until the door slammed shut behind him, but only just.

"How could you buy a pani, Cécile?" he asked in a low voice. "You know how I feel about such things."

"I told you, Papa!" she said hotly. "I tried to send him away."

"Do not raise your voice to me, Cécile," warned her father. "I will not have it."

"You will not have it! You will not have it!" she screamed. "I did it out of pity. If you could have seen —"

"Seen what?" Robert cried. "All I see is a slave, a pani, for the love of all the saints, standing in our house."

Cécile fought her tears. After that first week following her mother's death she had not cried again, not even when alone. It had seemed as though that part of her had dried up and blown away like fallen leaves. Now Cécile knew that she had not cried because if she had, she would never have been able to stop.

"You are soaked," said Robert. "Change your clothing before you take a chill." Her father, shaken by his lack of control, sat heavily as Cécile's slow steps faded up the stairs. He remained that way, his head in his hands, until she returned to the kitchen. "Cécile," he began. He was a proud man, a man who did not often apologize, but he had hurt her. "Forgive me."

"I have done nothing wrong, Papa," said Cécile, lifting her chin, "but I should not have shouted at you. Shall we forgive each other?"

He nodded to her. Then briskly, his attention on the indien, he asked, "What is your name?"

"Lesharo," came the soft answer.

"You are free to go from here, Lesharo. What she told you is true. There will not ever be a slave in this household. I will put food in your belly, and you may have a roof over your head this night. Then your life is your own. Now, I have work to do." His eyes flicked to his daughter then back to Lesharo. "I will be just behind the house, so call if you need me, Cécile."

Robert stood. As he passed, he squeezed her shoulder gently. Then he left the kitchen to see to their canoe, which was stored at the back of the house.

"Maistresse," Lesharo began, "it is my fault that your father was angered, not yours. Perhaps it might be better if I leave." But when he saw her flush and press her lips together, he faltered. He seemed shy; he was not. The watchfulness, the quick thought with which he weighed each of his actions had been learned long ago. A wrong word or deed was often paid for with unpleasant coin. He waited for what she would say, for the outburst that was sure to come as it always did from whites, given enough time.

"Cécile," she said stiffly. She tied an apron around her waist and pinned the square front to her bodice. "It is my name and you may use it. Mademoiselle Chesne would be ridiculous, and I am not your maistresse."

"Give me work, then," he said, and then he tried it on his tongue, "Cécile."

Lesharo cut the turnip and cabbage with the knife she gave him, concentrating on the task. He was not accustomed to kitchen labor; he had not been a house slave. The knife slipped and nicked his finger a little, the blood staining a piece of the turnip. He sucked at the wound and began again. His discomfort was intense with this girl so near, reaching past him for a bowl on the high shelf. Her fingers only brushed it, he saw.

"I will get it for you," he offered.

Lesharo wiped his hands on his shirt — his extremely worn, dirty shirt, Cécile noted with distaste, all spotted with blood in back — and took the bowl from the shelf. He met her eyes steadily as he handed it to her. If she means this, he thought, if

I am free, I need no longer turn my eyes away in shame from anyone.

Caught like a fly in honey during the branding's horrible display, Cécile had not really seen him well yesterday. He was younger than she had first thought, perhaps seventeen, and so only a little older than she, with long, black center-parted hair that he had tied back. His skin was a shade she had not seen before in an indien, a deeply tanned bronze. His eyes were dark, and his nose slightly crooked, with a small bump on the bridge where she was certain it had been broken at some time. He was not handsome, but his features, angular and sculpted, were pleasing in an odd way.

"*Merci*," she murmured. Though he could not have guessed it, her discomfort matched his own precisely.

They worked in silence, Cécile running up and then back down the narrow staircase with clothing, Lesharo adding the vegetables to the soup of salt eel that simmered in a pot over the fire. He found the woodpile behind the house and loaded his arms with as much wood as he could carry. The man, making repairs on their canoe, watched him. Robert said nothing as he passed, but gave a slight nod of approval.

When Cécile wiped her hands on her apron and went to the door to call in her father for the evening meal some time later, the light snow had finally stopped. A dog's barking shattered the quiet, and then the sound faded. The early evening was still and dull, filled with the coming promise of long winter nights.

Robert washed his hands in a basin of hot water. Lesharo, uncertain of himself, did the same. With a grunt, his hands shielded by leather potholders, Robert lifted the pot from the fire and set it on its three little feet in the center of the table. He sat while Cécile filled a bowl and put it in front of him. Then she served Lesharo. She filled her own bowl last as her mother always had, then sat down on her mother's chair.

The spoon of soup part way to her mouth, she paused and said, "What are you doing?"

Lesharo was sitting cross-legged on the floor near the fire. They had not sent him to eat outside as his last master had been in the habit of doing. He had decided to take advantage of that, and warm himself while he could.

"You will not eat my food sitting on the floor," Robert said gruffly. "You will join us at our table."

Lesharo, accustomed to instantly obeying any command, stood, crossed the room and sat. He had not ever eaten at a table with whites. He felt his hunger slipping away, in spite of the fact that seconds ago the smell of the soup was the finest thing that had ever reached his nostrils. What would they expect of him? But they only fell to their eating, talking of their day, both of them wiping their bowls clean with chunks of fresh bread. His discomfort easing, he ate in silence, careful of his split lip.

Robert pushed his chair away from the table and belched softly. "You are a free man, free to go anywhere. Where will you go?"

Lesharo swallowed. Without asking him, she — Cécile — had filled his bowl twice more, to appease the hunger that returned to knot his belly. Where *will* I go? he asked himself. He thought of places he had lived since he had been captured, each new one taking him farther and farther from what he had once loved.

"I will go home," he said simply.

"Home. And where is that?"

"Far to the west, back to the Pawnee." He lifted his chin and said, "I am Pawnee; not pani. *Pawnee.* My people are the People of the Wolf."

Cécile started. Her dream; how odd that she should have dreamed of a wolf. "We are going west," she blurted before she could stop herself. She saw her father's brows draw down.

"The canoe needs some work," said Robert. He had skillfully changed the direction of the conversation, Cécile thought, as skillfully as he steered his vessel. "The damp has kept the bark supple. That is good, but there are a few more spots to which I must attend."

Three weeks ago, they had visited a spruce grove far from where most people walked. How she relished the clean air of the woods, the sweetish smell of the spruces as she watched her father make many cuts in the bark of the trees. A few days later they had harvested their work into a cloth bag: dozens of beads of amber spruce resin.

At home, Cécile had dropped the bag into a pot of vigorously boiling water. As she poked and stirred the bag, the purified resin floated to the surface. Tomorrow her father would again melt the resin and mix it with animal fat and crushed charcoal. The black sticky spruce gum would be used to seal any leaking seams.

Cécile lit a candle and placed it in a lantern, driving a bit of the gloom from the kitchen. She poked the fire, added another log and saw to the dirty bowls, spoons and cooking pot. That done, she added more water to the pot to heat, and sat down with a gusty sigh. The kitchen was in order once again.

Robert took down their snowshoes from where they had hung since the summer.

"Better we find a rotten sinew now than in the woods," he said.

"I can help with that," offered Lesharo. Seeing Robert's poorly concealed doubt he added, "I have made and repaired more than one pair while journeying. I can help with your canoe as well, if you wish."

"Tell me about yourself," said Robert. "Where did you journey?" Her father had handed Lesharo a pair of the snowshoes. Hers, Cécile noticed.

She began darning a mitten, her eyes cast down. One side of her faced the fire; light flickered over her cheekbone and turned her hair molten. Her other side was in shadow, but when she moved a bit, the red of her hair seemed alive, like a banked fire when the air moves over it. Her skin was so white.

For a moment Lesharo openly stared, and then he tore away his eyes saying, "All through the Illinois country."

Robert's brows rose, and his hands stopped moving over the snowshoe he held between his knees. "What happened that you came to be there?" he asked, already suspecting the answer.

None had ever thought to ask him — not for the entire story. Oh, a man who had just bought him might ask a question or two, but then Lesharo simply fell into his place as did a packhorse or a dog. He glanced at Cécile. She was watching him closely now.

"I was twelve summers old. It was the time of the buffalo hunt and the warriors were gone. I had remained behind at my father's bidding to protect my mother and my brother, who was but five winters old. A Sioux war party came to our village. I fought them hard, as we all did, but I was not a truly seasoned warrior. It was an easy matter for them to kill the old men and women and take what prisoners they chose."

"Your family?" asked Cécile.

"They killed my grandmother. My mother was heavy with child and could not have stood the journey, they said later. They slaughtered her in front of our lodge as she sang a death song for herself and the child within her. They took my brother and me with the others, but my brother died along the way. They would not let me build a burial platform for him — there was no time, they said — and so his body was left for the animals." Lesharo felt a stinging bolt of pain deep in his chest. He had not felt such a thing in a long while. "I was sold to coureurs de bois that fall, as was a woman from our village, and I worked for them for two winters all through the Illinois country. There I was bought by priests who tried hard to make me accept their god. On a journey to Montréal — you know the island of Montréal? We stopped at a place where the river is very narrow, a place between a big lake and a small one."

Lesharo's voice slowed then stopped. How oddly they looked at him.

"Go on," Cécile urged.

"We wintered there among the Miami, who had a small camp. One French-speaking man offered many times to buy me. They would not sell; they would bring me to love their god or know why, they said. The priests failed. Two springs ago they sold me to Ducharme to work as his servant when he was at Montréal. He brought me here."

"Ducharme," Cécile said very softly. The branding man, she mouthed. She saw just the tiniest flicker of distaste in Lesharo's dark eyes.

"I had thought the coureurs and the priests were hard men." He gave a short laugh, but said no more. All the while his hands had been pulling at the snowshoes, testing the tightness of the sinew, peering closely at the wood to see if there were cracks. He handed one across to her. "This snowshoe will see you though the winter. This one needs a new strap. You favor your right leg sometimes, do you not?"

Cécile's face grew brightly pink. "How did you ever know that?" She had slipped on a moss-covered rock two summers ago and cracked her ankle very hard. Sometimes it ached in the cold or damp.

Lesharo tensed, his attention fully on her father, he of the quick fists. Had he given the girl an insult? Had she taken offense at his words? No, she and her father were laughing.

"Anyone with a good eye could see it. It is the way the strap wears, and these marks along the bottom, there and there. A small enough repair," he finished lightly.

"She falls often," said Robert. "I expect her to take many tumbles as we journey."

"Enough, Papa! You have no right to tell him such things about me!" she complained, but she was still laughing. "Perhaps I should relate a few tales about *you*. Shall I do that, Lesharo?"

Something shifted, just then, the way snow will slide down a slope when the sun has warmed it. Lesharo had been told that he was free. The fact had taken all evening to sink into his bones, but their laughter had such open invitation in it. Whites laughed *at* a pani; on occasion with one, but here was the invitation from her to join in as an equal.

"If you would allow it, I could accompany you," he said in a rush. "I could be of service. I work hard, I am strong and I am used to doing with little." Lesharo expected Robert to wave him away, but the man only listened, his eyes wary. Braver now, Lesharo went on. "I speak Wendat and some Sauk. Miami as well. The man Roy — the one who tried to buy me so many times — he was allied with the Miami." The silence in the room, with only the low hiss of a slightly damp log to break it, shook his bravery for a heartbeat.

"It is an excellent idea, Papa," said Cécile. "An extra pair of strong hands is always important. And I wager you can shoot well, Lesharo."

"Not a musket, no, but I can learn. The coureurs saw to it that I had a bow and a sheath of arrows so that I could hunt, and then I hunted for the priests with the men who guided them. They said I was not to be trusted with their muskets." He recalled the sting of that as sharp as a whiplash. "I know that I could learn."

"Where is your bow?" asked Cécile. The water was hot; she stood and pulled it away from the flames.

"Broken. Gone. Ducharme likes his brandy, but when he is drunk he likes to break things."

"My father says it may be a difficult journey," said Cécile. She was unnecessarily wiping the table with a steaming rag. "It seems Sieur Cadillac will want to push hard to return as quickly as possible."

"I have done that many times. I can do it again."

"The weather may turn foul. After all, it will be November before we arrive."

"I am used to the cold."

"Nonsense; no one bears that sort of cold without warm clothing and stout footwear. You and Papa are of a size. I make all the clothing in this house, and I say you shall have some of his old things. There is an extra pair of snowshoes upstairs as well. They will be yours." Implacably, she went on. "The lakes breed dreadful snowstorms."

Leshary could think of nothing to say to that.

"But you will have Papa's old boites sauvages on your feet and a sturdy pair of our snowshoes. What will the weather matter then?" She thought to go on, to joke about the longhouses and the fleas, but she did not. Here was someone who had known hardships she could only imagine. To him a longhouse would be a lavish dwelling.

Robert shrugged his shoulders and let them drop with resignation. He was not entirely pleased with this; the young indien would bear watching — he was a stranger, much hardened by life — and yet for some reason Cécile, who did not take quickly to most, had warmed to him. The truth was that once she had her wishes fixed upon something, she would have it. She was so much like himself. He slapped his thighs and stood.

"Very well. We shall all sleep on it tonight — and do not give me that look, Cécile. You will not be held to anything, Lesharo, if in the morning the plan looks different to you and you wish to set out on your own. I am to my bed."

"You will have a place here before the fire where it is warmest," said Cécile as her father thumped up the stairs. "Here are some blankets. The water is hot and you may wash if you wish. The soap and cloths with which to dry yourself are there."

His last glimpse of her was the brown wool of her skirt swishing around her ankles. Then she was gone. There was the sound of her walking on the wooden floorboards above his head, the faint wishings of "sleep well," and then quiet.

Lesharo poured hot water into the deep copper basin she had left for him. By habit he was no cleaner or dirtier than the next. He had swum in the river near his village when he was a boy. He had done the same when he could after being taken as a slave, scrubbing his body and scalp with sand. His unwashed hair and the greasy dirt that accumulated on him must be endured through the winter, but as soon as the river or lake was free of ice, Lesharo would wash himself once more.

He had a memory of sitting in a sweat lodge with his father the day before he and the other warriors had left on that last buffalo hunt. The warm cleansing air that swirled around him had been misted with the scent of sweet grass. They had stepped out into an early dawn under a sky tinged with shades of tender pink and violet. There, low in the west was the Morning Star, that reddish glimmer of perfect beauty that had once again overcome the Evening Star. Lesharo had felt a great rush of love for his father. Four days later the attack had come.

He undressed, first stripping off his mitasses and breechcloth. He untied the leather thong he used as a belt and pulled his shirt over his head, grimacing as he did so. A small leather bag hung on a strong braided cord around his neck. He removed it and set it near his clothing. The hot wet cloth on his skin felt wonderful as he washed his body, his neck and under his arms and his chest, avoiding the brand with lingering anger.

Lesharo dried himself with the rough cloth and quickly tied on his breechcloth, conscious of the whites who slept above him and their strange ideas regarding nakedness. It would not do to offend them. He untied his hair, leaned over the basin and washed it as well as he could. Rubbing it briskly with a cloth, he combed it out with his fingers and tied it with the thong. Water still dripped down his back as he carried the basin outside to toss the water into the street.

Lesharo was just bending to pick up his shirt, when he heard a floorboard creak. He did not face her at once. She would have had a clear look at him with his back to the firelight. Her silence said that she had, and shame filled him, hot and uncontrollable.

Cécile had heard the water splash into the street and so knew he was finished. It would be safe to come down and get her journal. "Who did this thing to you? Who gave you this beating?" she asked.

His back was criss-crossed with thin scars, the smooth skin laid over with a tangle of lumps and silvery welts. There were fresh slashes as well. He had received a vicious beating perhaps yesterday; dried bloody lines were there among the old scars, and in a few places where the wounds had reopened, blood was beading up.

Lesharo turned around. She was holding a roll of woolen fabric and a shirt, clutching them to her chest as though to protect herself from what she had seen. "Which beating?"

Cécile's hand went to her mouth.

He looked up to the ceiling as though he was reciting a verse. "Ducharme, mostly. He did it often if he was taken with drink or if his business did not go well. The coureurs? Not as often as Ducharme, but often enough. And the priests beat me because I would not accept their god. This last? Ducharme beat me yesterday."

Cécile let her hand drop. "Why?" Lesharo said nothing, and so she said firmly, "Tell me why he beat you."

"He said I had given offense."

"To whom?" Lesharo began to pull the shirt back over his head, but Cécile ordered, "You will not put that filthy thing on again. To whom did you give offense?"

I am a free man. She wishes to hear it? Very well, she may hear it. "Ducharme said that I was an offense to you. If I had not run, he would not have branded me and you would not have seen him do so. Only offal such as myself would have caused such distress to a French woman." He saw her stiffen. The joy he had felt in the freedom of being able to speak as he wished was gone. "That was only what he said. He beat me for his own enjoyment. It was not for your sake."

"Papa!" shouted Cécile. "Are you awake?"

"I am now," came the answer. "Get to your bed, Cécile."

"He was hurt, Papa, before he came here," she called, setting down the cloth and shirt. "I must tend to him."

Lesharo heard the floorboards creak above his head. There were footfalls on the stairs, and then Robert was in the doorway of the kitchen clad only in his knee-length shirt. More shame, thought Lesharo. Now *he* will see.

"He is injured, Papa," Cécile repeated. She would have much preferred to keep her eyes downcast, but she knew it was best to meet those of her father. "It will not take long." She gestured to Lesharo's arm.

Robert watched Cécile pleating and smoothing a fold in her skirt with her fingers, her eyes troubled, her cheeks red. Lesharo held his shirt in his hands and stared steadily off to one side, his mouth a straight line, the burn on his upper arm swollen and inflamed.

"Give him some ointment. He may tend to it himself."

"His back is also injured, Papa."

Her father stood in the doorway, bare hairy legs visible, toes lifting and wiggling in defense against the cold floor. A flogging then, was that it? "Very well," he said.

Robert crossed his arms over his chest and leaned against the doorjamb.

"Papa, please," begged Cécile. "Go to bed. I can do this."

"When I struck you," Robert said, lifting a shoulder, "it was only that I thought you meant to do her harm."

"I know that," said Lesharo, touching the tip of his tongue to his lip. "You will not do so again, though."

Robert raised an eyebrow at that. "Really?"

Lesharo knew how to fight; he had defended himself often enough against other slaves. It might cost him, but he would not take such treatment again from anyone. "You need have no fear of that," he said, matching Robert's cool tone. "I owe your daughter the debt of my freedom."

"Papa and you, Lesharo, there will be no fighting in this house! No arguing. I forbid it!" warned Cécile.

"Then we must obey," her father said airily, and he held out his hand to Lesharo in the manner of the whites. Feeling absurdly pleased, Lesharo clasped and shook it.

"See to his wounds, then," said Robert. "I shall remain awake until you are in bed, Cécile."

When her father was on his way back up the stairs, she swept past Lesharo, took down a small, green earthenware pot from the shelf and removed its lid. Cécile sniffed the contents of the pot and held it out to him. "This is an ointment of yarrow, burdock and plantain that is good for burns and cuts. My maman used to make it; now I do. Put some on your lip as well."

Lesharo scooped some of the salve out with a finger. It smelled of beeswax and something green and fresh. He dabbed it on his lip. Then he rubbed some around the burn and, steeling himself, directly upon it.

Ducharme had branded him with the letter P for pani, she saw, as she took a length of linen from her sewing basket and cut a long strip from it. Her chest was tight with anger as she carefully bound up the burn.

"Sit, please," she said. "On the bench here, with your back to me, and pull your hair away."

Again, the shame rushed over him and settled in the pit of his belly like a hot stone, but he sat and there was only a soft cloth patting his back dry, and then her warm hands applying the salve gently, but in a competent manner. She did not cluck her tongue or make sounds of either pity or disgust, for which he was grateful.

"They will fade," she said as her fingers moved over his back.

"How can you know such a thing?"

SISTER TO THE WOLF

"Papa's did."

Lesharo twisted around and gaped at her. "Your father was a slave?"

"As a young man he signed a contract and was an *engagé* for three years when he first came here from France. The merchant for whom he was obliged to work was difficult to please. Papa does not talk much about it, but that is why he loathes slavery. You will see the marks some time when he takes off his shirt to work. They do not shame him, he has said many times; they shame the man who beat him."

Lesharo felt something twist inside himself. Just then he did not dare face her, so moved was he by her father's wisdom.

"There. You may have this clean shirt and breechcloth of Papa's," she said, briskly wiping her hands on her apron. "Leave your old shirt there and I will wash and mend it tomorrow, and make new mitasses for you. No need to bank the fire; feel free to add logs if you wish to." Then he was alone in the kitchen — rather dazed — and she was climbing the stairs once more, a book in her hand.

Lesharo put the leather bag back around his neck. He shut his eyes and squeezed it, fingering the few objects within. It was his medicine bag, though not the one he had made for himself when he was still among his own people. That one had been taken and burned by the priests, its sacred herbs and objects blackening and rising as smoke into the air. This was a new bag he had made in secret since he had been in Ducharme's possession. He had kept it hidden, and only today had he slipped it over his head before following the girl into the street. Would she scorn it as the priests had? Lesharo wondered uncomfortably. I will risk that, he decided, for I will never hide it again.

He slowly dressed himself in the clean clothing and, with a rush of pleasure, added a log to the fire and tossed his old breechcloth into the flames. Then he made up a bed with the blankets in front of the hearth, and lay down on his right side to spare both his torn back and throbbing arm. He could hear low conversation come from the second floor; the girl laughed once and then it was quiet.

Lesharo pillowed his head on his arm and watched the flames. He had not been treated in this manner before by any of his masters. The grease-spattered hearth in Ducharme's filthy kitchen had been forbidden to him. He would steal food, he had been told, and so his bed had been a nest of old blankets and straw in a locked closet. Lesharo lifted his arm and held it to his nose. This shirt and the blankets smelled of soap and the fresh air in which they had been dried. This house was clean, the food rich and good.

Lesharo rolled carefully onto his back. The salve had not eased the pain much yet, but it was allowing him to move without reopening the wounds. Cécile. He whispered her name. No one had touched him

in kindness since he had been taken as a pani. An image flashed through his mind: his mother, stroking back the jumble of his hair, hugging him to her so that his unborn sister — his mother had insisted that the child was to be a girl — had kicked in irritation. Sometimes he could still hear the way his mother's laughter had rung out across their village.

Now he could try to return, somehow retrace his journey, find his people and salvage what he could. Because of the girl, Cécile. He turned again with a deep sigh, favoring his branded arm, letting the fire's heat warm and soothe his back. I owe her my life, he thought. And then he slept.

Chapter 3

What allows such cruelty to exist in the world? I some-times saw cruelty among the indiens, but for them it was almost always born of war. Papa said that I must learn to try and hide my feelings, that I must not show sympathy when prisoners were brought in. It was not easy, but to be accepted among them it was necessary to accept their ways.

Leshalo sleeps below in our kitchen, and I think perhaps it is the best bed that he has ever had, other than what he would have shared with his family. How fortunate I am to have Papa asleep in a room not far from me. Leshalo will have far to go if he is ever to regain what he has lost.

• • •

"This is madness," said Soeur Adele the next morning. She had finally stopped storming back and forth across the kitchen and had now planted herself in front of Cécile, who was hacking a chicken into pieces with a cleaver. Robert was studiously taking no notice of the old nun. It was partly, Cécile knew,

that he was pouring molten lead into a musket-ball mold; he did not wish to burn himself. It was mostly because it was always best to let her grandmother tire herself out.

"I am not remaining behind, Grandmère," said Cécile calmly. She whacked the carcass in two and put it in a pot of water with the neck, wings and legs. "We are staying together."

The old nun leaned forward, the palms of her hands on the table. "Cécile, you are fifteen years old. It is unseemly for you to be wandering in the wilderness in the company of only men, even if your father is with you."

Cécile began to peel and chop an onion, blinking rapidly to stop the tears that were already coming. "That is nonsense. The men may not always be respectable, but I am. Besides, we do not wander; Papa knows precisely where we are going."

"Is it nonsense? You say you have no vocation and that I can accept, for not all are suited to become nuns. Even I, who am so content now, would not ever have considered doing so had your dear *grandpère* not died, may he rest in peace." She crossed herself and kissed the crucifix she wore around her neck. "But you! Do you not wish to marry, Cécile? Do you not want a husband and children and a home of your own?"

Cécile paused, half an onion in her hand. "Who am I to marry, Grandmère?" She attacked the rest of the onion and dumped it all into the pot.

"No one, if you continue to damage what reputation you have left. Who will have you for a wife then?"

"That is enough, *ma mère*," said Robert more sharply than Cécile had ever heard him speak to her grandmother. "My daughter's reputation is unblemished and will remain so. As for who will have her as a wife? Any man who needs a strong girl who can shoot nearly as well as I can, who is able to tan skins, who can cook, sew expertly, keep accounts and who does it all uncomplainingly. That is who."

"What of the finer things, Robert?" Soeur Adele came around to the other side of the table and embraced Cécile.

"You will stink of onion," warned Cécile.

"What is that to me?" She took Cécile's face in her hands and studied her. "You are so much like your mother, child. She would have wanted you to have a better life than this. My dear Jeanne was a cultured woman. She could sing; she was well educated. No one was lighter on her feet when she danced."

"And look what it got her," said Cécile's father. "Me."

"Papa!" cried Cécile. Then, she could not help it, she burst into laughter.

He rubbed the back of his neck. "Ma mère, Cécile has more practical talents. Jeanne — may le bon Dieu and his Holy Mother protect her soul — was meant for a life in the town."

"My point exactly, Robert," said the old woman. "Cécile could be meant for it as well, with the proper training. But what opportunity will there be for that in the wilderness? And you have not even made a commitment to Sieur Cadillac or signed a contract," she added accusingly. "That bit of foolishness means you must provision yourself."

"We can afford to do so, as you very well know, Grandmère, with the money left to me by Maman. It is mine, and I will use it as I please," said Cécile, straining for calmness.

"That money and this house are your dowry, Cécile!" cried the nun in horror, clutching at her heart.

"The money will be replaced when we are at work," assured Cécile. "And Papa has not signed a contract because he is a careful man. If the fort turns out to be as promised, then he may sign a contract there if he chooses to do so. Until then, he has given his word that he will work for Cadillac for a time."

The door opened. Lesharo walked in bringing crisp, cool air with him.

"Yes. Then there is the matter of the slave," said Soeur Adele tightly. "Oh, I heard. It is all over town, how Robert Chesne's daughter bought a pani. What well-bred girl would do such a thing?" Her attention was now focused on Lesharo. "Have you been baptized? I thought not. Do you plan to take instruction? No? I am not surprised, but I am shocked you would have an unbaptized sauvage under the same roof as your daughter, Robert!"

Cécile did not care much for the word she had used. Sauvage. The term had once been reserved for those who were not part of the Church — it was a favorite of Soeur Adele's — and it was commonly applied to the English, but that, after all, made sense. Les sauvages, though, was used by many to refer to all indiens.

"Stop it!" Cécile's cheeks and neck were flushed and her eyes blazing. "Leave everyone else out of this. It is only about me. I will not be separated from Papa! I appreciate what you did for me, and I do love you, Grandmère, but not when you are like this."

"I simply want what is best for you," said Soeur Adele. And suddenly she looked very old and tired to Cécile.

"I know that," said Cécile as she put her arms around the elderly woman. "You will not change my mind."

"I will not cease trying, though. You will at least let me write a letter of introduction for you to Madame Cadillac," the nun insisted.

"Yes, but only if I may read it before it is sealed."

"I will write it now, then. Bring me paper and a quill and ink."

Soeur Adele settled herself at the table. She stared down at the blank sheet for a few moments, and then she began to write.

"I found what you sent me for," said Lesharo, feeling it was safe to enter the kitchen. "I think I bargained well for the knives, sheaths and toma-hawk. There are still three livres and some left in the purse. And here is the bread, Cécile. Two fresh loaves, as you asked for."

Soeur Adele sat straight up when she heard him call Cécile by her first name. She made a strangled noise in her throat and paused in her writing. "Cécile, is it? In my day a young lady did not permit a man to call her by her Christian name." She gave Robert a black look. "Neither did her father. What have we come to?" The pen began its scratching again.

"It is my name, Grandmère," said Cécile as calmly as she could. She was carrying the heavy pot to the fireplace crane. Lesharo took it from her and hung it over the fire himself. "It is for me to say who uses it and how."

"Do you see what I mean, Robert?" Soeur Adele had stopped writing once more. "No sense at all of what is appropriate." She sighed hopelessly, shaking her head as she finished the letter, signed it with a flourish and sprinkled sand on the ink. "I will spare your clean floor, Cécile. If you will, please? Then you may read it."

Lesharo had been warming himself at the fire; he stepped aside so that Cécile could dump the sprinkling of sand into the hearth.

"My dear Madame Cadillac," Cécile began. "May God and his Blessed Mother find you well and safe.

We sisters of the Congrégation de Notre-Dame pray for you and for the conversion of les sauvages each day. Although we have not made each other's acquaintance, your reputation precedes you and sets my mind at ease. I therefore commend my granddaughter, Cécile Jeanne Chesne, to you. She is a girl of excellent reputation — Now my reputation is excellent, Grandmère? It is confusing! — and admirable qualities too many to number here. I ask that you take her under your influence, since there is so much that you may teach her. Yours in Christ, Soeur Adele Fleure."

"Swear you will deliver it," said the old nun. "Melt wax for me, Robert, and fetch me a small glass of brandy. Perhaps I shall perish of all this and fall down upon your doorway. Will you cruelly step over me, Cécile, and return to the wilderness?"

"Probably," said Cécile. "It will be excellent practice for climbing over the fallen logs in the woods."

"Bah!" the old woman snapped. "Well, if you have nothing else, you have your impudence. It is no substitute for the training you could receive here, but in a pinch it may get you by." She sipped delicately at her brandy and patted the chair next to her. "Sit here with me, child. No. Back straight, hands folded in your lap. There is no boning in that corset, is there? Just as I suspected!" She sighed, and shook her head. "So little time to ready you to meet

Madame de Tonti and, of course, Madame Cadillac. Swear you will not disgrace your family!"

Cécile groaned inside herself and said, "I swear it, Grandmère."

Soeur Adele softened then and cupped her hands around Cécile's face, studying her. "You are a good girl, Cécile. I will pray for you and this path you are choosing. Do not forget what you are and do not lose faith, no matter where you are. Your faith in le bon Dieu and your beliefs will protect you."

Lesharo, squatting at the fire, listened to their conversation but said nothing. Cécile's beliefs are the same as the priests were, he thought, and theirs were terrible to me. It cannot be so, for what she has in her heart holds no cruelty. She is so good. Once we are away from here, the old holy woman says that Cécile's faith in her god will protect her. That may be so, but until we part I will be there to protect her as well.

Chapter 4

Papa gave the knives and tomahawk to Lesharo last night. He also presented him with knife sheaths, a well-made bow and a quiver of arrows with fine metal arrowheads. Lesharo said nothing at first, and I thought perhaps he would refuse the gifts. Papa announced that this was no charity, and that he expected squirrels and rabbits for the cook pot, since I refuse to hunt unless I must. Lesharo assured Papa we would be well fed.

He is so very proud. Slavery must have been a terrible burden.

. . .

Three days later, two canoes floated just off the beach among other small craft, tugging at the towing lines that held them tethered to stakes. Both rode low in water that was spangled red by the sun just lifting above the edge of the forest. Walking toward the shore with Lesharo, Cécile could hear the maples creak as a brisk wind roared through them, the branches rattling and tapping against each other, the breeze strong enough to keep the fragile birchbark canoes away from the shore. She pulled the blue wool *capot* she wore more closely around her neck. There was the promise of a fine day in that cool wind. It smelled of adventure, and Cécile felt her spirits lift.

The *Canoterie Royal,* where the Crown's canoes and equipment were stored, was a busy place this morning. Cadillac's men moved in and out of the building carrying the stores that they, unlike Cécile's father, had been accorded by the Crown. It irritated Cécile that they must provision themselves, but Robert had refused to ask for even one thing.

Her father had been at work for hours loading the canoe. Sacks of flour, corn and dried peas, rolls of fabric and canvas, salt pork and lard in small casks, Robert's tools, Cécile's sewing basket and coils of rope had been packed so that the weight of it all was evenly distributed.

Robert looked up at their approach and wiped his forehead with the back of his hand. "Your grandmother took it reasonably?" he asked.

"Well enough," said Cécile. They had said farewell to Soeur Adele the evening before, but to please her, Cécile had agreed to attend one last mass at the convent chapel. Lesharo had accompanied her there before dawn, at her father's request, for Robert would not permit her to walk out alone at that hour. Lesharo had stood uncomfortably at the back of the chapel while the mass droned on beyond him. The smell of the incense, the indecipherable prayers, the chanting and mournful singing had disturbed him deeply.

"She made me promise to always sit up straight." Cécile shook her head hopelessly and smiled. "She is Soeur Adele; she will never change. And she gave me this." Cécile pulled it out from under her clothing. It was a scapular, two squares of wool connected by cords to be worn around the neck, with one square in front and the other behind. On one of the squares was the image of the Virgin Mary. Some people, like her father, wore a simple cross; others wore the scapular as the sign of their devotion to the Mother of God.

"Whosoever dies wearing this scapular shall not suffer eternal fire," Soeur Adele had recited as she placed it over Cécile's head. "It shall be a sign of peace and a safeguard in times of danger." Lesharo had touched his hand to his shirt beneath which lay his medicine bag. If the cloth held such power, it was a good thing for Cécile to wear it.

"Well, you may practice the sitting up straight very shortly" laughed Robert. He was soaked to above his knees, from wading back and forth to the canoe. "We are ready to leave when Cadillac gives the word."

"Mademoiselle!" said Cadillac, turning to her and bowing. "You are prepared for the voyage, I see." He was dressed for the journey in plain warm clothing, although the cloth of his coat and breeches was expensive and far finer than what her father wore, and he had not been able to resist lace for the cuffs of his shirt. "How charmingly you are attired, Mademoiselle. Perhaps you may set a new fashion at the fort."

"That is doubtful," said Cécile with a feigned haughtiness. "This capot? A man's coat? It is for warmth only, Monsieur. A cloak flaps about so, and as for skirts — while traveling in a canoe, I believe that the indien way of dressing is best." Beneath the hooded coat she was dressed in garments she had learned to make from the women of the tribes with which they had traded. A long blouse belted at her waist, a knee-length wool skirt and high mitasses would keep her warm.

"My Marie-Thérèse thought differently. All the way to the fort dressed as a lady. She was with child when I left; it was due to arrive any day, and still she was a picture of womanly loveliness. Ah, well, who can know the minds of females, eh, Robert?" he sighed. "Now, Mademoiselle, we need only get you into your canoe and we may be away." He snapped his fingers. "You! You are her pani they tell me. Carry your maistresse to the canoe." He bowed to Cécile. "There is no need for you to become wet at all, Mademoiselle, with such a creature to serve you."

"He is not my creature, Monsieur." She glanced at Lesharo, who was holding himself very still, his face blank.

"I am a pani no longer," Lesharo said quietly. He turned to Cécile. "There is no reason for you to wade out. I will happily carry you, if you wish."

Before she could answer, her father had scooped Cécile up into his arms. "She looks light, but one may as well be hauling a bag of rocks about, Lesharo," he said over his shoulder. Splashing through the cold water, he set her down in the canoe. Her father took his place at the stern, Lesharo sat at the bow and Cécile made herself comfortable between them. Cadillac's men cast off the canoe's lines, turned their vessel upriver and hoisted themselves in.

They paddled hard until evening, stopping only a few times — once to break their fast and twice so that Cécile could go ashore to relieve herself and stretch her aching muscles, which meant that their canoe had fallen far behind the others. When they again rejoined Cadillac's party, his men had eaten and were lounging about warming their toes by the fire.

"This will clearly not work," Robert admitted after they had eaten a quick evening meal. "You are five men to we three, Cadillac. Cécile paddles, yes, but I will not exhaust her, and I *will* make certain concessions for her."

"Papa!" Cécile snapped in extreme embarrassment. "There is no need for this."

"No, Mademoiselle; your father is correct. You deserve concessions," Cadillac said magnanimously.

"My dear wife, Marie-Thérèse, and Madame Tonti were properly treated when they journeyed to the fort. You deserve no less, but it is important that I return as quickly as possible. I trust Tonti, and of course Arnault and Radisson are there now representing the Company, but the fort is still my responsibility."

"Do not concern yourself, my friend," said Robert. "We have traveled alone before."

Later, when they were all settled for sleep, Lesharo lay in the darkness watching the stars. He had tried to pray, but in time his prayer had turned to other musings. The women of Québec had been what Ducharme called ladies. They would step aside when Lesharo passed, sometimes crossing themselves with the sign of their god. Some did no work at all, he had learned, having servants to see to their households for them.

He looked over at Cécile, asleep beneath the canoe that her father had tilted on its side to make a shelter for her. Garbed like a woman of one of the tribes, she labored beside her father, uncomplaining. It was her father's tender treatment of the girl at which he wondered. Cécile was no chattel to be worked and then married off to be worked yet harder; instead, she was loved and treasured. There was a fierceness and determination in her that he had not seen in any white female before. It was so much like his memories of his own family that he could have wept for it.

Instead, Lesharo gazed up into the sky and whispered to Tirawa, who made all things, that he watch over and protect the Chesnes. Then he gave a prayer of thanks. Until he was home again, until he had found his father, it was possible that he could be content.

• • •

It seems long ago — more than three weeks, if I counted correctly — that I was relieved to see the end of the St. Lawrence River. Had I known what lay ahead, perhaps I might not have rejoiced quite so openly. Lake Ontario is fearful. Papa says the waves can be very high and the storms terrible. You cannot see to the other side. A ship could easily cross the lake, and indiens will do it when the conditions are perfect, but we will remain close to the shoreline, which reassures me.

Lesharo says that the Pawnee do not use canoes. They travel on foot or on horses. He had not ever seen a canoe until he was sold into slavery, and he had not ever seen whites, either, for that matter. Once his grandmother told him that her mother had spoken of traders with skin as white as the milk of mares. Lesharo believed her only because she was his grandmother.

He has not forgotten his people. He has kept his memory of them alive by telling himself the stories he was told as a child, he said. How hard that must have been.

• • •

It was a long journey to Détroit, and for all his talk of concessions, Cécile's father did not offer her many. He could not, she knew perfectly well, if they were to avoid being stranded during wintry conditions. Fortunately, the weather remained good for traveling; it was cool and dry with only four continual days of miserably chilling rain. Every stroke of their paddles brought them closer to the safety of the fort.

Lesharo hunted at dawn each day — he used his weapon with a deadly accuracy that impressed even Robert — and so there was usually fresh meat. When the water was not too rough, they sometimes fished with a net as the canoe moved along. Minding the net was Cécile's task, as was hauling in and subduing any trout, pickerel or salmon that found its way into the mesh.

So they pressed on, with geese and flocks of ducks winging their way overhead, the sharp vees of their passage and their calls somehow rather lonely. The last of the leaves blew from the trees until the branches were but black lace against the sky. Still the weather held. Cécile's muscles were loose and fit from many days of paddling. Her palms regained the calluses they had lost, she slept well and deeply each night. If her hair was tangled and her linen less than clean, what of it?

It was early in November when they reached the mouth of the Niagara River on the afternoon of a mild, windless day. There were villages on the beaches on each side, but they were abandoned and not a soul was visible. Her father steered the canoe over the sandbar and through the powerful eddies that swirled all around it. They stayed close to the shore where the current was less swift, but Cécile was soaked with sweat, the muscles in her arms trembling when they finally stopped at a place Lesharo showed them.

"We can go no farther," he had explained, as they brought the canoe near the shore where an enormous fallen tree cut the current. "No one does, for the water moves so swiftly no canoe, even with the strongest of paddlers, can manage it."

Cécile waded in to shore, then knelt by the river's edge and lifted water to her mouth with her cupped hands. It was cold and sweet. She ran her palms over her face and splashed water on her neck, not minding at all when it dripped down to dampen her chemise and shirt. Her father and Lesharo tied the canoe's bow and stern to tree branches, and then they all helped unload the gear. There was less of it now, with some of the bags of peas and corn having been emptied and folded away, since nothing could be wasted. Finally, they untied the canoe and carried it ashore. Laying it on its side on the bank, Robert checked to see if there were any repairs needed — as he did each day — while Lesharo found firewood and Cécile prepared a meal.

The sun set, although its glow lingered rich and red in the west; stars were coming out and the evening sky was clear. Later, the waxing moon would rise, misshapen and a little less than full. If no clouds came it would be large enough to give a great deal of light. By the time they had eaten the squirrel stew and flatbread, by the time Robert's pipe was lit, it was doing just that.

"The Pawnee say that the moon and the sun were the parents of the first male child on Earth," said Lesharo. He was on his back, head pillowed on his blanket roll, his arms behind his head, watching the sky.

"And what of the first female baby?" asked Cécile, who was propped against the trunk of the fallen tree. She leaned forward and poked a long twig into the fire until its tip burst into flames.

"She was a child from the union of the Morning Star, her father, and the Evening Star, her mother," he explained patiently. "It is from those two that the Pawnee people came."

Grandmère would not like this, thought Cécile, but she herself was quite accustomed to hearing such things. Unless they had been converted, unless they were baptized Christian and brought into the Catholic Church, indiens viewed the world in a different way and had their own beliefs. Even if one did not agree with such things, it was wise to keep one's opinion unspoken.

Cécile sat up then and dug into the leather pouch that held her personal items. She pulled out her journal and a cow horn, something her father had made for her long ago. Cleverly crafted, it came apart into three pieces with the bottom section forming a stoppered inkwell, the middle for quills and the top containing sand to sprinkle upon the wet ink. Selecting a sharp quill, she opened the journal to where she had last left off and looked thoughtfully up at the moon for a moment.

"Silence. The scribe is at work," warned Robert in an ominous tone. Cécile hid her smile. He had slowly, cautiously begun to trust Lesharo. Even such a small joke said that perhaps his reserve was continuing to melt.

Lesharo rolled on his side and watched her. He could not read or even write his name, but the marks she made upon the paper fascinated him. Ducharme had kept a ledger. His writing was sloppy and the pages stained with food and wine. Cécile's marks were graceful and even, full of loops and swirls like the path of a tiny dragonfly. The sound of her pen scratching on the paper was like the claws of mice in a cupboard, secret and small.

"What will it say this time?" he asked her after a while. What she wrote was magical to him.

"The day's events. Papa's feeble paddling." Her father made a rude noise. "The eagles we saw just before the mouth the river, the way we had to fight our way up here." She paused. "And what you just told me." His eyes widened at that, and so she quickly asked, "You do not mind, do you? If you mind I will not."

They were his people's stories and stories were lost if no one told them. Perhaps if she set them down in the book they would live on in a different way.

"No, I do not mind. I will tell you more tomorrow if you like," he answered.

Cécile put away the journal, quill and ink and crawled into her bed under the canoe. "Yes, I would like that," she said quietly.

Robert tapped the ashes of his pipe into the fire; he rolled himself into his blankets.

"Listen," Cécile whispered. From the distance came a low rumbling.

"*Onguiaahra*," Leshao said sleepily. "Niagara speaks to us. You will see it tomorrow, Cécile."

All that night the river flowed past and the forest was very quiet as the moon crossed the sky. Just before false dawn a wolf padded silently into the camp, its silvery-red fur thick about its neck, its tail lush. For a time it watched Leshao, who was asleep, the blankets pulled up over his nose. Then the wolf turned to Cécile. It stared at her for a long while with its slitted yellow eyes that gleamed like slivers pared from a harvest moon. Noiselessly it moved into the forest and far up the hill.

It looked back once over its shoulder, back toward the hidden camp and the sleeping girl. Then it sat in the fallen leaves and howled.

Chapter 5

They stopped several times on the way up, resting for almost a quarter of each hour. It was to spare her, Cécile knew, and though it embarrassed her, she was secretly grateful. An indien woman would have gone on with the warriors, carrying as much as the men, if not more, and perhaps carrying a baby as well. She had no wish to make her father sorry she had come along, and so she gritted her teeth and went on.

Cécile carried as much as she could. Robert had slung the lighter sacks of food and clothing over her shoulders. She rolled all the canvas and cloth into her blankets, and he tied that on as well. Rather than sling his musket over her shoulders, she carried it, since it would be the only weapon quickly available should danger strike. Lesharo and her father had slightly lighter loads, but they would bear the canoe over their heads. By this time tomorrow it would be over. For now, though, the escarpment loomed above them.

"They call them the Three Mountains," explained Lesharo. "It appears as one big hill, but it is three and the last is the steepest."

The trail was clear; the Seneca had used it for untold years, and who could say how many pairs of moccasins had passed over it? Now ours are added to that number, thought Cécile. She worked her shoulders to ease the strain of the weight she carried, and then she shifted the musket into a more comfortable position.

Near the base of the last steep rise, her father called another rest. She dropped down and simply lay back; to remove the load was too much trouble. Lesharo shrugged off his packs and unslung the hollowed gourd he carried. He had filled it with cold water this morning.

"Will you drink, Cécile?" he asked. A year ago he would not have dared to offer a white female what he had touched to his own lips. Now he offered it with no discomfort; she had already asked him for it herself, earlier.

Cécile drank and passed it back, glancing at her father as she did so. He was not openly watching, but she knew he was aware of each thing that passed between them. His trust went only so far, particularly regarding her.

"An hour, perhaps a little more, and we will be to the top," assured her father. "Then we will camp." He pressed his lips together. "I see it again. Perhaps I should shoot the cursed beast."

It was a wolf. The creature had been following them all day, staying well out of range, disappearing for a time; and then there it would be again on a rocky ledge or standing on a windfall log. Now it was motionless in a pool of sunlight, its tail up and its ears perked forward.

"Do not shoot it," cautioned Lesharo. "It does us no harm at all."

"It is tracking us," said her father impatiently. "Would you wait until it attacks?"

"It is a wolf. The Pawnee do not kill wolves."

"I am not Pawnee, Lesharo, and if this thing is mad, then think of Cécile."

"I think of her," said Lesharo. "I think of the wolf as well."

"Papa," said Cécile. "Look at it. Surely we are in no peril, since it never comes close to us." The wolf was panting, and even from this distance it seemed to her that it smiled a lupine smile. Unconcerned, it yawned and trotted off.

"Very well," said her father, watching it weave in and out of the trees. "I will spare the thing if I see it again, as long as it does not threaten us."

The backs and underarms of their shirts became soaked with sweat. Cécile used every bit of her will to set the pace, walking, as she had all morning, in the lead. There were anthills dotting the earth and chunks of rock to trip over; Cécile slipped once, but she did not fall.

The forest was thick here. The old oaks and maples with their massive trunks and thick towering branches would create deep shade in the summer. Now they were bare of their leaves, and sunlight

patterned the forest's floor. There would be different
sounds as well, thought Cécile, keeping her eyes on
the trail, trying to think of anything that would
focus her mind away from the pain in her shoulders
and legs. Then it would be birdsong and the petulant
whine of squirrels high in the branches. Perhaps the
wind would rise and set each tree rustling as it swept
by. Today, though, there was only the sound of her
heart thumping and the noise of the waterfall.

They had been able to hear it all along, even far
down where the portage had begun. It had been
growing louder, like the roar of a great beast or river
serpent. In the sky to the right was a huge cloud of
mist that rose and moved like the ghost of the river
itself.

There was an end to the climb at last, and when
they stopped Cécile could have wept for the sheer
pleasure of it. A cooling breeze came from the
northeast; she put down her father's musket — her
palms smelled of iron — then removed each pack
from her shoulders, groaning while she did so. She
sat down and leaned back, her weight upon her
hands so that the thick braid hung away from her
neck.

Cécile wrinkled her nose. It was not only her
palms that smelled; her entire person had an unpleasant odor. She had washed this morning as well
as she could, the river's current dismissing any
thought of swimming in the cold water, but the
heavy work had soaked her chemise and blouse

many times over. Perhaps later she would draw and heat water from the river, she thought.

"We must see this amazing spectacle," said her father, wiping his dripping face with a rather dirty handkerchief that he stuffed back up his sleeve. "Lead us to it, Lesharo."

He took them through the spruces and maples to a place where there were no trees at all. She would see it again many times in her life, but this first time she saw the falls of Niagara would be locked in her memory forever. Swirling columns of mist rose from the foaming waters of a deep gorge, and the sun made a rainbow of them. The falls roared deeply, ceaselessly; Cécile could feel it inside herself as though the waterfall was touching her soul. No one spoke. They only stood and watched while what seemed like an ocean of water flowed by. Finally, not wanting to break the spell of it, they began to walk back, silent for a few moments.

Her father cleared his throat and asked, "How much farther, Lesharo?"

"Not so far to where we put in the canoe tomorrow," Lesharo answered. "And," he added, "we are fortunate that the weather is as cool as this."

"Why might that be?" asked Cécile.

"Because the rattlesnakes sleep now. When we passed here in summer they were everywhere, warming themselves wherever there was sunlight."

"Did you hear that, Cécile?" called Robert. "Snakes. Big snakes!"

"You know very well I am not afraid of them," she said, very conscious that there were great patches of sunlight here, and large bare rocks.

"I am fond of them myself," said Lesharo. He had stopped and was fitting the arrow he had pulled from his quiver to the string of his bow. "Be still, Cécile, so it will not strike."

Cécile had not heard anything above the roar of the falls, but Lesharo had caught the small deadly rattling. She felt sweat break out on her back, and the flesh crawled on her arms.

"Where is it?" she breathed.

"Do not move. Be very still," Lesharo repeated. He edged forward, placing his feet carefully until he stood just ahead of her. Then his arrow flashed in the sunlight. Lesharo took a few steps ahead and held up the limp body on which she would certainly have stepped. He worked the arrow from the rattlesnake's head.

"I am in your debt," said Robert softly. "I did not hear it, much less see it. If she had been struck —" He shook his head and shuddered. "There is no manner in which I may truly thank you for this."

"I owe her my life, as I said, and while we are together I will do all I can to see that her own is protected. No harm will come to Cécile as long as I am near her. Did you doubt me?"

Robert's eyes met Lesharo's. There was no longer any judgment in them. "I do not doubt you now."

Lesharo and Robert were silent for a moment, and Cécile felt something unspoken pass between them. Then Lesharo pulled out his knife. "Yes, I am fond of these things," he said once more. "They have a fine taste when grilled over a fire." He whispered a prayer over the body of the snake, then gutted and skinned it, exposing the gleaming white flesh. "I will eat what you do not want, Cécile," he offered, grinning at her expression.

Later, her father and Lesharo wrapped themselves in their blankets. Just before she did the same, Cécile sat writing one last sentence in her journal by the light of the dying fire. Earlier she had heated water and washed herself behind a blanket draped over a low branch. With a clean chemise under her clothing, she felt pleasantly tired.

"Now I owe you *my* life," she said quietly to Lesharo. "I have no way in which to thank you except to offer my friendship." What would he say? Was it too daring, too forward?

Lesharo, who had been watching the stars, turned his head to her. She had not thanked him yet for what he had done. At first, she had been white with the shock of what had nearly happened. Then she had grown quiet. He had seen her struggling with the manner in which to speak to him all evening. It had pleased him that she had given such careful thought to what she would say. But this. He had no friends. How could Cécile know that it would be the most precious of gifts?

"I will accept it only if you accept mine in return," Leshara said, his voice thick with emotion. She nodded. Each of them smiled, and then he turned his face once more to the heavens and whispered, "Do you know why the Pawnee call my tribe the *Skidi*, Cécile?"

"No, I do not," she said softly. "You will tell me though, I think."

"Our word for wolf is *skiri-ki*. So strongly have we always admired the wolf that we became the Skidi, the people of the wolf." He turned his face to her once more. "And can you guess what it is we most admire in them?"

"No, I cannot," whispered Cécile, as she packed away her journal and writing tools.

"It is their loyalty to the pack, to the family. It is a quality to be admired above all others."

"I admire silence," Robert said grumpily. "Talk in the morning."

Cécile lay awake for a while, thinking about family, and the pain of losing it, and then she was asleep. When the single howl of a wolf, long and infinitely mournful, rose into the night a long while later, only Leshara was awake to hear it.

Chapter 6

The south shore of Lake Erie is behind us, as is the Niagara River. Papa has driven us so very hard these two weeks, not trusting the weather to stay as fair as it has, if cold damp days may be called fair. We have gone from island to island at the west end of the lake so that we may not be caught too far out on open water by a sudden squall. Tomorrow, from this small island, we will set out on the last few legs of our journey, into the mouth of the Détroit River.

Our supplies are low. There is not much to be done with corn and peas that may tempt the stomach, even with fresh meat added. I think I would truly welcome another meal of grilled rattlesnake meat, for it was the feast Lesharo promised. But alas, the snakes are all tucked into their burrows.

There are thin clouds in the sky tonight, and behind them dozens of stars are falling. It is so beautiful. Lesharo says it is a powerful sign. Papa says he hopes it is a good one.

• • •

When they woke in their camp at sunrise, the eastern sky was lurid with blood-red color. The weather had turned sharply cold. To eat breakfast upon rising was not her father's habit when traveling; they would usually stop at mid-morning and have something. But this bitter dawn, Cécile made coffee and flatbread. When the canoe was loaded they stood on the beach watching the sun come up, warming their hands upon the cups they held.

"I do not like the look of the sky," Robert said when they were well beyond the beach. "We can make landfall in a few hours if we paddle hard."

Out on the lake the sun came up, but only dull light shone upon the water through the heavy cloud cover. The sunrise had given way to a deep purple edged with pewter. There was no wind, but there were long rolling waves coming in from the east. Their canoe would ride up and tip just a little, so that they had to lean to the side and correct the motion.

"Something stirs the lake," said Lesharo, and Cécile's skin prickled.

A line of cormorants passed directly before them, low on the water, winging west — flying to shelter, Cécile thought — and then another, rushing above the tops of the waves. The shore crept closer, and then they were at the mouth of the Détroit River. Cécile tried humming a tune, the first verses of "En Roulant," but it sounded hollow, so she gave it up. A few flakes of snow drifted down, sticking to knitted caps and mittens. Cécile felt their cold kisses upon her cheek.

When the storm came there was no warning, only a low deep sound from the east as it raced across the unbroken distance of Lake Erie. Robert turned the canoe, and Cécile gasped as the first blast of wind hit them. Icy wind and flakes of snow as sharp as tiny knives raked her face. Slowly, slowly, her father steered away from the wind, urging them to paddle hard toward the shoreline while snow hissed down on the water and pelted the side of the canoe.

Thick sheets of snow whipped across the water, the wind blowing so hard that Cécile paddled with her face turned from it. The very air turned white, the shoreline disappeared and then there was only the icy wind sucking the heat from her body, stealing the feeling from her hands.

The ghostly image of a vessel appeared, shooting out of the whiteness, rimed with snow, its bow coated with frozen spray. Swallowed once again by the storm, it disappeared.

"There was a canoe, Papa!" she called back.

It came into sight once more, closer now, heading toward them, plowing through the choppy water, the storm whirling all around it. Four men rode in it, scarves wrapped across their faces and heavy blanket coats over their bodies.

"This way!" called a man in French from the stern of the canoe. "The wind has shifted. This way or you will head out to the lake and be lost!"

Cécile turned and looked past Lesharo to her father. He hesitated, wanting to trust his own judgment, she knew, rather than the words of a stranger. His eyes glittering within his hood, her father nodded and turned their canoe.

"We follow them," Robert called above the wind.

The canoes went on side by side, staying the same distance apart. Cécile's eyes flicked to the indien vessel repeatedly, but each time the men were facing forward, paddling in unison as though driven by clockworks.

"Not far now!" called the stranger.

Cécile could see a darker gray drifting in and out of the blowing snow as the curtains of whiteness lifted and fell. It was a heavily treed island. Then they were at the shore, with Lesharo and her father leaping into the freezing water to stop the canoe and walk it in. Her father lifted her in his arms and deposited her on the beach. Their canoe was unloaded; then both vessels were carried high above the waterline and hidden in the bushes.

"We will help you with your gear, Monsieur," said the stranger. Cécile could not see his face well, for a scarf was pulled up to his nose and a knitted cap covered his head. He called something to the other men in an indien dialect that Cécile did not recognize. Each man picked up something and they were led wordlessly into the dense forest, into the blessed shelter of the trees, where the snow came down more gently and there was only the heavy moaning of the branches to say that the storm raged on.

There was a camp with a single longhouse standing in a clearing. The men filed inside. Cécile and the others followed, the very act of bending to enter the dim interior of the longhouse bringing back a flood of memories to her mind. It was smoky within, but not terribly so, since the fires that burned in two open pits in the center of the floor were drawing well, with most of the smoke leaving through the smoke holes in the roof. A warrior had risen to his feet at their entrance, his hand on his tomahawk. The young woman who remained seated by the fire only watched them, her eyes wide.

"What is it that brings a canoe to us out of such a storm as this?" asked the stranger. He pulled the cap from his head and unwound his scarf. "Monsieur, you must be on an undertaking of great consequence. That, or you are very foolish." He was perhaps three and twenty, tall and broad shouldered with long light-brown hair and a pleasing smile, but behind the smile was wariness.

"As foolish as you, since I note that your canoe was also out in the storm," said Lesharo.

"Lesharo!" cautioned Robert angrily.

Cécile's hands flew to her mouth as the man's head whipped around. His companions, all young strong warriors, grew very still. The man frowned darkly and then he slowly walked toward Lesharo until the two of them were face to face. His hand flashed up and snatched the cap from Lesharo's head. They stood silent and unblinking. The crackling of the fire and the steady drip of melting snow falling from garments were the only sounds to fill the tense silence.

"They say even the foulest of winds may blow in something of interest now and again," said the man in a low voice. Then he stepped forward and gripped Lesharo's shoulders. "By the bell of Ste. Anne, you have returned!"

"I have," said Lesharo, and then they both burst into hearty laughter. "Robert Chesne, this is Pierre Roy, the man who tried to buy me so many times. Pierre, this is Robert and his daughter, Cécile." Pride touched his voice as he added, "She is my friend."

"It is my pleasure, but no more talk now unless you want to lose toes," cautioned Pierre. Cécile swallowed hard, the branding man's threat rising up in her mind, but Lesharo seemed undisturbed. "You have dry stockings? Good. See to yourselves and then join us by the fires." The young woman, who still remained seated, cleared her throat pointedly. "By all that is holy, have I forgotten you, my beloved? Could such a thing be? I shall throw myself upon your mercies and do penance for it when we arrive at the fort. Cécile, Robert, Lesharo, this is my wife, Marguerite Ouabankikove of the Miami."

There was the smell of wet wool, wood smoke and unwashed bodies in the longhouse, those odors and something savory simmering in a pot. No one said much at all until they had hot food in their bellies. Cécile looked up from her bowl once to see Marguerite watching her. She smiled, and Pierre's wife smiled shyly back. Finally, relaxed around one of the fires — the warriors having chosen the other — Pierre began again.

"You were a boy when I saw you last, Lesharo," he said. "You are a man now." He drew on the pipe he had lit and passed a bag of tobacco to Robert, who nodded his thanks. "Many things have happened to you, I would suppose."

"Many things," Lesharo agreed. He sat cross-legged, his elbows on his knees. He had grown very fit on this journey, Cécile thought. All traces of the pani he had once been were gone.

"Who are you to him?" asked Pierre, his attention now on Robert. "His master?"

"No, he is not!" said Cécile quickly. "That was me."

"You!" Pierre's expression grew angry. "He is your pani now?"

"Not now. I am a free man now, Pierre," said Lesharo quickly. "It is a long story."

"Is it an interesting one?"

"A very interesting one," Lesharo assured.

"Good." Pierre settled back against a bale of furs. "Marguerite, there is cider in the jug on our sleeping platform." He blew a smoke ring and then gestured to Lesharo with his pipe. "And you, my friend, will pay for your dinner by entertaining me. Proceed, if you will."

• • •

He is Pierre Roy, a coureur de bois of sorts from La Prairie near Montréal, who has lived among the indiens for years. He was there at the site chosen for the fort when Cadillac arrived with his men in their 25 canoes. Pierre's wife, Marguerite, is a year older than I am and wedded already, but such are the ways of her tribe. They are the Myaamiaki, she has said, which means The People in her language. It is the French who call them the Miami.

Lesharo told Pierre everything — of being sold at Montréal, Ducharme, the branding — he left out nothing. Pierre was quiet for a while when Lesharo finished, giving me a very hard stare. You are fortunate in friendship, was all he said.

I am not certain whether it was me to whom he spoke or Lesharo.

• • •

A powerful wind continued to blow, heaping the heavy snow into a dense, high drift against one side of the longhouse. It made the building warmer, for now the storm could not poke its icy fingers into a structure that had really been built to serve as a summer fishing camp.

They went outside only to bring in firewood or to relieve themselves. Pierre would reenter the lodge, shuddering and grimacing, to make some crude remark under his breath that Lesharo found infinitely amusing no matter how many times it was repeated.

"Why do you encourage him?" Marguerite would ask each time the performance took place.

"He makes me laugh," Lesharo explained with a quick smile. "It feels good, and it is better to laugh than not to when so many share the same place."

The longhouse was crowded, but not unpleasantly so. Cécile stayed close to the fire where it was warmest, talking with Lesharo, enjoying the peace of it, listening to her father and Pierre discuss the fort in thoughtful voices. People simply called it Détroit she learned, the name suiting the place.

The Miami warriors kept to themselves, sometimes inviting Pierre to join them.

"They know a victim when they see one," called Lesharo when this happened.

They gambled with flat bone dice in a bowl, for their brass trade rings and bracelets, the cheap ornaments changing hands to laughter and moans. Now and then one man or another would uncoil himself from his place at the fire, glance meaningfully at Pierre and leave the longhouse. When he returned, stoic and unruffled — though rather snowy — Pierre would applaud and Lesharo would laugh once more.

It was good to hear him laugh, thought Cécile. He was serious and quiet by nature. Here in the longhouse, though, among other indiens, Miamis with whom he could converse and joke, he was entirely relaxed.

One morning two days later, there was a lull in the wind.

"We should hunt," announced Robert. "You have been generous in sharing your supplies with us, Pierre, but I think we should set out in search of game. The fresh meat will not last another day."

The men all wrapped coats and blankets around themselves. They gathered hunting bags, powder horns, muskets, pouches of shot for birds and ball for larger game.

"Someone must stay with Cécile and Marguerite," said Robert firmly as he pulled a wool cap down over his head. Pierre nodded.

Lesharo hesitated. He wished to hunt, to put food in the pot as the others would. His disappointment carefully hidden lest Cécile should see it, he unslung the bow and quiver from his shoulder. "I will remain behind," he said cheerfully.

Robert nodded in satisfaction. "Good. I had hoped you would do so. It is unfortunate that he will not hunt with us, Pierre. He is the best shot with a bow that I have ever seen. Quick and very accurate. Moreover," he added as he turned to pick up his musket, "I suspect he would be merciless in battle. I trust in their safety completely if he is with them."

Cold air and a rush of snow swept in when the men left the longhouse. Cécile tied down the deer-skin that acted as a door, and then she crawled onto their sleeping platform, one of four that lined the walls of the longhouse. She had slept in such a cubicle when they wintered among the indiens, wrapped snugly next to her father, sharing the space as whole families did. There had been a moment of awkwardness the first night, Lesharo being uncertain of where his place would be. Cécile would be ever grateful to her father that he had insisted Lesharo sleep next to him.

When she emerged, it was with her sewing basket and a roll of cloth.

"You do not bring out your book?" asked Lesharo. Settled now to the task of refletching arrows, he was fitting narrow strips of feathers onto the ends of the shafts. He had found blue jay feathers as brilliant as jewels while they were traveling, and he favored those.

"I could, I suppose," mused Cécile. "Though I would only be tempted to write in it, and the sewing is more important."

"What is this thing of which you speak?" asked Marguerite. She had sewing in her own lap: the first moccasin of a pair she was fashioning for her husband.

In the few days they had spent together, Cécile had felt herself warming to Marguerite. In every way she was Pierre's opposite. Small and dark-haired, she met Pierre's teasing and rowdiness with deep sighs and meaningful rolls of her large brown eyes, as though he were some overgrown child with whom she must deal.

"I have a book in which I write my thoughts. I set down stories and draw pictures as well," Cécile explained. Lesharo leaped up and got her journal; he handed it to her with something near reverence, and she passed it across to Marguerite.

"What story does it tell?" asked Marguerite, turning the pages. "My people make pictures upon rocks to tell stories. Do these marks do the same?"

"Yes," Cécile said. "It is the story of our journey, and there are also stories that Lesharo has told me."

Marguerite handed the journal back to her.

"Will you tell of us?"

"Yes," said Cécile carefully, "if it would not offend you."

"It would not. What will you say?"

"That you have made a long journey, as we have. That you are going to live among strangers, as we are. That you and Pierre and the others have been so kind to us."

"That Pierre is a terrible gambler and that he tells tales of his skill as a hunter that are filled with nonsense," added Lesharo, and Marguerite burst into laughter.

"Yes! You must say that. If he shoots a squirrel, sometimes in the telling the squirrel becomes a bear," she said. "And you must tell that we are to be married!"

"But you are married." Cécile's eyes went back and forth between Marguerite and Lesharo.

"I understand the way of it well enough," Lesharo said quietly. "It is the priests, is it not? I saw such things when there were priests in the villages. She must listen to their words and call only their god hers. They will pour water upon her head and make her one of them."

"You are to take instruction and be baptized, so that you may be married within the Church," Cécile said slowly.

"I will not be permitted to live with my husband inside the fort unless I do this thing," Marguerite said calmly.

"Our ways are not good enough for them." Lesharo shook his head in disgust.

"I do this willingly, Lesharo. Pierre has told me many things about his god and his god's Holy Mother." She shrugged her shoulders. "I will admit they do not make much sense, but perhaps in time they may become more clear to me. If not, well, I will be with Pierre, anyway."

Lesharo said seriously, "If he has been telling you stories about his god, Marguerite, I now see why they make no sense."

Then he began to laugh, and Marguerite laughed helplessly with him. Cécile tried very hard not to join in. What dreadful things they had been saying about the priests and the Church! If Grandmère ever knew that she had found such words to be amusing she would — what would she do? Fall over in a faint? Begin a novena? But Grandmère was not here, and it really was so very funny that Cécile could not help but join in.

"Enough!" she said breathlessly. "Marguerite, I will explain what is not clear to you if I can. I have been a Catholic all of my life, and I will admit there are many things that I do not understand either. One accepts them on faith. Perhaps we will be able to help each other."

"I thank you," said Marguerite with a wide smile.

Picking up her sewing, Cécile glanced at Lesharo. She knew very well that he loathed the priests. They had beaten him in the name of le bon Dieu, which was a shameful thing, because he would not accept their god as his own. Le bon Dieu is my god as well. Lesharo does not reproach me at all because of my own faith, but he will have no part of it. Whoever the priest is at Détroit, she thought as she threaded her needle, he had best treat Marguerite gently. And he had best leave Lesharo alone.

Their clothing had taken a great deal of abuse during the journey, and although she had been unable to wash any of it until now, she was determined to keep it from falling apart. They worked in comfortable silence for a long while, listening to the fire pop, sometimes standing to stretch or walk to the hide and look outside.

"The priests said your god died and then rose up from his grave. My people say it is not polite to speak of the dead," Lesharo said suddenly.

"As do mine," Marguerite replied.

Cécile looked up at him after she snipped a thread. "We do not feel the same way. It is like the stories you tell me. If we talk of those we have lost, it keeps them alive." She rethreaded her needle and picked up a shirt of her father's that looked as though he had survived a bear attack while wearing it. "He did have to lead us through the brambles. He could not have gone around."

"Not your father," Lesharo laughed. Then his smile faded. "I know nothing of your god, but maybe you are right about the dead. I think of my mother often."

"I will write of your mother if you will tell me things about her," said Cécile gently. "If you wish to do so some time, that is."

Lesharo nodded. "Perhaps some time. What of your own mother?"

Cécile stopped sewing. He had told her so many things about himself and his past. It was not her nature to be too open with others, but she sensed that if she were to deny him the closeness he so clearly needed from their friendship, that she would lose it.

"It is hard to talk about her even now, Lesharo. I miss her so much." She stopped and swallowed. "But then you know how I feel."

"I do."

"Papa was among the indiens trading. Maman was returning from the home of a friend who lives on Ile d'Orlean not far from Québec; Madame Toussant's baby had been born the week before, and Maman had assisted her with the birth. She was nearly home they told me. The canoe in which she was crossing the river was caught in a sudden violent thunderstorm. Maman could not swim."

"It is not polite to say too much among my people, but then I am no longer among them, am I, and I suppose I will have to learn at least some of the ways of the whites," said Marguerite. "My mother also is gone, Cécile, and I have only my brother, whom the French call *Le Pied Froid*. Have you put your mother's stories down in your book? The happy stories of when she was alive?"

"No, I have not."

"If you do, she also will always be remembered," Lesharo offered gently.

Cécile said nothing at all for a moment, and he feared he had pushed her too far, but then she looked up at him and smiled. "I think perhaps I will."

Just then, a hand reached in and untied the leather thong. The wind blew open the deerskin and the hunters hurried inside, stamping their feet.

"There were rabbits everywhere," said her father. "They should have been sheltered away in this storm, but there they were, offering themselves to us." He held up a brace of plump rabbits, as did three of the other men.

"We will skin them," said Cécile. Lesharo, saying nothing, began to help her and Marguerite, ignoring the looks cast his way by the Miamis, who would not lower themselves to do women's work when there was a female around to do it.

"We have come to a possible arrangement, your father and I," said Pierre, as he removed his snow-crusted clothing. He focused his attention on Cécile. "I do not intend to travel on to Détroit until spring. This longhouse is comfortable enough, and the hunting is better here than around the fort where there are now so many indiens living. If we take care with the rest of our supplies we will have enough."

"I agree with Pierre," her father said. "I know I drove you hard to get this far, but we would be no more comfortable there than we are here."

"I have a house within the fort, although I do not own the land upon which it is built," Pierre went on. "The Company has not yet permitted Cadillac to cede land to anyone, but when the time comes, I will be ready. You may live within the fort with Marguerite there, until you have a house of your own."

"That is most generous of you," said Cécile, her hands dripping with blood. Yet she was certain her father would change his mind and take her when he left in the spring. "Papa?"

"Pierre and I will set out to the Miami village to trade on Cadillac's behalf, Cécile," said her father firmly. "That is my work; you will have yours."

"Marguerite's brother, Le Pied Froid, is a great chief there," Pierre quickly went on. "I will try to convince him to move the village to Détroit, which would make Marguerite happy. She longs for her people and her family, although she does her best to hide it. Until we return, I will not leave her alone at the house, Cécile. I ask only that you remain a companion to Marguerite."

Cécile had immediately seen the trap that had been set for her, but there was no escape. Pierre had been so kind to them; she could not possibly refuse. She gave her father a fiery glance, which he did not acknowledge. "Of course I shall do this for you. It would be an honor."

"What of me?" asked Lesharo.

"What of you?" Robert asked in return. "Your plan was to go west, to return to your father. It would please me to have you travel with us. You could be a great help."

"Nothing would please me more," Lesharo said quietly. "Yet perhaps I may help in another way." He drew in his breath slowly. "I could remain behind with Cécile and Marguerite. Then you may rest easy and have no worries at all as to their safety." Guilt suddenly wore at him like a bond that chafed and burned. It would mean delaying his journey and the reunion with his father. Once before he had given his word to protect someone. He had failed, and his mother and family had died. He would not fail this time, and he somehow knew that his father would be pleased.

Cécile worked, listening while the others talked, and her father considered the plan. In spite of

Lesharo's offer, she grew more and more angry. The rabbits skinned, quartered and in a pot, she rinsed and wiped her hands. Then she snatched up her capot from where it was bundled on their sleeping platform.

"Is it still snowing?" she asked Pierre.

"Not as hard, but the sky says it will begin again."

Cécile brushed past her father, who only gave a resigned sigh at her irritation. It was not until she was out of the longhouse, striding toward the beach, her eyes filled with tears, that she realized Lesharo had followed her.

"Leave me be, Lesharo." She brushed the tears away, her hands stinging with cold.

"You left these behind." Lesharo held out her mittens. "You should not walk out alone, even here." He was armed with his bow and quiver of arrows. "I will walk with you."

She took the mittens from him and pulled them on, murmuring her thanks. They walked out to the river where steam was rising into the air from its surface. Skiffs of ice, small floes that had come down from Lake St. Clair and Lake Huron to the north, floated by in the distance. On one, dozens of gulls rode, facing into the wind.

"That would be the way to travel," said Lesharo cheerily.

"He did not ever have any intention of taking me with him," said Cécile, as though he had not spoken. "He treats me like a child. Did he tell you of his plans?"

"He treats you like a daughter. Would you have him do less? And your father said nothing to me. Can you not see that it is for the best?"

"What does that matter to me? I shoot as well as he does," Cécile raged on, "and yet he would have me remain behind in that wretched fort, probably under the watchful eyes of precious Madame Cadillac, like some slave." The moment it came from her lips she regretted it, her carelessness sending a bolt through her. She reached out and put her hand on his arm, hoping he would take no offense at her forwardness. "I should not have said such a thing. I am so very sorry, Lesharo. Nothing that I experience at Détroit could ever compare with what has happened to you. I ask your forgiveness, my friend."

She had tears in her eyes once more and it was not from the wind, thought Lesharo. My friend, she had openly called him. "You have it, Cécile. There is no cruelty in you. I meant what I said. You will not be alone, for if you will have me and if your father agrees, I will remain at the fort." When she nodded, Lesharo, in spite of the cold that was blowing through his clothing, felt quite warm inside. "Your nose is running," he whispered, hoping to make her smile. "It is also very red."

Cécile pulled off her mitten and wiped her face as well as she could. "Yes. Please. I do like Marguerite, but I barely know her. Surely a closer friendship will come in time, but until then, if you are with me I could bear Papa's absence." She sniffed. "Not that it makes me any less cross with him. Come. Let us walk along the river."

The frozen sandy beach was hard beneath their moccasins. Above the waterline were high drifts pocked with animal tracks, some old and blurred, but some fresh. Lesharo paused and crouched down, examining them casually. He pulled off his mitten, dug out a pebble and put it inside his medicine bag. A few gulls, vigilant in search of dead fish, stalked quickly away from them on stiff yellow legs to launch themselves into the air. They wheeled off and called down their annoyance as the wind took them.

Cécile picked up a flat stone and skipped it across the water. "Tell me," she said without looking at him. "What of your father? What of your own plans?"

"He will be there waiting for me," he assured her with as much conviction as he could. "I know that in my heart. Now let us return. There is rabbit for our dinner, but if we do not hurry Pierre will get our share."

No more was said of the arrangement that had been made until they had eaten. Feigning disinterest, she listened to Lesharo's quiet words and watched her father's face as he turned the idea over in his mind. Finally he nodded, clapped Lesharo across the back and offered his thanks.

"This sets well with you, Cécile?" asked her father, his concern for her clearly visible.

Her anger was suddenly gone. "It does, Papa," she said lightly.

"As it does with Marguerite and myself," said Pierre. He paused a moment, his head on one side. "You know, I have thought about the story you told me, Lesharo. You are on a new path now, but the other is not ended. There is one thing left." He, Lesharo and her father had been sharpening their weapons with small stones, honing their tomahawks and knives to razor sharpness.

"What do you mean?" asked Lesharo. "What is left?"

Pierre examined his knife, turning it this way and that, catching the firelight on its gleaming surface. He pushed the blade deep into the hottest of the coals. "The brand remains. It need not."

Cécile shook her head. She was staring at the knife blade in the fire. "No," she said. "You cannot even think of doing such a thing to him."

Her father silenced her with a hard look. "That is not your choice to make, Cécile," he said.

"A little pain and then Ducharme's mark is gone," said Pierre. "There will only be a scar. What is that? Nothing at all."

Lesharo pulled off his shirt and Cécile shut her eyes tightly.

"Robert, fetch snow in that bowl, and Marguerite, find a cloth. Cécile, you will assist me."

"I will not!" she snapped, eyes open and flashing. "And I will not let you do this to him, either."

"I want the brand gone, Cécile," Lesharo said quietly. "I have no wish to have Ducharme's mark on

103

me. If you will not permit Pierre to do this, will you do it?"

"Ducharme said I should put my own mark on you," she recalled, turning her face away at the memory. "I cannot do what he did."

"His mark is the mark of a pani, set upon me by a man who was less than an animal. I would proudly bear the scar you gave me, for it will be something done to me in friendship."

She stared wordlessly at Lesharo, seeing in her mind the image of him tied to the wall. He smiled at her a little and lifted his brows in a silent question. Cécile took the knife from the fire.

They sat facing each other, Lesharo's eyes on her face, his body still, and when the red-hot blade of the knife came down on his arm with a hiss and then another, he did not blink. One of the warriors grunted in approval.

"Hold this on your arm," said Robert. He handed Lesharo a cloth filled with snow.

"I will do it," Cécile said, setting down the knife. His throat moved once when the cold touched his arm, and a muscle in his cheek jumped. "Papa, the little bottle in my pack, please."

She did not ask him if it hurt and for that Lesharo was grateful, for his whole arm was aflame and his stomach close to emptying itself. Instead, she held the snow-packed cloth on his skin above the burn, letting the icy water trickle over it, her tightly pressed lips and flushed cheeks the only sign of her dismay.

Finally, she took away the cloth. It hurt her to see the deep burn, but Cécile made no sound of pity, fully aware of how he would react. "I think it is best wrapped with no ointment on it. This instead." She dabbed a liquid on the burn. "I will leave the bottle with you. Wych hazel is very soothing."

"As is this," said Robert, producing a green glass onion-shaped bottle. He poured amber liquid into a cup. "Drink it straight off."

Lesharo, unaccustomed to so much attention, took a great swallow to cover his discomfort. When he had stopped coughing he gasped, "What is this?"

"The most excellent brandy," said Robert. He held it out to Pierre, who accepted a cup.

"No need to offer it to the Miamis. They do not partake. Many do, but not these fellows, who are far more sensible than most. Sit a while, Robert, and I will tell you all that I know of Détroit. If we are both to work for Cadillac, then it's best to be armed with as much knowledge as possible."

· · ·

There they are by the fire, Papa and Pierre, the rest having gone to bed. I could not sleep after all that had happened, and so I got up and now sit here. Papa thinks nothing of it, and although Pierre cast me a few odd looks at first, he has resigned himself to my strange ways.

Lesharo rests as comfortably as he may with his burned arm. He is asleep; his breathing tells me so. I know he saw what I saw in the snow, though he said nothing. Among the old tracks of gulls and rabbits were fresh prints, those of a wolf. In the very center of one of the prints was a round reddish pebble upon which it had stepped. That pebble is now inside Lesharo's medicine bag.

There are wolves everywhere, surely, and yet I wonder about those tracks and what wolf made them.

Chapter 7

The days passed quietly, all muffled in winter's cold blanket. Cécile let herself slip into this tranquil world, moving to the slow rhythm of days so different from the manner in which they had been living while they traveled. There was a comfort in that, for it kept her thoughts from the future and the uncertainty of what awaited her at Détroit.

The winter weather was as harsh as any she had experienced, but it was also frustratingly unpredictable. There was a pervasive dampness in the air. It touched everything with its clammy fingers. Cécile would wake in the morning to find the forest laced with frost, the branches and twigs of every tree coated white and sparkling in the pale sunlight. It might melt and drip a little, then bitter cold would sweep down from the north. The wind would moan and rage around them for days. When it was gone the dawn might be still and so glacial, that tiny ice crystals would freeze and drift through the air.

Now and again they heard a wolf howling. The haunting sound disturbed her for some reason, especially if she lay awake at night in the darkness. But it pleased Lesharo.

"It is the sound of my people, Cécile. It makes me feel close to them."

It makes me feel uneasy, she would think, but she said nothing.

Lesharo's arm healed slowly. The burns she had inflicted upon him were deep ones, but in time the flesh crusted over, and then the scabs dropped away bit by bit until only a scar, raw and ugly, was left. But he was content with it, turning his arm this way and that when there was no one but her to see him do it, studying the mark with satisfaction.

Cécile came to enjoy Marguerite's gentle company during those quiet days. She and Pierre's wife would busy themselves inside the longhouse, not being permitted to wander about on their own. On sleepy afternoons, Cécile would record the stories Marguerite and Lesharo told her, and sometimes, when it was very peaceful, she would write about her own mother. She was content.

It was the nights, though, that she came to treasure.

If the weather was foul, if the wind blew cruelly and snow swirled around them, they remained tucked inside the longhouse. Robert had a small chess set he had made for himself long ago; now and again she and her father played, inventing strange games for their own amusement. But on clear evenings, she and Lesharo would walk to the beach.

He would tell her stories about the stars and why they were important to the Pawnee people, stories that she would later record in her journal.

"There," Lesharo said one night, pointing through his mitten, his breath puffing in a cloud around his face. "The chief star, He-Who-Does-Not-Walk." And Cécile looked up at the North Star, small and unmoving, set in the inky blackness of the sky. "Long ago, Tirawa, who made all things, said to this star, 'You shall stand in the north. You shall not move; for you shall be the chief of all the gods that I have set in the heavens and you must watch over them.' It is how our chiefs are to live their lives and watch over their people; how my father has always lived his life. All the other stars gather around He-Who-Does-Not-Walk; in the same way, we draw close to the warmth of a fire or to the love of our family."

Lesharo began to go out before dawn. He was watching for something, he told her. One morning he shook her awake, and Cécile followed him out to where they could see the eastern sky. It was dark, with only the faintest hint of the dawn that would come later.

"See them? Follow where I point," he said with satisfaction. "The Swimming Ducks." Patiently, he helped her find the two tiny stars. "The Pawnee say that when the Swimming Ducks can be seen, the year has begun. Now look above you. Those seven small stars — yes, just there — we call them the Chaka. They mean that spring will come soon,

Cécile. At my village, there will be celebrations and ceremonies today."

Spring did come in its own good time. Snow-drifts began melting. Geese and swans winged across the sky, up the river to the marshes where they would nest. Ice floes no longer drifted by, and the days began to grow warmer. It was on a crisp morning in early April after a sudden heavy snowfall — Cécile prayed there would be no more storms — that they set out for Détroit.

Pierre had described the fort to them many times. She knew it was small and simply constructed, but his words had not truly prepared Cécile for her first sight of it late that afternoon. Squatting on a rounded hill above the north shore of the Détroit River at its narrowest point, the palisade enclosed what Pierre had told them was one *arpent* of land. A small creek ran to the west of it, emptying into the larger river. A palisade of vertical, twelve-foot-high logs encircled the buildings, and four bastions — small raised log structures from which soldiers could defend the fort — stood at each corner. Smoke rose into the late-afternoon air from the houses inside. The blue flag of France with its three *fleurs de lis* hung from a pole, rising and falling gracefully. To the fort's west beyond the creek crouched the palisaded Wendat village; to the east was the village of the Abenakis, and farther off that of the Odawas.

A party of a dozen soldiers was slowly emerging from the woods as the canoes approached the landing. Cécile knew from what Pierre had told them that they were men of *La Compagnie Franche de la Marine*, the company of soldiers who had come out with Cadillac and who still garrisoned the fort. Some of them were dressed in much the same fashion as Cécile's father and Pierre, their uniforms having been folded away and more practical garb adopted. Six of the soldiers were pulling three *traines* heaped with firewood; axes and saws lay atop the logs. The rest had been working as well, for their coats were dusted with woodchips, but these men cradled muskets in their arms and watched the approaching strangers carefully.

Cécile pushed back the hood that shadowed her face. Most of the hair had come loose from her braid, and the wind caught and lifted the strands. She had washed it last night as well as she could before going to bed, not wanting to appear before Madame Cadillac in an entirely filthy state. Her indien clothing put away, she was once more dressed in a skirt and bodice that were the best she had, though beneath the skirt she wore her high mitasses over her stockings for warmth. She was excited, and anticipation had flooded her cheeks with color.

Two young soldiers at the front of the group slowed and then stopped, their mouths hanging open. The men behind them had their eyes on the ground, watching their footing as they pulled the traine, and so did not expect to collide solidly with their companions. Nor did they expect to see them careening down the embankment through the snow, one on his rump, the other sliding head first on his back to come to a stop at Cécile's feet.

"Your servant, Mademoiselle," one of the soldiers said with great dignity.

"I bid you welcome to Détroit, Mademoiselle," said the other, looking up at her with a wide grin.

"Our reception at Québec when we returned from the wilderness was not half so impressive," Cécile assured them with an embarrassed laugh.

"We are expected by Sieur Cadillac," said Robert, mentally shaking his head over the way the two young men, and now all the others on the embankment, were openly gaping at his daughter. "Is he within?"

"You would be Chesne then, would you not?" asked the sergeant who was with them. He was an older man in a tricorne, but was no more able to contain his interest than his subordinates were. "We have been told to watch for you. Sieur Cadillac was at his house this morning when we set out for firewood, Monsieur. He may be anywhere, but try there first." He nodded to Pierre, whom he clearly knew, and without turning around bellowed, "Reaume, Menard, La Motte, and the rest of you not on the traines, give assistance here to Monsieurs Chesne and Roy. Have a care," he added wryly. "You will have noticed that the ground is a touch slippery."

The soldiers, even the ones pulling the traines, helped carry the supplies and gear up the slope, although the Miamis ignored them and shouldered their bales of furs and their own belongings themselves. Cécile walked carefully, digging the toes of her moccasins into the snow. When she did slip once, she felt Lesharo's hand firmly grasp her arm to steady her.

Inside the fort, the Miamis left them. They called out something to Pierre, who shouted back a reply and then said, "They are going to the *magasin*, the storehouse where trading is done, and I will join them at the Wendat village later. Let us go on to my home first."

How different this is from Québec, Cécile thought. The small houses were plain structures, built of squared vertical oak logs. There was not a single building made of stone. All the roofs were thatched, and none of the windows had panes of glass in them; there were only hides or greased paper to keep out the weather. In spite of the snow that had fallen yesterday, the streets were already muddy from the foot traffic. A small flock of chickens darted past, skillfully eluding the two little boys who were chasing them.

"There will be blood in the eggs if those boys are allowed to do that," said Cécile in disapproval. "What sort of people would permit their children to torment livestock?"

"That would be the Cadillacs," said Pierre. His tone was neutral. "Jacques and Toine are their sons, and they do what they wish. Let us not spoil this homecoming with a discussion of those brats. You will find them as annoying as everyone else does soon enough." Pierre had stopped in front of a small house. "Only Cadillac's home and the church are finer," he said proudly.

Unlike the others near it, it was built of horizontal logs laid between vertical posts set into the ground, all well chinked with clay. The roof was made of thick sawn planks that overlapped. There were shutters and a solid door of wood that he unlocked and pushed open so that the soldiers could help them carry in their belongings.

"We will seek out Cadillac," said Robert to Pierre, who was preparing to light a fire in a hearth made of smooth river stones. "Marguerite deserves to be alone with you, so that she may see her new home."

"For a while only, Robert," said Pierre, giving his wife a huge smacking kiss.

"Ah, yes. We do not want to set the tongues of Madame Cadillac or Madame Tonti wagging," Robert said dryly. "We will provide a distraction, and you may have an hour's peace here."

"Distraction?" Cécile asked. "Are they such gossips then?"

"Within the walls of this house I will tell you that, yes, they are," answered Pierre. "And they look always for a new subject, as some women will. Take care, Cécile. Their curiosity is insatiable."

"Perhaps Cadillac's woman does not have enough work to do," whispered Lesharo out in the street as he walked beside her. He knew the telltale signs of her anger well enough by now. "It would cause his wife shame to see how well you work and how strong you are. I will help by leaving all the skins of all the creatures I shoot at her doorstep. Scraping them will keep her hands busy and her mouth quiet."

Cécile gave him a sideways look of amusement. "Somehow I do not think so. I suppose I should take care not to appear any more scandalous than necessary. At least not upon the first meeting." She laughed a little then. "You cheer me, Lesharo. Thank you, my friend."

He heard Robert ask for directions but paid little heed. Warmth had filled Lesharo at her words, and he was still basking in it, thinking of what small thing he could do to please her, when Robert rapped at the door of a house, the largest one on the street. *Perhaps I will tell her a new story for her book tonight,* Lesharo thought. *The Medicine Grizzly Bear might be a good one.*

"Welcome! Welcome!" boomed Cadillac when he opened the door. In the room beyond him stood a young officer of perhaps five and twenty years, a fair-skinned fellow with pale blond hair, dark blue eyes and a poised bearing. He was able to contain his surprise at Cécile's presence, but just barely, as

Cadillac went on. "Finally you have arrived. Come in! Come in! By the saints, that was a winter, was it not? I am hardly surprised that you are arriving only now. Did you have any difficulty with les sauvages along the way?" He ushered them inside, Cécile first and then her father, with Lesharo following.

"We had no trouble," said her father. "In fact, it was a party of Miamis and one of your people, Pierre Roy, who led us to shelter during a storm last November. He has offered us the use of his home until I can build our own."

"He has returned with his woman, has he? She will be a new convert for Père Nicholas in time. Splendid," said Cadillac, rubbing his hands together briskly. "You," he said pointing to Lesharo, "will likely have no difficulty finding a place in the Huron village. The Miamis have a longhouse there."

"What do you mean?" Cécile asked slowly, not trusting her own ears.

"It is the Company's policy now that no indiens remain within the palisade after dark," explained the young officer. "Pierre Roy's wife is one thing, but as for any others, they do have their own villages. There has been thievery, you see, and even if that were not so, Monsieurs Radisson and Arnault, who represent the Company, believe it to be safer." He bowed to Cécile and said, "Mademoiselle, Lieutenant Edmond Saint-Germain at your service." He tried to take her hand and lift it to his lips. Cécile stepped away and put both hands behind her back. Unruffled and quite unoffended, the officer only smiled with amusement at her odd behavior.

"This will not do," said Robert slowly. "It had been my intention to leave Cécile here at Pierre's house with his *woman*, as you call her, while we journeyed west to the Miami village."

"She has a name, Sieur Cadillac, as do you," Cécile broke in. "She is Marguerite, and she is his wife, not his woman."

"Now, now, Mademoiselle, let us not go into that," Cadillac soothed, holding up his hands as though to fend off Cécile's burst of temper. "We are all good Catholics here, after all, and only doing what the Church expects of us."

"I also have expectations. Under no circumstances will I leave Cécile here alone, even in the company of good Catholics. Lesharo was to remain with her here for her protection."

Lesharo said nothing. Cécile could see how tightly he held his fists and knew the humiliation he was feeling.

"I have no wish to stay here, Papa," she said.

"You will not need to, Cécile. My friend," Robert went on to Cadillac, "Pierre will not like the thought of his wife left on her own here. I cannot answer for what he will do or say when I tell him that we are leaving."

"Nonsense. Calm yourself, Robert, and do not be quite so hasty. An exception could be made," said Cadillac smoothly, with a confident smile. "Are we to let such a small misunderstanding as this come between us? Your Cécile would be perfectly safe here. Besides, I see that I must remind you of your promise to me, my good friend. You did not sign a contract, but you did give your word to work for me for a reasonable period. I recall that there was a time when your word could be trusted."

"My word is still to be trusted," Robert snapped. "Is yours?"

"How amusing, Robert. Of course it is; your daughter will be in no danger here. I am, however, somewhat surprised that you would leave her without a female chaperone of any sort. Perhaps my wife might assist and take her under her wing."

"Cécile knows very well how to conduct herself properly; she does not require a chaperone. As for Lesharo, he is my friend as well as Cécile's. I trust him utterly, and if he remains with her and Marguerite, it will suffice until I return."

"Very well. This is not Québec society after all, I suppose, and allowances may be made. Robert, your daughter's pani may stay inside the fort."

"He is not my pani!" cried Cécile. "He is a free man. He is my friend, and if you call him that again I will —" She sputtered, trying to think of something particularly horrible with which to threaten Cadillac, and then suddenly she burst into tears.

Cadillac pinched the bridge of his nose while Robert closed his eyes and tilted back his head as though searching the heavens for guidance. The lieutenant pulled out a silk handkerchief and pressed it into her hand. Lesharo, conscious of the fact that he was the cause of her weeping, stood there in misery.

"You will do what, Mademoiselle?" asked someone lightly. In the commotion, no one had noticed the handsome woman who now stood in the doorway. "Boil him in oil? Skin him alive? Sell him to les sauvages? The saints know, I have thought to do so often enough, but for making you weep, poor child, he surely deserves it this time. Come with me. Antoine, you beast, offer Monsieur Chesne refreshment and a better welcome than I overheard, or you will be very sorry."

And, with a reluctant Cécile in tow, she swept her out into the next room.

"Well," sighed Cadillac. "Now you see who truly sets policy here. Not I, nor the Company." He laughed then and lifted his shoulders with feigned hopelessness. "It is my wife, Marie-Thérèse."

• • •

Marie-Thérèse Guyon — she has asked me to call her only by her Christian name — was kindness itself, and not at all what I expected. How she smiled over Grandmère's letter of introduction, saying that I had introduced myself well enough and nothing could have surpassed such a spectacular and entertaining scene.

Papa spoke with Cadillac for a long while. Perhaps it is best, since we have come all this way. Lieutenant Saint-

Germain again offered his services to me through Papa. I should not have put my hands behind my back in the way that I did. Thank goodness he took no offense. I suppose he must think me a great coarse bumpkin, but if he does, I do not care.

No one has ever wanted to kiss my hand before.

• • •

A few days later, Lesharo lay awake on the floor of Marguerite's kitchen, his hands behind his head, watching stripes of sunlight brighten the deerskins that covered the insides of the shuttered windows. Robert had slipped away hours ago at dawn to meet Pierre at the Wendat village. It would be a long, grueling journey to the Miami village, and they had wanted as early a start as possible.

The night before, when Cécile and Marguerite were asleep in the bedroom they now shared, Robert had sat by the dying fire with Lesharo. He had said nothing at first, only smoked his pipe and stared thoughtfully at the flickering of the low flames.

"I trust you with her life," Robert had said finally.

"I will not betray your trust," Lesharo had assured him.

"I must be very frank. There will almost certainly be talk. Marguerite will likely be safe from rumors, since Pierre is well known here. They will marry, and the reality of it is that she holds less interest for them since she is an indien. Forgive me for that, but it is the truth."

"There is nothing to forgive. I know what they think of us."

"It is Cécile about whom they will gossip." Robert had examined the glowing bowl of his pipe and looked up. "And you."

"Why? Because I remain inside this house with her? I will never understand the ways of the French, Robert. In every longhouse outside this fort, many families live together. Married women, young girls and boys, the old, warriors. The earth lodges of my people were the same. What is wrong with it? If I must, I will sleep on the ground outside the door to spare her their gossip."

Robert had laughed softly and then his face had grown serious. "There is no need for that. She is white, Lesharo, and for the time being the only marriageable female here at Détroit. It is difficult for me to say that — to think that Cécile is no longer a child — but it is the truth."

"Nothing will happen to Cécile. Let the soldiers talk and let them look at her if they wish. Do not fear. I will not permit her to marry anyone."

Robert's eyes popped open, but then he saw that Lesharo was smiling and making a small jest, and so he smiled as well. "I trust you with her very life," he had repeated.

Lesharo heard the sounds of Cécile and Marguerite stirring in the tiny bedroom beyond the kitchen; the door opened and he stood. They breezed out and began seeing to breakfast, ordering him out of the way. Resigning himself to their burst of domesticity, Lesharo folded his blankets and put them and his pillow back into the chest from which they had been taken last night. Then he sat at the table in a chair that Cécile said was to be his place.

"I am to return to Marie-Thérèse's home this morning," said Cécile, after they had eaten. She sipped from her cup. There was no coffee in this household; rather they had brewed a hot drink made from roasted and finely ground indien corn. "It seems there are matters she wishes to discuss with me."

"I will walk there with you," said Lesharo. "Marguerite?"

"Yes. I will come along. This is a good house, but it is too fine a day to remain inside."

Leaving the kitchen in order, Marguerite and Lesharo donned capots and belted them with sashes. He considered his bow and quiver, then slung them over his shoulder and thrust his tomahawk through the sash.

Cécile did not question his actions. They were inside the fort and there was little chance of trouble, but she knew the seriousness with which he regarded his responsibility to them. She swept her cloak around her shoulders and they set out into the crisp morning.

The sun shone, and the wintry weather was again gone; all that remained was melting snow that

SISTER TO THE WOLF

dripped from the rooftops or slid with soft plops onto the streets. A flock of sparrows, pecking at grain that someone had carelessly spilled, wheeled off, peeping with irritation. Soldiers and civilian men eyed them curiously and a few bade them good morning, but they were left to make their way along the streets to Cadillac's house without incident. When Cécile pulled off her mittens and rapped on the door, they only waited a moment, their breath clouding around their faces, before it was opened by a small boy.

The child glared at them and made an evil face at Cécile. Then he said several very foul words and hissed, "Go away! You are not wanted here!" The door slammed in their faces.

Cécile was stunned, not believing that a child would ever say such things to her, but Lesharo was furious. He had been called many things during his slavery, but for the boy to have spoken to Cécile in such a manner was too much.

"He should be beaten," he said coldly. "My father would have sent me out to cut a switch with which to beat me had I ever spoken such things aloud to a woman."

The door opened again. Marie-Thérèse, her face red with embarrassment, her lips pressed into a thin white line, held the boy by the neck of his shirt and forced a smile. She tucked a loose strand of her honey-colored hair back up. "I see you have met our little Jacques. Say *bonjour* politely, my dearest.

Surely you can do that for your maman. And do apologize."

"Bonjour," he said and mumbled an apology. When she released him, he retreated into the room to where an older boy was slouched on a bench, pouting.

"Come in! Come in!" bubbled Marie-Thérèse, as though her son had not just been unspeakably rude.

"This is Mademoiselle Chesne, my dear boys. Cécile, I present my eldest son, Toine. Toine? Say something charming, *mon petit chou*."

Cécile, thinking that the boy did indeed hold about as much charm as a small cabbage, nodded when he grunted and then began to pick his nose with a vengeance.

"Oh! This must be Pierre's intended. Père del Halle," she called to the priest who was warming his ample haunches before her fire. "They tell me her name is Marguerite and she is to be your newest convert."

"Welcome, my child! Come and sit here by the fire and we shall talk. Call me Père Nicholas, if you will. Madame Cadillac enjoys formality and declines to do so, but Père del Halle reminds me of my old life in Québec. I will show you the way to God, but there is no harm in us being comfortable while I do so."

Marguerite gave Cécile a bemused glance and then did as Père Nicholas asked. Cécile and Lesharo followed Marie-Thérèse and her sons to another corner of the room. There was a small writing desk covered in neat stacks of papers and opened letters; several chairs with spindly legs stood around it. A few portraits hung on the plastered walls. She gestured Cécile to a chair, but she did not extend the same offer to Lesharo, who remained standing, his face unreadable.

Marie-Thérèse wasted no time. "I wish to hire your services, Cécile."

"To do what?" Cécile asked faintly. "I have no skills except those of keeping a house. I am to do that with Marguerite, and I cannot possibly keep two houses."

Marie-Thérèse waved away the notion. "Marguerite needs to learn to keep her own house here, as we all do, unless she is to have servants. And that is not likely. What I need from you is something of enormous significance. You read and write very well, my husband tells me."

"I am literate, certainly, but I am no scholar. I write letters sometimes and keep a journal for my own pleasure, and I keep my father's accounts."

"Excellent! Reading, writing *and* sums. You will be perfect."

"For what?"

Marie-Thérèse leaned forward, her hands on the desk and smiled. "For my sons' tutor."

"Tutor?" Cécile glanced at the boys, who were both sulking in a corner, the youngest with his thumb in his mouth. With their dark hair, thin faces and prominent noses, they both resembled their father greatly. She had a brief vision of Cadillac with his thumb in his mouth. She blinked hard and bit her lip. "A tutor?" Cécile gave a short laugh. "You want me to teach these little br — your little boys?"

Lesharo made a strange noise, and Cécile fought the urge to burst into laughter.

"Yes. Exactly. We all have a role to play at Détroit for the sake of the fort's success; we each have our place and this shall be yours. Otherwise, there is little point in your being here."

"No. I am sorry, but I cannot." Cécile rose to her feet, all traces of her amusement now gone. "My place, for the moment, is with Marguerite and Lesharo. My role is to assist with the successful running of her household. As to whether or not there is a point in my being here, I have great doubt that there is any at all now. Still, I intend to make the best of it. I appreciate that you must be very busy with the new baby, but I have other responsibilities and —"

"The baby died," Marie-Thérèse said flatly. "This is a terrible place, a horrible place to bear children. There are no midwives and, what is far worse, there are no wet nurses."

"The villages have midwives, and surely there are nursing mothers there," said Cécile softly, wishing very much that she could escape.

"You cannot seriously think that I would let my own child be put to the breast of one of those —"

Marie-Thérèse began haughtily, but then the cold disapproval in Cécile's eyes stopped her. "Enough! Enough!" she went on placatingly. "Mother's milk is not the topic I wished to discuss with you, after all. It is the tutoring of my sons. See here; I will pay you well."

"I am sorry for your loss," Cécile said stiffly. "However, it is still not possible for me to teach your sons and work alongside Marguerite. It is not a matter of the money. I think it is best that we leave now, Lesharo."

"How much?" asked Lesharo, leaning casually against the wall, his arms crossed over his chest. "I can help you with them, Cécile; I had a brother of my own once, a brother whose good behavior — he learned early to mind me — was the envy of many mothers in our village." His eyes fixed upon Marie-Thérèse. "My mother used to say that the strength of warriors passes to them not through their fathers but through the milk of their mothers. Is it so with the French?"

Marie-Thérèse's eyes narrowed at the touch of sarcasm in his voice, but she ignored him. She tapped her slippered foot on the floor and said, "I will pay Cécile twenty livres for the year."

Lesharo threw back his head and laughed heartily. "Twenty livres? I saw her pay thiry-one livres in Québec once for something that she wanted."

"Very well. I want your services," said Marie-Thérèse. "Thirty-one livres it is."

"And six deniers," Cécile said quietly, her eyes on Lesharo. "I paid thirty-one livres and six deniers for what I wanted that time."

"You drive a hard bargain but, yes, I will agree to it," said Marie-Thérèse, knowing she had made an excellent arrangement with this inexperienced girl.

"In coin," said Lesharo. "No card money."

Marie-Thérèse's brows lowered at that, but she reached into her pocket and counted out a handful of coins. "Here is one livre, then. You shall have the same amount every two weeks and the balance the same time next year. I would have Père del Halle — oh, very well, *mon père*, do not glare at me so. I would have Père Nicholas witness a contract, but I think none is necessary. I trust you with my children. Is this not exciting, my dears? Mademoiselle Chesne is to be your new teacher."

There was an unpleasant silence, punctuated by a great burp from Toine, and then he said, "We do not want a teacher."

"No! We do not want one," said Jacques, who had taken his thumb out of his mouth long enough to speak. Back in it went.

"We learn what we need to know from the voyageurs, the soldiers and from Papa," Toine added. "We do not want her."

"Well, you have her, and that is that!" shouted their mother. "You will remain upstairs in the attic today until you see the wisdom of my decision. Go. Now!" She turned to Cécile, who had stepped back to avoid the boys as they charged across the room and up the narrow stairs, screaming all the way. "You will begin tomorrow?"

They were rude little boys, spoiled and clearly impossible, but Cécile did not care for what she was seeing. The woman had lost a child. Did she not treasure the two that she still had alive? "Since I have accepted your money, I suppose that I will, but on my own terms. I will return after midday tomorrow."

"I will keep you and the success of this wonderful plan in my prayers tonight," said Marie-Thérèse.

"Merci," said Cécile. But she thought, I will need it.

Chapter 8

We went to mass this morning. Afterward, Père Nicholas said most bluntly that it is common knowledge Marie-Thérèse cannot instruct her sons herself, since she has no patience. It seems that Toine was spoiled and headstrong and bad enough before he left for Détroit with his father. Now he is impossible. Jacques worships his brother and so behaves in exactly the same fashion. Cadillac, though he loves them, has no time for anything but the affairs of the fort.

Poor Marguerite. She is to take her instruction each morning for an hour after mass. She is already extremely confused by what she is being told. Père Nicholas has given her a brass Jesuit ring that has begun to turn her finger green, and a rosary that she insists upon wearing around her neck. This amuses Lesharo no end. I have offered to teach her her prayers, so that she may use the rosary properly.

As for Toine and Jacques, I am certain I will manage them. Marguerite says I am mad to take on this work, even if Marie-Thérèse is paying well. I say, "Bah," as Grandmère would. They are only children, after all.

• • •

It was truly horrible. Neither boy could sit still for more than a minute. Toine had a loathing for books and writing. He could read reasonably well, but his little brother could not; nor could Jacques even write his name in a decent hand. Marie-Thérèse had a few books in her home; they and many other things not accounted for in Cadillac's reports, letters and inventories had been spirited to Détroit for her comfort and pleasure. The volumes, either religious works of great difficulty and seriousness, or romances — Cécile had examined several of those and snapped them shut, her cheeks flaming — were hardly suitable for children.

"Have you a blank ledger of some sort, Marie-Thérèse?" Cécile asked her thoughtfully.

"Several." She was just draping a cloak over her shoulders in preparation for visiting the only other French woman at the fort, Marie-Anne Picotte de Belestre, the wife of Tonti, Cadillac's second in command. "Use what you wish. Quills and ink are here and my penknife —" She stamped her foot and hissed, "Give that to me at once, Toine. It is a chair, not a carving stick." She snatched the knife from the boy, handed it to Cécile and then departed.

"This red one will be your practice book, Toine, and this green one will be yours, Jacques." Stung by the unexpected scolding and the loss of the penknife, Toine had tears in his eyes and Jacques's bottom lip was trembling. Wanting to fend off a bout of whining and weeping, she quickly said, "Please write your name and your age on the first page, Toine. Jacques, I will write yours and you shall copy it. That will be the end of our first lesson."

The boys looked at each other doubtfully. "Maman said we were to study hard," said Toine. "She said we were to read what you gave us."

"I can hardly read! And when I write, I hate it. The letters make no sense," wailed Jacques. "What am I to do? She will shout at me again."

"No one will shout at you unless you deserve it. You will learn to read in time," Cécile assured him, "but first we must go back to the house and get something."

"Your book?" asked Lesharo.

"You have written a book?" asked Jacques, wiping his running nose on his sleeve. "What is it about?"

"It is a story of great adventure," whispered Cécile in a conspiratorial tone. "I will read it to you and you shall see. First, though, you must write your names for me."

Toine labored over his script, the tip of his tongue poking out, and produced something blotched and smeared that Cécile could barely decipher.

"Antoine Cadillac. Eleven years old," he read to her. "It is my real name. I am only called Toine so as not to be confused with Papa."

"Jacques Cadillac. Eight years old," said his brother, beaming proudly at what he had messily copied as he repeated what Cécile had told him the words meant. "Will he learn as well?" All eyes went to Lesharo; he simply shrugged his shoulders.

"If he wishes to," Cécile said carefully. Lesharo had no use for such skills, here or where he was going, but she had no desire to embarrass him in front of these boys. "If he does, it will be in the evenings. This time is for you alone. Now get your capots and mittens, and we will walk to the house."

They had not been outside their own home for nearly a week before yesterday, Cécile learned. Then, they had been sent back inside by Père Nicholas for chasing the chickens. Perhaps that was the reason for their pasty complexions and their extreme rest-lessness. Children needed fresh air and exercise, and so, when they begged her to take the long way, Cécile agreed. They went past Tonti's house and Ste. Anne's Church and then west to the magasin.

There was another, smaller gate there and a party of what Lesharo said were Wendats coming in with furs to trade. Toine made a snowball. Before Cécile could stop him, he threw it and hit one of the warriors in the back of the head. The men whirled around to see who had done such a thing, their eyes ablaze with fury. When they saw it was Cadillac's son, one of them whispered something to the boy's victim. Brushing snow from his partially shaved head and scalp lock, the man followed his companions inside.

Cécile caught hold of Toine's hand and dragged him shrieking into the magasin. Lesharo picked up

Jacques, who was now making more noise than his brother, and flung him over his shoulder.

"You will be quiet!" Cécile ordered Jacques, when they were inside the building. Jacques, hearing a tone no one had ever used to him before, shut his mouth with an audible click. "And you, Toine! You will apologize."

Toine stuck out his tongue at her but nothing else came from his mouth. Lesharo, who had felt mild disapproval at the childish prank, went cold with anger. It was because of him that Cécile was to spend part of her day with these boys. It would be because of him that they treated her with respect. He dropped to one knee next to Toine, held him firmly by the upper arms and whispered to him. Toine went pastier than ever.

"You would not dare!" he said haughtily, but he could see that Lesharo, whose face had taken on a fierce expression, was quite serious.

"I would. Nothing could save you. Now repeat after me." He said a few words, glared at the boy and then nodded when Toine repeated them. The Wendats, unsmiling when he began, were making vain efforts not to laugh when he had finished. The recipient of the snowball said something in response, and then they all turned to their business.

"I had heard you were to tutor the boys, Mademoiselle. Was this their first lesson?" Lieutenant Saint-Germain was standing in the doorway and had witnessed the entire scene with delight. He gazed pointedly at Cécile's right hand with a small smile. Then he inclined his head to her and this time, when he moved to take her fingers and brush them with his lips, she did not pull away.

"It was not their first lesson but an important one, Monsieur," she said. "To show respect for all others is a lesson of which I believe their father and mine would approve."

"Mademoiselle, your father, in spite of the fact that he unwisely brought you all the way across New France, has my respect and admiration. I suspect that he will serve Sieur Cadillac effectively here at the fort."

"I brought myself across New France, Monsieur. My feet work quite properly. And it was not simply my father and I who journeyed; Lesharo was in our party as well," said Cécile.

"I see," Saint-Germain answered with a speculative look at Lesharo. "He was your pani, they tell me. You freed him. Why?"

Lesharo, disliking the fact that this officer was talking around him as if he were not present, broke in, "She did it out of kindness, and what she does for me now she does out of friendship."

"Friendship is a good way to begin," said the lieutenant smoothly. "May I offer you mine, Mademoiselle, along with my services? You are here on your own, I have learned."

"I am hardly alone, Monsieur," Cécile said as politely as she could, not wishing to offend him. "I have Marguerite and I have Lesharo, but I thank you for your consideration."

"Lieutenant Saint-Germain," said Jacques. "Toine wishes me to ask if you are going to hold Mademoiselle Chesne's hand all day."

Saint-Germain dropped her hand and gave the boys a withering look, which they met with mischievous smiles. "Bonjour, then, Mademoiselle. If there is anything you require, please do not hesitate to send for me." Yet another bow, and then into the magasin he went.

"That was dreadful," scolded Cécile once they were outside and walking down the street. "You are both very naughty."

"The officer looked as though he had picked up a hot cooking stone," said Lesharo thoughtfully. "And the bowing. It would make me dizzy."

Cécile began to laugh until she had to stop, bent in two holding herself around the waist. The boys smiled and laughed with her, not understanding the joke but eager to join in. They ran on ahead, shouting and skipping.

"What did you say to Toine inside the magasin?" asked Cécile when she could again speak.

"That if he did not show respect for you, the indiens here, and all other living things, that I would take him to the Wendat village clad only in a breechcloth and leave him there in the snow. I assured him that although I am a sauvage, as some say, I am an honest one."

"Why were the Wendat laughing?" She could feel her own laughter bubbling inside herself once more. "What did you make him repeat?"

"They found it amusing that the boy said he was not worthy to lick their moccasins, but would do so if they wished."

"That is terrible, Lesharo," Cécile whispered, but her mouth was twitching. "If Marie-Thérèse learns about it she will faint!"

"Perhaps, but I think he will not throw snow at a warrior again."

The boys ran back to them and resumed their chattering, naming the streets and explaining who lived in each house. Although Toine kept his brother between Lesharo and himself, there was no other sign that only minutes before he had been terrified of him. Eventually, he abandoned even that, and caught hold of Lesharo's hand to pull him outside the fort to show him something. They went all around to the east side of the palisade to where a building stood close to the wall.

"It is the big barn," Toine said. "There is another small barn inside where the chickens and some crates are kept, but this barn is our favorite. Come inside."

Two young oxen stood each in separate stalls, placid and liquid eyed. One lowed when they entered, but when Toine approached them, they backed away. The cat that lay on her side on a pile of rags nursing her kittens growled and then hissed.

"They do not seem to like people in here," said Cécile. "Let us leave them alone. Come now."

"They like people," piped up Jacques. "They like me if I come here by myself. It is Toine they hate. He screams and shouts to frighten them, and he chases the kittens."

"You lie! I will tell Papa that it was you who put the dead mouse in the holy water font at the church."

"You made me!" screeched Jacques, bursting into tears. "He poked me with a stick until I did it."

The kittens scattered, the cat stood her ground, back arched and spitting, the oxen pressed against the backs of their stalls and above it all the boys kept screaming. Cécile held herself very still. She said nothing, only waited until the boys' weeping had ended and the animals had quieted. Then she said, "A dead mouse? I trust you found it and did not kill it yourself, but the manner in which you have treated these creatures sickens me. Do not deny it! They cannot speak and yet they tell me how dreadful you have been with them. I despise cruelty. Anyone who hurts something so helpless is worse than an animal. You know the way. Go home and take this to your mother. I do not want it." She took the coins from her pocket where she had put them, threw them to the barn's floor and stormed out. Lesharo turned on them.

"You called her foul names yesterday and there was no punishment for you. Still she was good enough to set aside her pride, forgive your disrespect and agree to be your teacher," he said stonily. He paused, his eyes on Cécile, who was walking as quickly as she could. He added, "Now you again distress her. Go to your mother and do not come anywhere near Cécile. What I said to the Wendat? It was in jest. If you disturb her again, I promise I will punish you for it. Stay far away from her."

"Wait," said Toine when Lesharo began to leave. "Please!"

"Go back to your mother," repeated Lesharo. The boys had to run to keep up to his long, fast strides. "I have no time for you."

"We cannot," whispered Toine, close to tears again. "We must not."

"We sneaked out of our bed last night and listened to them argue in the kitchen," Jacques confessed. "They did not hear us."

"Papa said that we are to return to Québec, that it was an error for us to have come here," said Toine listlessly. "The affairs of the fort occupy him, and since Maman cannot make us behave, the priests back home surely will. Maman said that there would be no more problems with us in the hands of Mademoiselle Chesne." He sniffled and wiped his nose on the hem of his shirt. "If she will not teach us then I know we will be sent away."

Lesharo sighed as they entered the fort through the water gate, some distance behind Cécile. "You blame it upon her? You would be sent away because your behavior is shameful. Your father is the chieftain here, and you could grow to be warriors." He shook his head doubtfully. "You act like children."

"We are children!" sobbed Jacques. "But we do not want to go away."

"Cease this crying," said Lesharo rather reluctantly. "Come with me."

Back at Pierre's house, he made them knock and then stand quietly until he had called Cécile to the door. Marguerite, her expression curious, stood behind her listening.

"These boys have words for you," said Lesharo.

"We are sorry," said Toine.

"We are very sorry," said Jacques from around his thumb.

"They are selfish boys," Lesharo explained. "They apologize only because they know that if they misbehave for you they will be sent back to Québec by their father." Cécile's eyes met Lesharo's and he nodded. "They think only of themselves, but I myself believe that perhaps they could learn to think of others. If not, there is always the Wendat camp."

"You said that was a joke," said Jacques fearfully.

"I have changed my mind."

Toine held out his hand. In it were the coins Cécile had thrown to the stable floor. "This is yours, Mademoiselle Chesne. Please do not send us home."

"I will give you one more chance," said Cécile, accepting the coins. "You will behave and work hard for me. One chance only. Do you understand?"

"Yes, Mademoiselle," they said in unison.

"Very well, then," said Cécile, knowing she had made a terrible mistake. "Come inside and wash your faces."

Chapter 9

A few days later, Cécile and Marguerite attended mass at Ste. Anne's on Sunday. Lesharo again refused to enter the church, and Cécile, knowing his strong feelings, did not press him. He waited outside, pacing restlessly back and forth while the sounds of the mass, the strange prayers and songs flowed out of the building and over him like an unpleasant, tainting smoke.

Inside, Father Nicholas's voice muttered on in Latin. The church smelled of incense and damp wool; the closeness of the crowd was beginning to make Cécile's head throb. She had confessed her sins the day before, and so she would take communion. Lightheaded now, she had fasted since midnight as was necessary to receive the sacrament. It had been months since she had done so, but neither food nor water could pass her lips before she received the sacred host. Her stomach rumbled loudly in complaint. She looked up from her prayers to see Lieutenant Saint-Germain's eyes on her, a smile on his lips. Cécile dropped her own eyes to her rosary and left them there.

Outside the church after mass, Marie-Thérèse caught Cécile's hand and pulled her away. "Cécile, you have not yet met Marie-Anne Picotte de Belestre and her husband, *Capitaine* Alphonse de Tonti. My friends, this is Cécile Chesne."

Cécile curtsied. "Bonjour," she murmured politely.

"Ah. So this is the girl who defies all convention and for whom you have made the exception, Antoine," said Tonti silkily, looking her up and down. He was tall and thin with long dark hair that he wore swept back off of his forehead. "Keep your pani — oh, my; it actually does offend you, I see. You were serious about this, Marie-Thérèse. How truly remarkable. Rather, then, keep your sauvage under close rein, Mademoiselle. There are no other sauvages within the fort at night, and so if there are problems, I will assume he is to blame. That would unfortunately implicate you, as you see."

"You will have no trouble from me," Lesharo said softly, but his hand was resting on his hip, very close to his knife. "And Cécile need not concern you."

Tonti frowned, the smile disappearing from his lips. His eyes drifted over Lesharo. "Did I address you? I do not recall doing so. Take care, sauvage, and stay out of my way." With a bored sigh, he turned to Cadillac. "This is tiresome, Antoine. You have let this sauvage quite spoil my Sunday. Only beating you soundly will improve my humor. Will you join me?" He tapped the hilt of his sword. "An hour of practice before I hunt?"

"Certainly, Alphonse." Like Tonti, he had a rapier belted at his waist. "Outside the fort, though. If Père Nicholas catches us at it on a Sunday, our penance will be horrible."

"My dear," said Marie-Anne, as the two men strode away with Toine and Jacques following at their heels like puppies. A small woman, as fair as her husband was dark, she embraced Cécile and kissed her lightly on both cheeks. "Do call me Marie-Anne and dispense with formality, for now we are three females here, though if Marie-Thérèse's suspicions are correct, we are actually four."

"I am once again with child, you see, Cécile, and I am certain I carry a girl," Marie-Thérèse explained. "You must pray for me that this child lives."

"Madame." It was Lieutenant Saint-Germain. "May I offer my congratulations? Your husband shared the happy news with me only yesterday."

"Merci." Marie-Thérèse blushed prettily.

"And Mademoiselle Chesne, may I have the pleasure of your company this fine morning? I will walk you to Pierre Roy's home, if you will permit me."

Lesharo had been waiting patiently. Cécile had given him a brilliant smile when she came out of the church, but Tonti's words, which had not surprised him, had reduced Cécile to stunned silence. Cadillac's wife had then captured her, and now this officer was leaning over her like a fox over a rabbit. I will see her to the house, Lesharo wanted to say, but he did not. Instead, with a few quick steps he placed himself close to Cécile.

"I also offer my congratulations, Marie-Thérèse," she said quietly. "I will certainly pray for you and the child." Then to Saint-Germain, "Lieutenant, I have an escort, as you well see. I am under the protection of Lesharo, but I do thank you. And Marie-Anne, you cannot count, for Marguerite is quite obviously female as well."

Saint-Germain's eyes fixed upon Lesharo, but it was Marie-Anne who spoke. "Ah, yes. Pierre's intended. But excuse me, Cécile — the matter of your sauvage? I wonder at such an arrangement."

"I do not." With the utmost patience, Cécile took a deep breath. "Must I repeat it yet again? There is no question of ownership here. Lesharo is my companion and remains with me not only out of friendship, but because my father has asked him to do so. You would not have me disobey my father, would you?"

"I, well, of course not!" stuttered Marie-Anne. "You must naturally heed your father's wishes in all things."

"I knew you would understand," said Cécile with a smile that she did not feel at all. "Come, you two." She linked her arm with Marguerite's. "I am nearly starving."

"What is it the whites say?" Lesharo asked. "Wait! I recall it now. Your servant, Mademoiselle Chesne."

Saint-Germain laughed, the corners of his eyes crinkling. "Her servant, is it? *Touché*, Lesharo." He turned again to Cécile and said, "This is a small place, Mademoiselle. It will not be possible for you to avoid me forever." He bowed and strolled off, as though not a bit of it mattered to him.

The two older women watched them all walk away through the crowd of soldiers and other men, a scowl of displeasure on Marie-Anne's face, a far more shrewd expression on Marie-Thérèse's.

"We definitely have our work set out here, Marie-Anne," said Marie-Thérèse. "She holds great promise."

"Indeed, but her manners and the company she keeps leave something to be desired, I must say. You said she was a lovely creature and she is, but 'unfinished' and 'naive' barely describe her. She has no sense of discretion at all. That direct manner would put off any man, yet if she could ever learn to flirt properly and to lead one on, then it would be a different matter. And her clothing! She looks as though she does not have two deniers to her name!"

"She has property back in Québec and a decent dowry, if what my husband tells me is correct, my dear. I will admit she is a bit unschooled in the finer womanly skills, but that may all be remedied. As for the clothing, leave that to me. When I am finished with her she will be a wonderful match."

"For whom?" whispered Marie-Anne, but Cadillac's wife was focused upon Lieutenant Saint-Germain, who stood engaged in conversation with several soldiers. "Clever, Marie-Thérèse; very clever.

There is the distasteful matter of *his* background, though. Would he even be interested? He has resigned his commission, so it is only a matter of time before he leaves here. And what will Cécile ever think when she learns of his past?"

"It will take forever for the king to give his permission, if indeed he does. It could be months. Years! If Edmond is not interested now, he will be by the time we are finished with her, I assure you," Marie-Thérèse promised. "As for Edmond's background, I believe he prefers to pretend that it never happened. I have only once heard him discuss it with Antoine, and that was only because my husband wished to make certain he was suited to being here surrounded by all these sauvages. I hardly think that any of the soldiers are likely to take Cécile aside and reveal *that* scandal to her. No, she will suspect nothing."

"Is it true about his skin?" Marie-Anne leaned close and whispered. "They say it is dreadful."

"Please! I do not even wish to think about that," Marie-Thérèse replied with a small shiver of revulsion. "Now, come along back to my house. Cécile and I are close enough in size, and I certainly will not be wearing tightly fitted gowns for a while. I will sacrifice several to the cause."

"An excellent idea," said Marie-Anne with satisfaction, toying with a curl of her hair. "What fun this will be! This place is so boring; it will be a perfect diversion. A fall wedding, perhaps, do you think?"

"Time will tell," said Marie-Thérèse slyly. "Time will tell."

• • •

The day passed peacefully enough. A letter arrived from Cécile's grandmother. The winter had been long and cold at Québec, it seemed, and Soeur Adele had suffered from a lingering cough. They were in her prayers each day, and she hoped that they were returning the favor.

"And that I continue to sit up straight," laughed Cécile with a niggling touch of worry. Her grandmother was strong in spite of her age, and it was spring after all. Surely the cough would have disappeared by now, she thought that evening as she wrote back.

For the next weeks, Cécile spent each afternoon with Cadillac's sons, and life fell into a pattern of sorts. If the boys' behavior did not improve entirely, at least it was no worse. In Cécile's presence, they restrained their tantrums and boorish manners; a single glare from Lesharo saw to that any time they considered misbehaving. They were not really bad children, Cécile came to see; they had simply sought their father's attention in the only way they knew. Cadillac had no admiration for gentleness and re-straint; he was a loud, active man whose aggres-siveness was well known. Little wonder Toine tried to emulate him, and Jacques, of course, worked hard to adopt each of his brother's unpleasant habits.

"Sieur Cadillac says that the little fellows are becoming somewhat more manageable," Lieutenant Saint-Germain tactfully observed one morning after mass, out of the hearing of Marie-Thérèse. "I believe I can see it for myself; not once did I hear their mother's scolding. What have you done to them, Mademoiselle?"

"Nothing, really," Cécile admitted, although she was secretly pleased by his praise. "They needed order in their lives and things to keep them busy. Sitting still all day? No boy does that very well. We take long walks in the woods or by the river to tire them out each afternoon, and they are rather easier for her to control."

At first, it was Cécile who was exhausted after struggling with the boys. Lesharo, with his endless patience, was a great help. He made small bows and arrows for Toine and Jacques and showed them how to shoot.

"The trunks of trees will be your targets for now," he told them. "Yes, we will hunt in time, but not until your skill improves."

Afterwards, the boys having returned to their mother, Lesharo's quiet manner and gentle humor soothed her. They would sit each evening and he would tell her stories, tales that Cécile was writing into one of Marie-Thérèse's ledgers — one that was a lovely blue the color of a robin's egg — for Toine and Jacques to read, since she had decided against allowing them to handle her own journal. She would look up from the page to see him staring off at nothing as he spoke, his face filled with loss that the bittersweet memories of his childhood brought back to him. There was longing there as well, and it tore at her, for Cécile knew that he would leave when her father returned.

The two men who represented the Company, Monsieur Arnault and Monsieur Radisson, kept strictly to themselves, and Cécile saw them only at mass. Both angular and bookish in appearance, they would scuttle away to the house they shared to pore over accounts and write reports. It was clear that Cadillac disliked them. When Cécile occasionally saw Tonti, he was markedly polite to her but ignored Lesharo. Tonti's wife, on the other hand, was often at the Cadillac home when they arrived. She and Marie-Thérèse would sip chocolate and gossip lazily, while Cécile tried to disregard their cloying voices and shrill laugher.

One afternoon, she and Lesharo were just preparing to leave after their walk with the boys. The children were pink with exertion; their noses were running as usual and their hair was standing on end from the knitted caps they had pulled from their heads. Smiling at their happy chatter, Cécile suddenly realized that she had not had to be cross with them for quite a while.

"We made people from the snow, Maman! There is still snow in the forest," called Jacques to his mother. "Cécile said mine was the tallest."

"And mine was the fiercest. Was it not the fiercest, Lesharo?" asked Toine.

"It was. No Pawnee warrior could be fiercer," Lesharo agreed. "The sight of it struck fear into my heart." He clapped a hand to his chest and staggered back as though he would fall, and the boys shrieked with laughter.

Marie-Thérèse's brows drew together and her eyes narrowed. Cécile, who now read the older woman easily, knew that a reprimand would come. Yes, she will scold them, she thought. She will complain about water on the floor or wet mittens used instead of handkerchiefs, and the day will be ruined. I have no wish to witness it.

"We must be on our way, Lesharo. I have promised to help Marguerite with baking bread," she began, "and I must finish another letter that I am writing to my grandmother so that the men who are leaving for Québec tomorrow may take it with them. She has not been well, Marie-Thérèse. I must not neglect her."

"Wait, Cécile," Marie-Thérèse said. "Lesharo, would you excuse us? It is a female matter."

He was not certain what a female matter entailed. He understood the importance of the traditions and secrets of indien women, and why they would shut themselves away from the men for a time each month in a special longhouse. He had never seen Cécile do such a thing, but the customs of the whites were different and he did not wish to interfere.

"I will wait outside, Cécile," Lesharo said quickly and withdrew from them, flustered and a bit embarrassed.

Cécile was not pleased. What could Marie-Thérèse want that could be so important?

"There!" said Marie-Thérèse when the boys had been banished to the second floor and the door had closed on Lesharo. "Any matter between women is a female matter, my dear. Will you have a glass of wine with me, Cécile?"

"Thank you, but no."

"Well, then, I will get to it. Would you take an early supper with us tomorrow evening? Antoine and the Tontis and myself. A small gathering, my dear; it will do you and us good."

"That is all?" Cécile asked suspiciously. "That is all you want?"

"What more could I possibly want?" said Marie-Thérèse with a slow smile.

• • •

The invitation was not, naturally, extended to Lesharo or to Marguerite. I should not have been surprised, the Cadillacs and the Tontis being who they are.

I suspect Lesharo and Marguerite will have a pleasant enough evening. I cannot say what will happen to me.

• • •

"What do you mean there are to be no lessons?" Cécile stood outside Cadillac's house, her hands on her hips. She had arrived quite late today, household work having kept her.

"Maman says that Lesharo is to take us out into the woods instead," explained Toine. "She wants to see you, though, Cécile."

"If there is still snow, let us make snow people and shoot them with arrows!" shouted Jacques, waving his bow above his head.

"There will be no walk, nor any snow people, and definitely no shooting," Cécile countered. "Lesharo does not work for your maman. I do."

"It is only so that we may talk for a while," said Marie-Thérèse cheerfully. She had opened the door and stood there smiling. "An hour or two. Where is the harm in that?"

"It is I who am the tutor, not Lesharo," Cécile reminded her. "Lesharo has work he would much rather be doing at the house if he is not to keep me company here."

"I will pay him for his time," said Marie-Thérèse quickly.

"I do not want your coins." Lesharo's face was blank. "Come with me then, Jacques and Toine. You will practice with your bows if you wish, but the snow people will remain undamaged. I will return when the sun has gone down to the tops of the trees, Cécile," he tossed over his shoulder as he followed the excited boys.

Inside the house, Marie-Anne was standing at the fireplace. "Cécile!" she gushed. "Just the girl I hoped to see this afternoon. Are you ready for our little supper?"

"I suppose so," Cécile faltered. "I think I will bring a good appetite."

"Is she not amusing?" laughed Marie-Anne, clutching at her sides. "Do not make me laugh so, Cécile. I will burst my corset!"

"What she means, my dear, is have you prepared your *toilette*?" Not surprised to see Cécile's confusion, she went on smoothly, "Your toilette! Your gown and perfumes, your slippers, and an appropriate manner in which to dress your hair."

Cécile touched a hand to her long thick braid. "I have no gown and as for my hair, I know of no other way to dress it than this, unless I leave it unbraided or tied back with a thong. I do not own any perfumes. As for slippers —" All of them looked down at her well-worn moccasins.

"Precisely!" said Marie-Thérèse. "Which is why you must come with us."

With Marie-Anne leading the way, Cécile was marched through a doorway into one of the bedrooms. It was the one Marie-Thérèse shared with her husband, she quickly realized as the door shut behind her. She stared at the walnut bed with its fine canopy and curtains of white serge bordered with yellow silk ribbon. In her mind's eye she saw the low narrow bed she shared with Marguerite, one Pierre had made himself. Then came the image of Lesharo asleep on the kitchen floor, a plain blanket over him. A tiny flame of irritation lit within her.

"*Voila!*" cried Marie-Anne, gesturing toward a copper tub that stood in the center of the floor, wisps of scented steam rising from it.

"What is this?" asked Cécile uneasily.

"Can it truly be?" whispered Marie-Anne. "Has she never seen a bath before?"

"Of course I have seen a bath," Cécile snapped. "I meant only to ask why it is here."

"So that you may bathe, of course!" laughed Marie-Thérèse. "This is my bath, and I will tell you that it was not listed on any of Antoine's tiresome inventories, nor will it be." She sniffed. "It was one of my conditions if I was to come out here, that I have my bath, even if I chose not to use it. I would wager you have not bathed properly in months. Who does when it is so cold? Come now, Cécile, you would not wish to put this gown on over dirty skin, would you?" Marie-Anne was holding up a skirt and a bodice of pale green wool. "There are slippers that match and a lovely chemise all trimmed with lace."

"No, thank you," said Cécile, furious with herself at the blushing she was unable to control. "My own clothing is not new, but it is clean and so am I. Please let me pass, Marie-Thérèse."

"I will do no such thing, Cécile Chesne. We will leave you here and you may bathe in privacy. Then we will help you dress, arrange your hair and voila! You will be beautiful."

"No, thank you," repeated Cécile. "My own clothing will suffice, and if it does not, then I think I will decline your invitation to supper."

"This *is* your clothing now," argued Marie-Thérèse. "I am giving it to you as a gift. I am too big for it with this child inside me and will remain so for a good while after the baby comes. See reason. You must dress properly as we two do and set a proper standard."

"Only try them on, Cécile, and if you do not care for the garments, then certainly wear your old things," urged Marie-Anne.

"I need only try them?" she asked.

"Yes, but first a bath. Come along, Marie-Anne; let us leave her to it." And the women retired to an adjoining room — one Cécile supposed was the boys' — closing the door behind them.

She had seen a bath just once in the house of a wealthy Québec matron to whose back door her mother had delivered eggs. It had stood empty in the kitchen, the copper gleaming. Cécile, who had been only six, had wondered what it would be like to immerse herself in hot water like a cooking chicken.

I can find out if I get into it, she thought. What harm would it do? And I need only try on the clothing; there is nothing wrong in that. She reached down and put her fingers into the water. It was very hot. She cupped some in her hands and let it run out between her fingers. It would be wonderful to wash her hair in it.

In moments her clothing was on the floor, and she was carefully stepping into the bath. The hot water stung at first when she lowered herself, breathing in shallow gasps as it crept up over her body. Cécile held herself still for a long while, her eyes closed, tiny beads of perspiration popping out on her upper lip. She moaned with contentment, with the sheer pleasure of being entirely warm all over. When the water cooled enough for her to move, she slowly sat up and reached for a cake of soap. It was not the harsh, homemade lye soap she used for cleaning, or even the better Marseilles soap that she had for bathing. This was unlike anything she had ever seen, frothing up creamy and slick on her hands. Cécile washed thoroughly and then wet and washed her hair.

When it was rinsed, she leaned back in the water. Marie-Thérèse could do this every day if she wished. Not that she would; such excessive bathing would cause her to become ill or perhaps even to die. Oddly, the indiens did not believe that to be so. The men used sweat lodges to cleanse themselves, and they all swam in the hot weather. Cécile herself had swum in the summer, alone with the women. But this! It was wonderful, and not at all like swimming in a lake or cold river.

"Are you quite finished, Cécile?" called Marie-Thérèse. "You will be cooked red like a boiled crayfish, and that would be a truly horrible sight. We will not come in, you modest creature. Use the linen sheet I have left for you on the chair to dry yourself, and call when you are ready."

Grudgingly, Cécile rose from the bath, shivering as the cold air hit her skin. She rubbed herself briskly with the sheet, toweled her hair and then pulled the fresh chemise over her head. How fine and soft the fabric was. She tied her linen pockets around her waist, suddenly aware of how shabby they were.

"I am finished," she called nervously, not entirely at ease with having them see her in only a chemise.

"Come to the fire," Marie-Thérèse ordered as she hurried across the room. "Another sheet, Marie-Anne, so that we may dry this glorious hair thoroughly. And a shawl, since we do not want to see her take a chill." She rubbed the linen briskly over Cécile's scalp, and then combed and fluffed her hair until Cécile felt that she might fall asleep. It was so soothing. Her eyes closed; when she opened them, Marie-Anne was standing in front of her studying her critically.

"Do you think she needs it?"

"Of course she needs it. The girl will have a waist as thick as a cow if it is not properly trained. On your feet, Cécile," commanded Marie-Thérèse.

"Oh no!" said Cécile holding up both her hands to fend off the horror that Marie-Anne was holding.

"I will not wear a corset. They are far too uncomfortable."

"Nonsense. All ladies wear corsets, and if you are to be a lady, you must learn to ignore discomfort. I will not lace it tightly, and besides, you must wear it if the bodice is to fit correctly," Marie-Thérèse explained.

A few minutes later Cécile said weakly, "I cannot breathe."

"Of course you can breathe, silly girl. If you could not breathe you would not be talking."

"Marie-Thérèse," said Cécile in a small voice. "If you do not loosen this thing, I will cut the strings. I have a clasp knife in my pocket. I vow I will do so."

"You are exasperating, Cécile, but yes, I will loosen it."

"More!"

"And you are hopeless. Look how small your waist is, even with it laced very loosely. Put on the stockings. They are lovely ones of silk."

"I cannot."

"Why ever not?" asked Marie-Thérèse impatiently.

"Because I cannot bend!" wailed Cécile.

The two women helped her into the stockings. They tied ribbon garters at her knees to keep the fabric from slipping down and slid the shoes of thin leather onto her feet.

"They pinch my toes," Cécile complained. "I cannot walk in these heels. They are far too high!"

"High! They are scarcely fashionable. And as for the fit, that is because of those *things* you persist in wearing. You will have feet like a duck if you do not begin to wear proper shoes," said Marie-Thérèse.

They helped her step into the skirt, eased her arms into the tight sleeves of the bodice and laced it closed, ignoring her glares. She said nothing as they led her to a chair and told her to sit. Unable to bend at the waist, Cécile perched, her back rigid, while they combed out her hair and pinned it up.

"A few tendrils hanging here and here. Perfect," Marie-Anne declared. "Now, Cécile, walk across the room for us."

"She said walk, not stride as though you are forcing your way through the bushes after some animal you have shot for your dinner!" cried Marie-Thérèse. "Do not swing your arms so!"

"You may help me out of this; I have had quite enough," said Cécile resolutely. "I have things to which I must attend before your supper."

"More nonsense," laughed Marie-Thérèse. "They will keep. Besides, can you not hear my guests arriving?"

It was true. How long had they been at this?

"What of the boys?"

There was a wild thundering as Jacques and Toine raced into the outer room and began pounding on the door. With an impatient sigh, their mother let them in. "We will go out first. Give us a few moments, Cécile, and then make your grand entrance. Hold up your skirts and walk gracefully, if you possibly can."

Cécile waited until the two women had shut the door behind them. The boys had said nothing at all since they had come in; they had only stared at her, their mouths open.

"Do I look so dreadful?" she asked them, uncertainty in her voice. Jacques was sucking his thumb — something he rarely did these days — and Toine would not meet her eyes. "What is wrong?"

"Will you be like Maman now?" Toine asked in a small voice. "You will. I know it."

"I know it too, Toine," mumbled Jacques from around his thumb. "No more walks in the forest. Too bad. It looks as though we will not ever shoot the snow people now."

"That is ridiculous," laughed Cécile. "Of course we will all walk in the forest. Not with me in this clothing, naturally." Then she frowned. "Where is Lesharo?"

"Papa sent him to Pierre's home. Lesharo wanted to wait for you, but Capitaine Tonti said he was not to be hanging about outside our house," said Toine. "There is a guard posted outside to make certain he obeys and stays away."

"We did not like that," Jacques added sulkily. "We wanted to stay away, too."

Furious, she pulled open the door and stepped out of the room, watching her feet so that she would not tumble down and disgrace herself. Although, if I do, she thought grimly, at least they will never invite me again. The boys, knowing full well how angry she was, followed a safe distance behind. So closely was she concentrating, that she did not notice how still the room had become. Marie-Thérèse and Marie-Anne were both smiling in satisfaction. The eyebrows of Cadillac and Tonti had shot up rather astoundingly.

"You have grown up all in an instant, Mademoiselle," said Edmond Saint-Germain with a small smile.

A rosy flush rose up her chest and neck and into her cheeks. "Grown up, because of a gown, Lieutenant Saint-Germain? Then I suppose I will have to revert to childhood once again. Excuse me, please. I must go back and change into my own clothing."

"Why would you do that?" he asked, his face quite serious. "You look magnificent. Besides, I believe a guard has been posted at the doorway to match the one that watches outside."

"So it has." Marie-Anne was standing there, determinedly blocking her escape. Cécile sighed. "I had no idea you would be here, Monsieur," she said awkwardly. The other men had been led away by Marie-Thérèse, wine was being poured and the conversation was suddenly loud.

"Nor I you," said Saint-Germain. "I suspect someone has been plotting."

"To what end?"

"To bring us together, Mademoiselle." Saint-Germain watched her expression change rapidly as what he had said finally became clear. By heaven, she was like nothing he had seen here since arriving from Montréal. She was lovely, yes, but there was more to her, far more than fine skin and those pretty eyes. She had spirit, and if Cadillac's and Tonti's interfering wives thought to restrain that spirit within the confines of the corset she obviously now wore, they would have little success.

"No," she said in a low angry tone.

"No to what, Mademoiselle?" He smiled, the question hanging between them.

"I have no intention of being a pawn in their game."

"You are no pawn, Mademoiselle Chesne."

"Are you?"

"A Saint-Germain as a pawn? How droll. Not a king certainly, but a knight? Yes, a knight would do nicely."

"Then I shall be a knight as well."

He stopped smiling then. "Not a queen? No. I suppose not, but perhaps a Ste. Jeanne d'Arc would be better."

"It suits. Jeanne is my middle name, after all; it was my mother's name as well. I will need a sword and banner, of course, Monsieur."

Saint-Germain tilted his head to one side. "What an image. Would you crop your hair?"

"And wear a suit of armor and be burned alive at the stake for what I believed and cared about, if I must. But not for this foolishness."

"Will you two share what you are whispering about?" asked Marie-Thérèse as she began to cross the room.

"White or black pieces? What shall we be?" Saint-Germain asked Cécile quickly.

"White." She tried to keep her face serious, but she could not help smiling at his clever allusions to chess and Ste. Jeanne d'Arc, the patron saint of soldiers.

"Then our dear ladies are black. Ah, Madame, how lovely you are this evening," said Saint-Germain, skillfully steering her away from Cécile. All during the meal he kept up a gentle interference, politely interrupting conversations, turning aside curious questions, shielding her from their probing. He was of the upper class, the son of a minor noble, she learned, and for that alone she might have dismissed him, but he had an honesty that she liked. And she found that he made her smile. In time, though, as the evening went on, even that charm wore thin. She was tired, and the corset was digging into her ribs and belly.

"The meal was excellent," said Cécile as she pushed back her chair and stood. "I thank you for inviting me, but I fear I must return home. I have household responsibilities as you surely know. I must be up early to see to them."

"Always work," Marie-Anne sighed. "Servants would make it easier, certainly. I would look for an *indien* woman to help me here, but I am not certain one could be trained to run a French household properly."

"Marguerite manages," Cécile said coolly. "She has no difficulty at all."

"But surely her standards are not the same as ours," laughed Marie-Anne. "Having lived only in a longhouse or whatever her people inhabit, you see."

"What an odd notion," said Saint-Germain airily. He twirled his wineglass by its stem and admired the liquid ruby of the wine through the candlelight. "I found the standards kept within a longhouse to be quite high when I lived in one."

"Really. When was that?" asked Cécile. Her irritation at what had been said was instantly replaced by curiosity.

"None of that dreariness and past history," Marie-Thérèse quickly interrupted. "Please. Let us end the evening pleasantly. If you must leave, Lieutenant Saint-Germain will see you home when you are ready. Say your goodnights to Cécile, my sons."

Cécile kissed each of the boys on their cheek. This they suffered with eyes rolling, making small gagging noises, but the way Jacques threw his arms around her neck for a hug told her it was the sham she knew it to be.

"I should change from these garments," Cécile said fingering the skirt's fine cloth. "The shoes will be ruined if I walk out in the streets in them."

"I have others for you, and you may get your old clothing tomorrow when you return for the boys' lessons," said Marie-Thérèse.

"May I escort you, Mademoiselle?" asked Saint-Germain with a small bow. He took his cloak from where it was hanging on a peg.

"I suppose so." I have no more energy for arguing, thought Cécile. A few minutes and I will be rid of him.

Cécile could barely wait for the door to close behind them. She walked past the guard, peering through the darkness for Lesharo, but she could not see him. It was very cool now, and though there was no wind, she was immediately chilled in spite of the anger that blazed through her. Saint-Germain draped the cloak over her shoulders without asking her leave.

"I have no intention of giving you the opportunity to refuse it. Here." He gave her his mittens. They were too large, but they would keep her fingers warm. Then he offered her his arm.

Cécile hesitated. It was a formality only — a gesture of deference, she reminded herself — but no man had ever made that gesture to her. She took his arm and he led her down the street.

"Lieutenant," she began.

"Edmond. My name is Edmond, and you would do me a great honor if you would use it."

"Very well. Edmond."

"May I address you as Cécile, Mademoiselle?"

"Of course. Even the boys do now," she said, her voice filled with exasperation. "Among people such as us, life is not very formal. What would be the point?"

"To be respectful and civilized is the point."

Cécile stopped abruptly and pulled away from him. "Respectfulness I can surely accept, but if being civilized is what I saw tonight then I find nothing to admire in it. She had the entire evening planned, from the way they tricked me into this ridiculous clothing to inviting you and to making certain that you saw me home."

"Take my arm again, if you please. You can be just as angry while you are walking and you will not be as cold." Cécile did as he asked, but only because her teeth were chattering. "Marie-Thérèse and Tonti's wife are devious — I will give you that — but they are also simply bored. You are a novel and brief entertainment, as am I. They think they understand strategy, but they forget, Cécile, that I am an officer and so by nature a strategist. They cannot outwit me." They were at the door of Pierre's house. Edmond released her, but then bent over her hand. "I think they cannot outwit you, either. Obviously you play chess, Cécile."

"Yes, but not well. Papa has a set of pieces that he made as a boy. He played with Maman, and we two play now and again."

"Might we play some time? You are like an open book, Cécile, and therefore your strategies are there for anyone to see. The entire world can read you and see exactly what you think. Chess might help you learn to veil those thoughts."

"I have no intention of trying to hide my displeasure or my opinions. Their thoughtlessness is unforgivable."

He sighed. "Your friend Lesharo. Is that it? I shall be candid. His treatment is really not very much different than any other indien receives here. There is trade with them, yes, but do you truly think anything other than that is wise or even safe for the French? The indiens are not like us, Cécile. Do you really imagine he would have been at ease at Marie-Thérèse's supper? Hardly. I have spent enough time among them to know that."

"I have lived among them, Edmond. Lived. Not passed time." She handed him back his cloak and mittens.

"As have I, Cécile. For three years I lived with the Mohawks."

For what reason would this man ever have lived among the Mohawks? Cécile wondered. Why would he ever willingly do such a thing? Then she understood. "As a prisoner," she said softly. "You were taken in war."

Edmond nodded. "It was before the Great Peace was signed. I was young and inexperienced, and I suppose that I thought I understood the indiens very well. What were they compared to armed French regulars and militia, after all?" He lapsed into silence yet again, his thoughts on the past, and when he once more began to speak, it was in a dreamy voice. "They took only me alive. All the rest were killed. At first, I did not consider myself lucky; I wished that I had died with my men. All I knew of the Mohawks were tales of their brutality, and I fully expected to be tortured and burned alive." He laughed a little. "As you see, I was not."

"Slavery? Or adoption?" asked Cécile.

"I was adopted as the son of a woman whose own son had died in battle the winter before. At first, to me, it was like slavery and for a person of my position, the worst sort of torture." He laughed ruefully. It was not a pleasant sound at all. "Can you see me, Cécile, with my head plucked bare and with only a scalp lock?"

She tried to picture Lieutenant Edmond Saint-Germain in a breechcloth, his face and body painted, with moccasins on his feet. She could not.

"At first I thought of nothing but escape; but one morning it was not the first thing I thought of when I woke and then I stopped dreaming of it. I began to dream in Mohawk; I spoke it quite well by that time, and after I married —"

"You wedded a Mohawk woman?" asked Cécile. "You married in the Mohawk fashion?"

169

"Yes. It disturbs you?"

"Not at all. Should it? Pierre and Marie are wedded in the eyes of the Miami, Edmond. It is a true marriage, as yours is."

He looked down at his feet and then back to her again; beneath his stock his throat moved as he swallowed. "As mine *was*. I loved her with all my heart, and there was no longer any need to escape. I was one of them, you see, and happier in a different way than I ever had been in Montréal. But then the Great Peace was signed and prisoners were exchanged. Can you imagine, Cécile, how it felt to be pulled from a life I had come to accept as my own and thrust back into one I had willingly forgotten?"

"You could have returned, Edmond," Cécile said. "You could have gone back to her."

"I did return. In my white coat and knee breeches and with a wig on my head. No one laughed. I was still the man I had been when I had been forced to leave. How my Mohawk mother wept with joy to see me that day."

"What of your wife?"

"She had been with child when they took me away, as I cursed the very heavens. They told me that she died in childbed, bearing my son," Edmond said in a soft voice.

"And so you are here now. Why?"

"Duty. There is little left but that for me. I have resigned my commission, but until the resignation is accepted by the king, I must press on."

"Doing something in which you no longer believe? Is this the civilization of which you spoke?"

"It is all that remains for the time being, Cécile, though who can say what may happen." Then his voice brightened a little. "Enough of this; it is all in the past now, and besides, you are shivering. Do go inside."

She simply stood there, and so he bowed slightly and walked off into the darkness.

"Edmond!" she called to his back, shame making her throat tight. Who was she to judge him? He had lost a child and a wife. She knew the depth of her father's grief and of her own and, she was certain, of Lesharo's. His would be the same.

He did not turn around. "Yes?"

I am so sorry for your loss, she wanted to say. "Thank you for escorting me home."

"It was my pleasure, Cécile." He began to walk once more, and then he slowed and said, "Inside with you now, Mademoiselle. I would never forgive myself should you take ill."

The house was quiet. Marguerite's soft snores came from the bedroom, but Lesharo was not there. Cécile poked the fire and added another log. If I do not remove this corset and the rest of these things I will shriek, she thought, and so she tiptoed into the bedroom. She left the door open and was just beginning to unlace the bodice, when a small looking glass caught her eye. It was a cheap thing, a trade item for which Pierre would have paid a ridiculous price at the magasin, but it was still a looking glass. She picked it up from the chest and carried it into the kitchen to the firelight.

It showed her a stranger, a girl whose hair was pinned up as a lady would wear it. The color of the gown made her eyes seem very green. Cécile had seen herself in mirrors before. She knew the shape of her face and that she was tall and boyishly slim. She did not own a looking glass, though; there had never been a need for one. Teeth could be cleaned with a willow twig, one's face washed and hair combed without the necessity of staring at oneself. If there was a reason, there were always pools of still water.

This stranger, though, would have a looking glass, something in which to preen. Cécile stood very straight and studied the way the bodice and corset had changed her figure, made her waist very slender and, she saw with a rush of heat, pushed up her bosom. It was then that the door opened and Lesharo walked in.

"Where have you been?" Cécile asked faintly.

"I waited for you where Tonti's guard could not see me," he answered. "I was not certain at first that it was you who came out with the officer." He made a vague gesture toward her gown.

"It is still me under all this," said Cécile, trying for a light tone she did not really feel. "It is only clothing, after all."

"It makes you look very different."

"I suppose it does."

"White."

"I beg your pardon?"

"It makes you look like a white woman, like the women I would see in Québec." The ones who would cross a street covered in horse dung rather than allow themselves to be too close to me, he thought.

"Is that a bad thing?" Cécile asked defensively.

"Perhaps not." Lesharo removed his capot and hung it on a peg. He took blankets and a pillow from the chest to make his bed. "It is what you are, after all."

"I am hardly a lady of Québec or anywhere else, and I can no more help being white than you can help being indien. If you think that this dress changes what I am, then you are a complete fool!"

She whirled off into the bedroom, shutting the door behind her. I have hurt her, Lesharo thought, and his shoulders slumped. I have wounded her, she to whom I owe everything, she whom I am sworn to protect. He lay down on his side and stared at the fire.

Lesharo flipped over on his back. Stay with us, the Miamis had often coaxed. Your world is not there with the whites. There is nothing for you there, but among us you would be a valued warrior and companion. He had refused all their entreaties, saying that his place was here with Cécile, and until this very moment he had nearly believed it.

Then Cadillac's woman had made her feast.

He had not expected to be included; what would he have had to say to them? The company of the boys had been enjoyable enough. He had stood for a few minutes after he had brought Jacques and Toine back to the house, although he had been warned by Tonti not to do so. Cécile's voice had lifted above the others. He would know it anywhere, and she had sounded happy. Why should she not? She liked a good meal and a good conversation.

But then he had seen her just now, and if he had ever thought for a heartbeat that he might have importance in her life, that had disappeared like mist in the sunshine.

The bedroom door opened. Lesharo sat up.

"Is this better?" The green dress was gone, her hair was loose on her shoulders and she wore the clothing of an indien woman. She had been weeping, he saw with dismay. "Do I seem less white now? Answer me!"

"Cécile, what you wear changes nothing. You are yourself, whether in the dress of a white woman or in what you now wear. Forgive me. I was wrong to say otherwise."

"But the fact that I am white. It matters now. Why?"

"It matters not."

"You are lying to me," she sobbed.

"If Pierre was here he would toss you both out into the night," grumbled Marguerite. She came wandering out of the bedroom, rubbing her eyes.

"Then you would not be white or any other human color. You would both be blue. What is this carrying on? Cécile, what has happened? Has she been hurt, Lesharo?"

"This is my fault," said Lesharo, unable to meet Marguerite's eyes.

"No, it is not!" Cécile cried, angry tears spilling down her face. "It is not that at all."

"What is it then, Cécile?" Marguerite asked gently.

"That gown."

"The clothing you tossed onto the floor near the bed? The clothing I tripped over?"

"I hate it." She shook her head. "It changed the way they saw me at Marie-Thérèse's supper, as though I was better in it." Cécile glanced at Lesharo. "As though I was more like them."

"What does any of that matter?" said Marguerite with a weary lift of her shoulders. "What does it matter how they think? Let them talk and say what they will. Let them gossip like old women if they want to. That is no different from the longhouse, Cécile, you know that very well."

"There is gossip there, yes, but not the sorts of things the Miami tell me are being said here," Lesharo said. He took a deep breath for steadiness.

"What are they saying?" asked Cécile.

"You will learn of this from me rather than anyone else first. I have heard that the soldiers say your father leaves his daughter in the hands of a sauvage, with no thoughts to her reputation," Lesharo said. Now an uncharacteristic flush was creeping up his neck and darkening his skin. "They have a name for you, it seems, Cécile. *L'Indienne Blanche*. And for me as well. *Le Chien Sauvage*, since they say I follow you around like a well-trained dog."

"Have you a key for your door, Marguerite?" Cécile asked.

"Yes," said Marguerite. "I wear it around my neck with my rosary. Why do you ask?"

"Pierre would not want you remaining here alone. You may want to lock your house tightly against thieves, since you must come with us. I will not stay in this fort an hour longer. Let us pack what we will take with us."

• • •

Edmond had not been able to settle himself after the supper party and so had simply walked up and down the quiet streets, turning his thoughts over in his mind. It was with surprise that he saw Cécile and the others standing at the west gate, rolls of blankets and clothing tied with tumplines hanging from their shoulders. At their feet were canvas bags and copper pots they had set down.

"You cannot pass, Mademoiselle," a sergeant was saying. "No one may leave here without Sieur Cadillac's permission."

"This is preposterous," fumed Cécile as Edmond approached. "Tell them to stand aside."

"Cécile, you cannot simply wander out into the night." Edmond took her arm. "Come," he said.

Lesharo seized Cécile's other arm. "She is my concern, not yours. Take your hand from her," he said in a low voice.

The muskets of every soldier were suddenly trained upon them, and Marguerite gave a gasp.

"Lower your weapons!" roared Edmond.

"Lieutenant?" asked the sergeant when his men were again at ease. "Shall I have him removed from the fort? Shall I have him put in irons? Lieutenant?"

"I hear you, sergeant. There is no need to bleat at me," Edmond said, releasing Cécile. "I must at least know where you are going, for although you do as you please, I still feel responsibility for you."

Cécile lifted her head with as much dignity as she could. "I do not intend to remain here. We will stay with the Miami people at the Wendat village. My father, when he learns what is thought of me, what is being said, will be pleased with my decision."

"If you have been treated with disrespect, I insist on hearing the nature of it. I will deal with it myself, and may every saint in heaven help the man who has given you the insult that drives you from the safety of this fort." The menace in his voice was unmistakable; several of the soldiers coughed or looked away.

"What is going on?" someone called, and Cécile's stomach clenched. It was Tonti and his wife returning late from Marie-Thérèse's supper. Marie-Anne was eating up the scene as though she were starving, as though gossip would be a far richer dish than any she had eaten that evening. "Ah. The pani. Why did I know he would be at the source of this commotion? If there is trouble, then perhaps a touch of the lash on his back would settle him."

Cécile heard the sharp intake of breath through Lesharo's nostrils. He will die before he lets any man do that to him again, she thought wildly. Edmond, his eyes resting on her, said in an even tone, "There is no trouble at all, Capitaine. They are simply setting out for a walk to the Wendat village."

"At this time of night, Cécile?" asked Marie-Anne incredulously. "Do you have Cadillac's permission?"

"I do not need Cadillac's permission; I am not subject to him. I do as I wish," Cécile said.

"Oh my, Cécile!" exclaimed Marie-Anne. "What shall I tell Marie-Thérèse?"

"That L'Indienne Blanche who taught and cared for her sons and Le Chien Sauvage who follows her around like a hunting dog have left the fort with Pierre Roy's wife," Lesharo answered. "The air is cleaner where they are going." And then he threw back his head and howled. The sound rose into the night to be carried away by the wind, and the wind, sharp and cold, brought back a reply. From far beyond the palisade came the answering howl of a single wolf. Most of the soldiers crossed themselves. One, frantic to pull out the cross he wore under his uniform, dropped his musket.

"Imbeciles," drawled Tonti. "Superstitious fools. You are as bad as this sauvage. Away with you then, Mademoiselle Chesne, though I suspect the lice and stink will drive you back in time." He turned his back on them and led his wife away from the gate, Marie-Anne's scandalized chattering fading as they disappeared into the darkness. Cécile pried Lesharo's fingers from her arm, they picked up their gear and she took Marguerite's hand. The soldiers stepped back and let the three of them walk out of the fort.

When he passed Edmond, Lesharo stopped. "Have no concern for Cécile's safety. No injury will come to her."

"I will hold you to that. If she is harmed in any way —"

"I know of Mohawk vengeance. There will be no need for it."

Edmond drew back a bit and looked down his nose at Lesharo. "It is common knowledge then, is it? Of course it would be. Sometimes I forget that there are no secrets within the longhouse. Guard her closely."

The sound of the wolf's howling echoed from the distance again, and behind them the soldiers muttered uncomfortably. "Another guards as well," said Lesharo.

Edmond said nothing. He straightened, once again the French officer. "Get back to your posts!" he called angrily to the soldiers, who were all leaning out watching from around the gate's opening.

Lesharo broke into a run to join Cécile and Marguerite, who waited in the shadows. It was not until they were well beyond the fort that Cécile dropped the copper pots she carried, letting them clatter onto the ground. She fell to her hands and knees and vomited. Her fear had been like something alive inside her, something of which she must empty herself. Not once in the years she had lived among indiens with her father had anyone ever raised a weapon to her in a threatening gesture. To look down the barrels of the muskets, to see Marguerite cringe in terror, had been horrible. But the thought that Lesharo might again suffer a whipping for her sake — that had sickened her as surely as the taste of rotten meat would have. She spat once, twice, and then climbed to her feet.

Since Lesharo was with them, the warriors who guarded the maze at the palisade's entrance did not challenge them. Lesharo guided them through, and led them to the longhouse where the Miamis were lodged. They would not be the only females, Cécile saw; there were a number of women here, and there were children. She thought of Toine and Jacques with fleeting regret. Who would help them with their lessons now? But that was not her concern; now only Marguerite and Lesharo mattered.

Miami women, whispering, asking questions and shaking their heads, immediately surrounded Marguerite. One matron, a baby at her breast, called something out to Cécile in an irate tone.

"If I am not welcome here, I have nowhere to go," Cécile said worriedly, small lines of concern visible between her brows. "How can I go back to the fort? I will not."

"No," Marguerite soothed. "She is angry for you, not at you. You are welcome in this longhouse, as Lesharo is. Come to bed, Cécile, and put an end to this day. The women have given us a place, just there."

"Not yet; I will never be able to sleep," she said. Marguerite shrugged and went off with the other women; Cécile wearily pulled off her capot and sat down on it near the fire. "I should have thanked Edmond. He lied for us, after all, so that there would be no trouble with Tonti. Now we will not see him again."

"He is not finished." Lesharo sat next to her, sharing the fire's warmth. "To have survived Mohawk captivity? His sort does not give up easily."

Cécile rubbed her face tiredly. What did he mean about Edmond not being finished? She blinked hard as the rest of his words sank in. "You know, then, that he lived among the Mohawk and was married to a Mohawk woman?"

"The Wendat and Miami have talked of it, yes. They see him differently than the other officers because of it, though some pity him."

"Why? For the loss of his wife and son?"

"For that, yes. There are other reasons. He is caught between the world of the French and the Mohawk, they say. He no longer clearly sees the path of his life." Lesharo cleared his throat. "That is not a good thing. You have spent time with him. Is this so?"

"I am not certain, Lesharo. It does not matter now, since I will be spending no more time at all with him."

"We are better here. I think I will more easily be able to understand what it wants and what path I will take if we are not inside the fort," Lesharo said absently.

Cécile said, "What do you mean?"

"The wolf," he answered simply.

"Surely you do not think it is the same animal that we saw at Niagara and heard on the island last winter?" She was not entirely easy with the thought. No wonder the soldiers had crossed themselves.

"I do."

"How can such a thing have happened? Why has it followed you?"

"Perhaps it is not me that it followed. Perhaps it is you."

Cécile looked toward the shadowy doorway of the longhouse where the wind was making the deerskin flap shiver a little. The wolf she had seen at Niagara had been beautiful, but it was a large, dangerous animal. To think of it stalking her, the pads of its feet moving silently over the ground until it was just there behind her — she shuddered.

She fears it, and I cannot have that, Lesharo thought. "The Pawnee are the people of the wolf, Cécile. You need not be afraid of it."

"I do not have Pawnee blood, Lesharo," she reminded him. "I am not Pawnee."

"Give me your hand," he said gently. Lesharo took his knife from its sheath.

She had seen it done before a few times when men wished to link themselves in loyalty or brotherhood. Never women, though. Such things did not involve women. Cécile could bear pain, but to voluntarily bring it upon herself was another matter. Yet there was Lesharo, patient, waiting, fully expecting that she would allow him to cut her. Cécile held out her hand. Lesharo made a slice across his own palm and then quickly slashed hers. He dropped his knife and clasped her hand in both of his, holding tightly for several minutes.

"I give you my Pawnee blood, Cécile. I am brother to the wolf as are all Pawnee. Now you are his sister."

"Does this make you my brother?" she asked when he released her hand. It was a small cut only, she saw, but it stung dreadfully.

She is as pale as new snow, he thought. Blood does not sicken her; I have seen her skin enough animals to know that, but this is her own blood. And mine. "No," said Lesharo, with a small laugh.

"Only the wolf is your brother. Now, let us go to our rest, Cécile."

Late that night, lying sleepless next to Marguerite, the events at the gate replayed themselves in her mind. When at last she drifted off, they crept unwanted into her dreams. Tonti's cruel face, his vicious words, Edmond's hand reaching out for her; and then she was running through the woods, running until she tripped and fell, cutting her hand. She lay on her back, her breath coming in deep, heaving gasps, and so she did not immediately hear the sound of footfalls. It will kill me, she thought. It will rip out my throat and my blood will flood out onto the ground for it to drink. But the wolf only licked the blood from her palm; its tongue was slick and warm against her cold skin. Then it lay down next to her and slept.

Chapter 10

Six weeks or so have gone by since we came to the Wendat village. When I look back at what I have written during that time, the words tell only of ordinary things often repeated. There has been feasting but no suppers, fine new clothing made of leather and plain wool, but no gowns, and if our lives are now quiet and uneventful, it gives me comfort.

Père Nicholas, most upset that Marguerite left the fort, now comes out every few days to continue her instruction and to say mass for us, since I will not return to Détroit even on Sundays or Holy Days. He brings news, naturally. Marie-Thérèse's pregnancy has become a difficult one. The thieving from the magasin continues, and Cadillac's relationship with Tonti is now strained, although Marie-Thérèse and Marie-Anne manage to remain friends. Toine and Jacques have been in dreadful trouble, for Marie-Thérèse cannot manage them at all. Cadillac has not yet sent them back to Québec, though. He fears that if she is upset enough, she may lose the child. Edmond appears to have fallen into disfavor with Tonti, but Père Nicholas is uncertain as to the reason.

Why am I not surprised that the news of the fort is seldom happy?

• • •

Cécile surrendered to the measured cadence of life in the village, something that was as constant as the changing of seasons or the falling of rain. She was not seen as a guest, although that had been her station in other villages during the years when she had journeyed out with her father seeking to trade. Now the village enfolded her. Here she had her place, and it was among the women.

There was a sharp division between males and females, deep and complex. Men did the heavy work. Where not long ago there had been only forests, nearly 200 arpents of land had been partially cleared beyond the village when the Wendats had arrived last year. The trees were girdled and a wide circle of bark cut from their circumferences; the brush was burned and the trees left to slowly die. There had been special prayers during the mid-winter ceremonies, entreating the creator to protect the children from falling branches.

The need for corn was enormous since, besides feeding the hungry people, it could be used for trading at the fort. It was not something the Wendat usually did, but early this spring before the planting the men had worked at burning out and felling trees.

With them entirely gone, the fields would be more productive.

Only the women worked the fields, though, planting corn in the center of small earth mounds, with beans and squash around the corn. Cécile knew that to French women like Marie-Thérèse and Marie-Anne it would seem like a life of drudgery, but it was not. She loved to set out with the other women, chattering and laughing, babies strapped to cradle boards on their backs, toddlers following along behind. It was pleasant to work in the sunshine, piling the dark soil into mounds, smelling its loamy richness. They labored at their own speed. With no men around except for a few of the older warriors to assure their safety, their days were their own.

Cécile sometimes did not see Lesharo from the time the sun rose in the morning until sunset, when people settled around their fires for the evening. He hunted with the men or worked beside them, painstakingly clearing yet another section of land for the women to farm. Cécile had Marguerite for company, and she slowly came to know the other young women, but she missed the close companionship of Lesharo. She could say nothing, though; it would have shamed both him and her.

There were many little boys and girls, both Miami and Wendat, and although their customs were different, they all behaved much the same. It was not the habit of either tribe to discipline young children harshly. Children helped with the work — the boys alongside the men, and the girls with the women — but they were often simply allowed to do as they wished and there was plenty of time for mischief and play. The women took turns watching the smallest of them; it was a task Marguerite especially enjoyed since she longed for a child of her own.

"Children learn by watching their elders," Marguerite sometimes reminded Cécile. "If we are lazy, our children will be lazy. The child of a deceitful person is deceitful as well." Cécile thought of Toine and Jacques and of their parents. What sort of men would those little boys become?

There were also elders among the Wendat and Miami, old people whose wisdom was treasured by their tribes. Some were shamans — powerful medicine men and women. Cécile enjoyed the company of the female elders; quick to learn, she could now understand a little of what they said.

She avoided the shamans.

She knew well the sound of their turtle-shell rattles, the burning of herbs and tobacco, their chanting as they prayed over the bodies of the sick or those who had a problem. They gave the people comfort, as her own beliefs comforted her. It was one thing to respect the religion of the indiens, but to go to the shamans and listen to their advice as Lesharo did was another matter. She was a Christian, and there it ended, with the marking in the sand of a fragile, tremulous line never to be crossed, as the shamans very well understood.

Yet strangely, two of them — one a Miami elder, and the other a Wendat — would continually seek out Cécile. These women were very old with heavily lined faces and fine white hair that drifted loose from their braids like cobwebs. Short, stout and rather unsteady, they were escorted here and there by strong young women whose task that day was to see that they came to no harm. Cécile would be working, scraping a skin, plaiting a basket or grinding corn. She would look up to see the old women comfortably seated on the finest of blue trade blankets edged with white stripes, studying her. Finally she could bear it no more. In spite of her reluctance to speak with the two shamans, her curiosity overwhelmed her and she pointedly addressed them.

It was late on a warm and lazy afternoon when the field work was done. Cécile sat with Marguerite in the fading sunshine, her journal on her lap. She was drawing a shell that Lesharo had found on the beach. It was a pretty thing, tiny and flawless, the outside white and its inner surface a deep glossy purple. He reclined beside her, his head propped on his hand. The shell would go into his medicine bag, but for now it gave him pleasure to see Cécile draw it in her book.

"What is it that I can do for you, Grandmères?" she asked the staring old women. It was what everyone called them as a sign of respect. Her quill motionless, she waited for their answer, half hoping there would be none. Lesharo sat up then, surprised that she was speaking to them.

"For us? Nothing," said one of the women in French. From her clothing and the patterns of the tattoos that covered her arms and face, she was a Miami elder.

"We may do something for you, though," said the other with a pink, toothless smile. Her strangely accented French told Cécile she was Wendat. "You must ask us what we may do for you. You must ask us for what you need."

"But I need nothing," Cécile replied in confusion. She closed her book with a snap and put it down.

How they laughed at her words.

"Everyone needs something," said the Miami elder with conviction. "The answer to a question, the way to find one's path in life. We women hold great power here. The longhouses and all that is in them are ours, but sometimes power is not enough. Sometimes advice is needed."

"Perhaps you need medicine," suggested the Wendat, nodding to herself. She squinted at Cécile. "You have the look of one who needs to call upon powerful medicine."

"I am not ill, Grandmère."

The old Miami chuckled. "Not that sort of medicine. Your body is strong and young, but perhaps you need medicine for your spirit. I speak of a charm."

"I do not believe in charms or that sort of medicine," said Cécile in a low voice, her posture stiff with discomfort. She twirled the quill between her fingers and then set it down next to her journal. "I am Catholic. A Christian."

"You are an amusing girl, even though you are a Christian! You are not to be blamed for being a Christian, however. You were raised to it," the Wendat said. "But of course you believe in medicine. You wear it around your neck, as he does."

Cécile touched the scapular beneath her blouse. Lesharo had been swimming and was still shirtless; the women could see his medicine bag. Who had told them about her scapular? She pulled it out and off, and then handed it across to them.

"It is not a medicine bag, as you can see. It is called a scapular, and it gives protection through God's Holy Mother."

Both women leaned forward and intently studied the squares of wool, poking them with their gnarled and crooked fingers. "I know nothing of this," said the Wendat elder. "Do you, old woman?"

"No," admitted the other, returning the scapular. "Perhaps there is medicine in it, but it will do her no good when she must make her choice." The Miami woman pointed at Cécile. "I think you are not ready yet to hear about that, are you? You are not ready to hear with anything but Christian ears."

MAXINE TROTTIER

Cécile had no idea what to say in return; she was completely confused by what sounded to her to be pointless babbling. She looked to Lesharo and Marguerite for help as she slipped the scapular back on and tucked it out of sight, but they only shook their heads. It meant no more to them than it did to her.

"Of course she is not ready!" scolded the Wendat elder. "In time she will be, but not yet. Now take us to our fires, you lazy girls. My stomach rumbles."

"I am old and my ears are ancient, but I could hear that rumbling from here," said the Miami shaman as the girls helped them up and folded the blankets. "Wait, you girls." The Miami turned and fixed Cécile with eyes as sharp and black as those of a squirrel. "Come to us when you are ready. We take no offense that you cannot find it in you to believe. We will wait." Then grumbling under her breath, she let the girls lead her away.

Cécile let out her breath; she had been tense and uncomfortable. These were not simply old women, filled with all the things they had learned during their many years on earth. They were what the priests called *sorcières*. She did not quite believe in sorcery or witches, but it was best not to tamper with such things.

"I have no idea what they meant," Cécile whispered. "Do you?"

"No, but what they were saying was not for us," Marguerite gently reminded her.

Lesharo picked up the shell and slipped it into his medicine bag. He stood and held out his hand to Cécile, pulling her up when she grasped it. "Dandelions," he announced. The shamans had disturbed her, he thought. She had concealed it as well as she could, and she had more respect for the ways of the people here than any white person he knew. Her god was a jealous one, though, and so Cécile could not open herself to the women's wisdom. It troubled her, but he knew a way to take her thoughts from it, at least for a while. "Dandelions," he said again, taking her journal and writing implements from her. He trotted over to the Miami longhouse and went inside.

"Now it is I who do not understand," said Marguerite. "Is he making one of his jokes? They are becoming nearly as bad as Pierre's."

"No," Cécile answered, brushing dried grass from her skirt. "When I left the field this afternoon, I waded into the shallows at the river to wash my face and arms and to cool myself. My hands stank from burying dead fish in the corn mounds, you see. I saw a large patch of young dandelion greens and I said that I wished to pick them. Now I shall. Will you come with us?"

"Not this time," said Marguerite with a grunt. A small girl, one of several who were playing with a collection of corn husk dolls nearby, had just settled herself in Marguerite's lap. She stroked the child's hair and exclaimed over the faceless doll. "It is my turn to watch the children, but I promise I will help when you come upon another patch."

"No need. I will pick some for you and for the shamans as well," Cécile told her, feeling she somehow had to make amends. Lesharo had returned, a shirt covering his upper body now, his bow and quiver over it, a willow basket in his hand for her. "The greens will be easy for them to eat when boiled up."

The dandelions were still there, well hidden from prying eyes and eager fingers by a grove of low bushes. Cécile picked only the most tender, sorting through them, flicking away small insects, pulling away even the smallest bits of brown. It was a large patch and she took her time, humming under her breath. Now and again she would pass a small leaf to Lesharo and take one for herself; the two of them would nibble, enjoying the sharp, green taste. The sun was nearly down when the leaves were loosely wrapped in a damp cloth in the basket and she declared the job done.

They walked along the riverbank, past the village, then scuttled down to where the water met the narrow sand beach. It was a clear evening, and Cécile and Lesharo sat at the edge of the river in the still-warm sand. He found kindling, a few chunks of driftwood, and with flint, tinder and a steel striker made a fire.

The stars came out, and with them came a group of Wendat men with torches. Light wavered on the river where they fished with spears. A few children splashed in the water or chased elusive fireflies. Crickets and nightjars began to sing. Cécile lay back in the sand watching the stars with Lesharo sitting beside her.

"The planting is finished," he said. "The men say that they will clear no more land until next year; now we will only hunt. It was a good day."

"Yes, it was a wonderful day." Cécile picked up a handful of sand and let it trickle through her fingers. "I just wish Papa was here to enjoy it all with us. When will he and Pierre return, do you think? It seems like so very many weeks since they left."

"It is a long journey. Not as long as the one I will make when Robert is safely back, but long enough." It had weighed on him, these weeks, the fact that he had delayed leaving. Sometimes at night it was like a vulture tearing at his soul, pulling him first one way and then the other. His father would surely have approved, and yet guilt worked at his heart, nibbling away the joy he felt when he was with her.

Something had twisted inside Cécile at Lesharo's words. It is his decision, she thought unhappily. He is not trying to hurt me; it is only that he does not want me to forget what will happen in time. No matter how I will miss him, it is his decision. She was trying to think of something cheerful to say, something to change what for her was a melancholy subject, when she heard a branch crack. Lesharo rose to one knee, his bow in his hand, an arrow fitted to the string, and Cécile flipped around to see who or what was there.

"I did not expect an entirely warm reception, but I am prepared to return the courtesy if it is extended," said Edmond cautiously. His hand was on his pistol; his body was braced and ready. One of the Wendat men called out sharply in alarm.

"Edmond!" she cried, with a nervous glance toward the warriors. "Tell them it is only Edmond, Lesharo."

"They can see for themselves, Cécile. You should take greater care than to come out of the darkness like that," Lesharo called, lowering his weapon. He sat next to Cécile once more. "Your white coat and yellow hair make a perfect target for someone who cares to use it."

"It was caution on Lesharo's part only," Cécile said in a rush, relieved that Edmond had taken his hand from the pistol. "No offense was intended."

"None was taken, Cécile. You are wise to be cautious. One never knows when an enemy may come upon you," said Edmond. "May I sit with you a while this fine evening?"

"Of course," she answered.

"I was uncertain of my welcome, given the circumstances under which we were all last together," he said, lowering himself next to her on the sand. "I see I was correct."

"That is all past," she assured him, feeling distinctly ill at ease between the two of them. "What happened that night is forgotten."

"Is it?"

Cécile looked from Edmond to Lesharo. Both of them were staring out at the river, watching the moon's reflection undulating on the water as though it fascinated them. "Of course it is." She willed Lesharo to speak, to say something to break the tension.

"Dandelions!" said Edmond with pleasure. "I have not eaten them in years! How will you prepare them, Cécile?"

"You have come out of the fort alone at night to ask a woman how to cook dandelions?" Lesharo broke in. He knew Cécile had definitely not forgotten their last night in the fort, despite her words, and neither had he.

"I have no fear at all regarding my safety and, yes, I do know how to prepare the greens. It was idle curiosity only. I must admit that I have another reason for being here." He picked up a handful of pebbles and tossed one into the river, waiting for the circle of ripples to die away before he tossed the next. "I am rather in disfavor at the moment, as you might know."

"The night at the gate," Lesharo said flatly. He did not like the officer and did not like that he was here now after all this time of peace, sitting next to Cécile. Still, he felt a twinge of shame nagging at him. "Tonti would have had me beaten, given a chance." He cleared his throat and said with as much sincerity as he could muster, "I have not thanked you

for standing in the way of that. You lied for my sake
— for our sake."

"A Saint-Germain lie? What a suggestion. I most
certainly did not!" huffed Edmond. He flung the rest
of the pebbles, and they hit the river with watery
plunks. "I only spoke the truth in that there was no
trouble."

"Well, trouble or not, you have my gratitude," said
Cécile. "I might still be there at the fort were it not
for you."

"Then may I beg a favor of you in return,
Cécile?" Edmond asked carefully. She stiffened as he
had suspected she would, instantly wary, and so he
held up a hand. "Only listen. My difficulties are
nothing compared with those of Cadillac. His life is
being made a complete and utter misery."

"What is wrong?" asked Cécile. "He answers to
no one except the Company." Edmond gave her a
meaningful look, one that she could read even by
moonlight. Her hands flew to her cheeks, and she
began to laugh in undisguised delight. "Marie-
Thérèse?"

He nodded, trying vainly to keep a serious
expression upon his face. "Cadillac's existence has
been nothing but torment since you left. Marie-
Thérèse has seen to that. Cadillac would never have
sent me out, except that his wife harried him night
and day until he agreed to do so." Edmond sighed.
"She asks that you return. Hear me out and then

argue, if you feel that you must. Can you imagine? I am not to return unless you agree to what she asks."

"You cannot return? Do you like sleeping in the woods, Edmond? I am not returning with you," Cécile said firmly.

"Sleeping in the woods is nothing to me. She offers more money, Cécile, which I know you do not want. She is truly desperate. The boys have been running entirely wild and will not obey even their father. In spite of her pleading, they are to travel back to Québec this week unless you return to the fort."

Cécile stood then, the basket of greens under her arm. "No," she said as Edmond and Lesharo rose to their feet. "Wish them a safe journey on my behalf, since I am fond of them. Guilt will not work with me this time. I will not go back, and I cannot believe that you are asking me for her. Do you hold her so highly in your regard, then, that you act as her courier?"

She saw his entire person grow rigid at that, and he reddened. "She did not ask me to come. I made the offer. It is her unborn child that concerns me," he said with tight control.

He lost a child himself, thought Cécile, wincing at the accusation she had just flung at him; he knows how painful it is, but before she could utter even a word in apology, Edmond continued.

"I have suggested to her that you might be willing to take the boys for a time."

"Cécile will not go back to Détroit," Lesharo said. His patience at an end, his tone was sharp. "Her place is here waiting for her father, not serving Cadillac's wife. That woman has her husband to care for her and her sons. She has her entire family around her. What does she need with Cécile?"

Edmond ignored him. Only the way his jaw tightened told of how Lesharo's interruption irritated him. "Cécile, she is quite unwell with this pregnancy. She lost the last child and prays that this one will live." He was certain that the tenderness in her would win out. "I think you would pray for the same thing."

"I will consider it," Cécile said vaguely, hating the fact that he could see through her, hating the tension that nearly crackled in the air between the two men. "I doubt very much if my father would approve."

Lesharo peered into the darkness, and a huge wave of relief swept over him. "Ask him yourself."

Someone was walking out of the shadows, someone whom Cécile longed very much to see. With a whoop of joy she passed the basket into Lesharo's hands and raced down the riverbank. Her father was almost knocked over when she threw herself into his arms.

"It is so good to see you, Papa!" she whispered to him. "I am so happy that you are back."

"As I am," Robert said quietly, studying her face. "Though I think I wish we had arrived sooner. The Wendat hailed us from the riverbank, so we made landfall there at the village. I was told the two of you were walking, and I thought I would come out to find you." He released his daughter and gave Lesharo a rough hug. "You are well, my friend?"

"Well enough, and happy at your safe return," Lesharo answered. "We have much to tell you."

"I wager you do." He nodded to Edmond. "Lieutenant Saint-Germain. You are out beyond the fort rather late, are you not? You have no escort?"

"I need none, Monsieur. And yes, I am out rather late, but I am on an assignment of great consequence — one from which I cannot return until it is completed."

"I suppose it involves you, Cécile," said her father.

"I suppose it does," said Cécile resignedly. "Will you come with us to the village then, Edmond?"

• • •

There was no unpleasant conversation while Pierre and Robert ate, groaning with approval over some of the tender dandelion greens. They spoke only of their journey to the Miami and the weeks they had spent there, answering each of Marguerite's eager questions in detail. She hung on their words, her longing for her family and village painfully evident.

"There are priests there at your village now," said Robert between swallows. "They are good men, and your brother approves of them."

"But he will not move your people here to the fort," Pierre said at last with regret. "A few families came with us, as you see, but Le Pied Froid says he has no wish for the Miami to starve. More tribes will come this summer, and Le Pied Froid knows full well that the hunting will grow no better here."

"That is the truth," admitted Lesharo. "Even now I sometimes see little or no game at all."

"You saw enough to think that you could provide for Cécile and Marguerite here rather than at the fort where supplies are available, Lesharo," said Robert, and the lighthearted feeling dissolved. "Or was that your decision, Cécile?"

Her cheeks red, Cécile told her father what had happened. She left nothing out, although it embarrassed her dreadfully to have Edmond hear the names by which they were now called. He himself had the good grace to blush when Cécile recounted the scene at the gate. When she stopped, there were a few minutes of brooding silence around the fire.

"Now that I think on it, I recall feeling like a turkey bone," Cécile said suddenly. "If they had both been pulling harder at me, I might have snapped."

At Cécile's words, Pierre began to sputter and then laugh aloud. "What did you wish for, you two?" he asked. Neither Lesharo nor Edmond had anything to say to his question.

"What indeed?" muttered her father. "The names mean nothing at all, Cécile; you know that very well," he went on. "The choice was yours to make, though.

I suppose it means that we will not live at the fort, and I admit that it does not necessarily disappoint me. Ah, well. There is land enough. I think we will find a place that suits us, and if not, we will go elsewhere."

"I understand, Papa." Perhaps we may go west with Lesharo, she thought as excitement bubbled up in her. I will introduce the idea to them both when I think the time is right.

Leaning toward Cécile, Edmond said, "You have not told your father of my mission."

When she had explained, her father again shook his head and said doubtfully, "It is up to you, Cécile, though I cannot understand why you would wish to do anything more for her."

"Those boys are foul-mouthed little fiends," warned Pierre. "My own sons — when they come one day — will be well behaved and have my exquisite manners." He hugged Marguerite, ignoring how she rolled her eyes at his nonsense. "Do us all a favor and let Cadillac send them back to Québec. The peace and quiet will be blissful!"

"I would not be doing it for her sake only," said Cécile. Lesharo saw the look that passed between her and Edmond. "I am thinking of Toine and Jacques, Papa, and more importantly, of Marie-Thérèse's unborn child. She is unwell and she has buried one baby here. It may not help if I take the boys, but it cannot hurt. She will surely be in her bed at this hour, Edmond, but tell her in the morning that I have agreed to what you have asked."

"I hope you will have her thanks," said Edmond, as he climbed to his feet. "You have mine."

"I misjudged you," Lesharo said abruptly. He looked away from Edmond and then back again. "I ask your pardon."

"Do you now? And what might be the basis for your sudden change of opinion, Lesharo? It is all too clear to me that you have resented my presence here for a variety of reasons." He crossed his arms, his face set. "You misjudged me? What makes you think you have the right to judge at all? Do you think we have a shred of anything in common, that our captivities would be enough to make us brothers of a sort? Or is it pity? Is that it?"

"Our lives have been nothing alike. I feel no pity for you and ask none in return."

"Then what can it possibly be?"

Cécile sat perfectly still. They will fight. Lesharo is armed and so is Edmond, and there will be blood drawn this night.

Lesharo stood and then walked slowly to Edmond, speaking as he went. "They say you lost an unborn son. You loved your wife and the Mohawk family that took you in. You love them still, I think, as I do my own family, even though they are gone and only my father remains. I will see them again — my grandmother, my mother and brother, and my sister who never knew the joy of life at all — and that will be a happy day. You will see your son and wife. Until then, we have the living in which to take comfort." He glanced at Cécile. "There is much to be valued in friendship."

Edmond said nothing. Then the disdainful anger that seethed in him slowly dissipated and he relaxed. A smile, polite and cool at first, grew slightly warmer and he nodded to Lesharo. "I can live with that."

• • •

They have made a pact of sorts between them, Edmond and Lesharo, which sets me at ease. Papa says he is not surprised, and that they have more in common than either of them will admit. For myself, I am only happy that there was no fighting. Somehow, though, I think their friendship, if that is truly what it is, cannot last.

I wonder at Edmond's words. Why would Lesharo ever have reason to resent his presence in the village? I will not ask, for I think it might shatter this harmony and my peace of mind.

• • •

In the morning, Cécile returned to Fort Détroit for the first time since the dreadful supper. Edmond met them at the west gate and there they separated; her father, Pierre and Marguerite headed to the magasin, followed by the Miamis, who were carrying the bundles of furs brought back from their village.

"We will meet you at Cadillac's house," Robert instructed. "We will go there when we have been paid for our work."

She, Lesharo and Edmond continued down the street. Curious soldiers and voyageurs stared, and once or twice there was whispering, but a single icy glance from Edmond ended that.

Cécile knocked at the door and waited. When it opened, both Jacques and Toine raced out and hurled themselves at her. They had both grown, she saw with pleased surprise, having shot up like spring weeds.

"We thought you would never come back!" Jacques cried.

"Were you held captive by the Wendat?" Toine asked. "Why did Lesharo not rescue you and bring you back to us? You had Lesharo's bow there. Why did you not shoot them?"

"She was not a captive," Lesharo explained. He shook his head in exasperation. "How can you think such a thing of the Wendat? She was there of her own will, and you know well enough that Cécile does not shoot people."

"Is your maman at home?" asked Edmond. "If she is, I would speak with her."

"Maman!" shrieked Jacques over his shoulder, reluctant to let go of Cécile.

"Lieutenant Saint-Germain is here!" Toine screamed. "Come out here right now!"

Cécile pushed them away, firmly but not unkindly. "I *know* without being told that you have not been practicing your reading and writing. That in itself is a disappointment to me, but your manners have disappeared entirely. Think of your poor maman."

"Cécile," Marie-Thérèse said weakly, as she came slowly out of her bedroom. "I thank le bon Dieu that you have returned. What could you possibly have been thinking to have left us?"

"I had my reasons, Marie-Thérèse. I am quite certain you know of them." Cécile gave her a warm smile, hoping that her shock was as well concealed as possible. The woman looked truly unwell. Little of the elegant lady remained; her hair had been hastily put up and her gown was wrinkled. Dark circles shadowed her eyes.

"Well, you are here and that is all that matters." Marie-Thérèse ushered her into the house, one hand on her enlarged belly, a small grimace of discomfort crumpling her features.

"For the time being only," said Cécile. Braced for the other's reaction, she was not surprised when Marie-Thérèse's eyes flashed and then slitted like those of an angry house cat.

"What do you mean?" She rounded on Edmond who was still in the street with Lesharo. "You promised, *promised*, I remind you, that you would ask her to take the boys. Now she says she will leave again!"

"He did exactly as he offered to do, Marie-Thérèse," Cécile said.

Marie-Thérèse started to weep noisily. "You cannot do this to me!" she cried, wringing her hands. "You cannot! I need your help!" Jacques was sucking his thumb and both boys were now close to tears, caught up in their mother's distress. "See what you have done to my precious sons! Do not cry, my darlings. She does not want to be with you, but I can do nothing about it."

"I have agreed to help you and I will," Cécile shouted above the uproar. "Now stop all this!" She waited until the distraught woman had calmed herself and only the boys' snuffling could be heard. "Marie-Thérèse, it is not good for the child or for you to carry on so. I will take the boys, but they will come out with me, back to the Wendat village. It will be an adventure for them."

"My sons living among les sauvages? Are you insane?"

"But we want an adventure with Lesharo and Cécile!" cried Toine. "It is so tedious here."

"We want to be sauvages," shouted Jacques. "We want to wear breechcloths and to be wild!" They began racing around the room, waving their arms, their attempts at war cries causing their mother to hold her hands over her ears.

"They do not need Cécile's help for that," Lesharo mumbled.

"Stop this or you can both stay here!" Cécile shouted. Toine and Jacques froze, and she resolutely went on. "Marie-Thérèse, those are my terms. I have lived there in perfect safety all this time. I assure you that no harm will come to them at the hands of the Wendat or the Miami."

"Or wherever else we are to go." It was her father, his business apparently finished. "Madame, we will spend only the night here. It is my intention to find a place beyond the fort where we will settle. Your sons are welcome to accompany us if Cécile has the patience to deal with them."

"How long will you be gone?" Marie-Thérèse asked. She was hiccupping and wiping her eyes with a delicate batiste handkerchief. Her voice had become soft again.

"A few weeks — perhaps less. It is my intention for us all to return for Pierre's and Marguerite's wedding."

"Very well." Marie-Thérèse sniffled and took a deep breath. "My sons will be ready to go with you in the morning. Come, darlings. Assist Maman back to her room, and she will help you pick out clothing that is suitable for travel." She gestured Cécile out and without another word, closed the door.

"She did not even thank you," said Lesharo. He was stunned by the woman's thoughtlessness.

"I do not like this," said Cécile when she was out in the street. She stared at the closed door of Cadillac's house, gnawing her lip thoughtfully. "Not her lack of consideration, for that does not surprise me at all. No. She gave in too easily."

"I cannot say I blame you, but you do have *my* thanks for your kindness," said Edmond. He picked up her hand and brushed it with his lips in farewell.

"I must leave you to it, though. I have work to which I must attend."

"She is planning something. I can tell. I can nearly feel it."

"Surely nothing that can affect you, Cécile." He dropped her hand, bowed and walked away, the men in the street stepping aside for him.

The fort, which had been quiet when they arrived, was now filling with voyageurs and indiens. Several canoes had come in at the beach. Men were bringing in furs: beaver, muskrat, fox, squirrel and — Cécile saw with a small flinch of distaste — wolf to trade. Some had rolls of deer, wapiti or moose skins. There was laughter and talking in indien dialects, some that Cécile recognized and others that were unfamiliar to her. A few men who knew how expensive the trade goods would be already grumbled among themselves. Someone made a joke and another shouted back in reply. It was then that Lesharo's head snapped around.

"You!" he called, and ran to a party of men.

"We want no trouble!" warned one of the indiens in French, dropping his roll of skins and lifting his hands in defense.

"You will have none," said Lesharo joyously. He picked up the roll and handed it back to the wary indien. "You spoke Pawnee! I am Pawnee, as you are! I am Lesharo, son of Iskatappe, and I was taken from our people years ago in a raid. Can you give me word of my father?"

"Follow us now or you will get no food tonight," shouted a voyageur. It was then that Cécile realized that this indien with whom Lesharo spoke was likely a pani.

"We will be in the Odawa village after his trading is done. Come and I will tell you what I know," said the pani. Wanting his supper more than conversation, he began to follow his master.

"At least tell me if my father is well," shouted Lesharo. Cécile could hear the excitement and elation in his voice.

The pani did not turn around when he answered, but his clipped words came clearly enough. "Your father is dead."

All the blood drained from Lesharo's face. He stood there blinking hard and swallowing again and again, as though something was caught in his throat. His lifeless eyes drifted over Cécile as though they did not see her. Then without a word, he turned and ran out of the fort.

"For the love of God, leave him be, Cécile! Let him mourn in peace!" called her father, but she paid him no heed.

Beyond Détroit's palisade, Lesharo was walking unsteadily. He tripped over something and fell. When Cécile reached him, he had risen to his knees as slowly as an old man. He set his trembling left hand upon the ground and pulled out his knife with the other.

"Oh no, Lesharo," whispered Cécile. "Please do not do that." He intended to cut off part of his smallest finger as a sign of mourning; the blade was already pressing into his flesh, blood welling up around its sharp edge. "I beg you, please."

Cécile put her arms around him. She could feel then how he was shaking, how his heart pounded. He dropped the knife. Lesharo slid his arms around her and wept. She rocked him for a long while, tears rolling down her own cheeks, until at last he grew quiet.

"All this time I have believed him to be alive. I have thought only of myself and what I wanted, when I should have thought of him. Mourned for him! I should not have remained here," he said dully. "I have no one now. My family is gone."

You have me, Lesharo, she wanted to say, but she did not. No words could possibly make a difference to such a devastating loss. Instead, she stroked away damp strands of hair from his grief-ravaged face.

"I must be alone, Cécile." He pulled away from her. She was shaking her head, red strands of her hair whipping about her face, and he said, "I will not cut myself. That I do for you. I need to pray for forgiveness. That I do for my father. And when the Pawnee comes out of the fort, I need to speak with him so that I may hear how my father died. That I do for myself."

It was very late when Lesharo returned to Pierre's house. His eyes were red and the skin around them puffed, but he had managed to compose himself and conceal his anguish. Cécile knew that no one would question him; she did not really expect him to say anything at all. When he sat and began to speak, his eyes on the floor, it was clear that he needed to. He could not keep this inside and bear the misery and guilt that were nearly consuming him.

"I did not know Taguayo — the man who told me of my father — very well. I would not have recognized him at all today if he had not spoken; he has changed so much since he has been a slave." Lesharo steeled himself, took a deep breath and went on. "He said that when my father and the rest of the hunting party returned to find the village burned and so many dead, their sorrow was horrible. Their rage, though, was greater. There was little to place upon the burial platforms. It had been a month since the attack, you see, and the vultures and scavenging animals were thorough. My father gathered what he could of my mother's remains, so that he could do what was proper for her and the unborn child.

"Then they rode out seeking vengeance, but the Sioux outnumbered them. Some of the Pawnee warriors escaped. Some were taken prisoner and sold into slavery, but my father was killed. Taguayo said he fought bravely." The room was entirely silent and Lesharo's voice had sunk to a faint whisper. "He died well. That was good to know." He looked up at her in absolute despair. "There is nothing left for me, Cécile."

"There is no reason for you to journey west any longer, is there? You will, of course, remain with us,

Lesharo," said Robert. "When we find the place where we will live, there will be a great deal of work. I cannot possibly do it alone before winter." It was only a small lie, but Cécile's heart swelled with love for her father as he continued. "There will be land to clear and a house to build. You are a good provider; we will hunt together and keep Cécile well fed through the winter." Robert squeezed Lesharo's shoulder and added, "You are like a son to me. I cannot replace your father and would never presume to do so, but I would honor him by having his son at my side."

"Please stay," Cécile said softly. I could not bear it if you were to leave me now, she thought. I cannot stand the idea of you being alone.

"You will always have a place with us here as well," said Pierre with conviction. "Let your mind be easy on that count."

Wordlessly, again close to painful tears, Lesharo nodded, his mouth working as he fought to control himself and rein in his emotions.

"Good. It is decided then," Robert boomed. He slapped his thighs and stood. "It is late, we have an early morning and I believe that my bed is calling to me."

"And mine as well," said Pierre with a gusty sigh. "Our friends will leave at dawn, and I do not want you to be alone here, Marguerite. Come to the village, my beloved. In two weeks we will be wed in the eyes of the Church. Until then, I must sleep among Miami warriors whose snoring is far worse than yours, and you must sleep among the Miami women. Life is cruel."

"Journey safely." Marguerite embraced Cécile. She paused only a bit, then she put both of her hands on Lesharo's shoulders and quietly spoke to him in her own tongue.

When they were gone, Cécile turned to Lesharo and asked, "What did she say, if you may tell me?"

He looked up at her, no longer able to hide what he was feeling, grasping at the crumb of hope he had clearly been offered. "That those of my own blood may be gone, but kinship need not be a matter of blood. Can this be true, Cécile?"

"It can," she answered. It will, she thought.

Chapter 11

Toine and Jacques were waiting for them with Cadillac down at the river the next morning. Cécile did not pay much attention to the voyageur who stood near them, talking to Tonti with his back to her. There were other men there, already working or standing in relaxed conversation before their day began. He was just one of many. It was only when the boys called to her and he turned that she recognized Edmond.

His uniform had been replaced with clothing much like her father's. The linen and wool were of far better quality, but his deerskin mitasses were stained by wear. The silk ribbon was gone from his hair; it was now tied back with a leather thong.

"Lieutenant Saint-Germain will accompany you," Cadillac announced before Cécile could even open her mouth. "Marie-Thérèse insists upon this, although he scarcely can be spared."

"There has been another episode of thievery from the magasin, you see," said Tonti, his gaze focusing upon Lesharo. "Powder and lead this time, and four trade muskets. We shall find the sauvages who are responsible, and when we do, they shall pay dearly. It is unfortunate that Lieutenant Saint-Germain must act as a nursemaid rather than an officer, especially since I feel we are so very close to discovering the serpent in our midst. But Madame Cadillac will not be denied." He bowed to Cécile and turned his attention to a party of soldiers.

Cadillac crouched down near his sons. "Your maman needs her rest and I am needed here. Do your duty like soldiers, my sons, and obey Lieutenant Saint-Germain and Mademoiselle Chesne in all things." He ruffled their hair and then hurriedly caught up to Tonti, who was already returning to the fort.

"So much for your strategies," Cécile said to Edmond, grinning when his fair skin pinkened. "She has out-maneuvered us both once again. I said that she gave in far too easily last night; I see now that it was only because her mind was occupied with how she might use you for her purposes. You were being so thoughtful and now it means that you must endure this, this — penance!" She flung up her arms in exasperation. "She has no shame."

"Endure? To journey out in such fine weather and in such splendid company is hardly a penance. It will be refreshing to escape the imbecilic idea that this thievery involves indiens." Realizing that he had been quite indiscreet, Edmond coughed and added, "That is, there is no hardship in this for me, Cécile."

He turned from her to Lesharo and said in a low voice, "I heard of your loss. Your father died a warrior's death, and so you surely must take comfort in that."

Lesharo, caught by surprise at Edmond's unexpected consideration, only gave a brief nod. He looked away as the pain of it all caught at him afresh.

Edmond had been given a canoe that had been provisioned at Cadillac's direction. Compared to their own light rations — which her father had supplied himself, Cécile thought crossly — it was heavily laden. They repacked the two vessels so that the weight was evenly distributed.

"I will need someone at the bow, since neither of these boys will be of much help," said Edmond. How Toine and Jacques howled in protest at that. "Perhaps Cécile would be willing?"

"We will separate the boys to reduce the chaos as much as possible," Robert said briskly. "It will be Cécile, Jacques and me in my canoe. You and Lesharo will take your canoe with Toine."

Edmond stood unmoving for a few seconds, his eyes riveted on Lesharo. He had thought to see displeasure on the younger man's face, but there was only the same silent misery of his mourning. Edmond felt a small twinge of guilt at having lowered himself to such thoughts. "Very well," he said brightly. "This is your expedition, after all, Robert."

They paddled upriver all that morning, staying close to the shore to avoid the strong current. It became a fine summer day, hot and cloudless with a steady breeze behind them. Now and again Cécile gazed longingly at the shady forest to their left that rang with birdsong. Her blouse was damp with sweat, and her braid stuck to her neck. She wished that perhaps they could stop somewhere and swim, but she kept her words to herself, for no one else complained.

The boys were little help; Toine dropped his paddle twice and Jacques three times, forcing them to turn the canoes. Finally, Robert could endure no more of it and ordered them to head for a small wooded island that lay ahead, just at the mouth of the river. They circumnavigated the island, finally steering the canoes into a little bay on its west side.

"It seems deserted. We will stop for the night, and if you two drop your paddles one more time before these canoes are beached, you will swim for them," Robert grumbled.

"We cannot swim!" Jacques cried in panic. "We will drown and be dead!"

"And worse than that, our clothing will be ruined!" whined Toine. "Papa will be very angry. I do not even want to think of what Maman will do."

"Oh, do be quiet," Cécile scolded. She kicked off her moccasins and leaped out of the canoe. "Take off your moccasins and stockings, both of you, and climb out. Why she sent you out like this in breeches and coats, I will never understand. Silk ribbons for your hair are also very useful in the bush."

"We are not allowed to go without shoes and stockings," Toine said. "Maman said you would carry us ashore."

"If I pick you up, it will be to toss you in," Lesharo threatened. His voice was husky; those were the first words he had spoken all day. Locked within himself, he had silently paddled, his eyes on the water or on the horizon as he struggled alone to come to terms with his pain. "Do as she says and help unload the canoes, or you will have nothing to eat tonight but what you find washed up on the beach."

Facing his threat of starvation, they quickly obeyed him and leaped into the water with a complete disregard for their clothing. Cécile gritted her teeth when Jacques dropped a sack of peas, but at least it was the only thing that became soaked, and with everyone helping, the canoes were soon unloaded and carried up.

"You may not be able to swim yet, but you can paddle about in the water and cool off," said Cécile to the boys. She pushed back strands of hair from her sweaty face, then pulled out a roll of cloth and took a pair of small black scissors from her pocket. Measuring the boys with her eyes, she cut two rectangles and two long strips. "Here are breechcloths and belts for you. You will go into the bushes and put them on. Help each other if you cannot manage alone."

The boys snatched the breechcloths from her hands and ran off behind the bushes, their shouts of, "Now we will look like les sauvages!" ringing through the forest. Robert quickly stripped to his clout and waded in. She saw Lesharo staring at her father's back, at the scars that marred his tanned skin. He pulled off his own shirt and his medicine bag, walked out until the water was to his waist and then dove in. The marks on his back had not faded much, and the ugly scar upon his arm was vivid, but they were only scars. Nothing more, she reminded herself with satisfaction.

Toine and Jacques ran past her, tossing their sodden clothing down on the sand. They flung themselves into the water and began splashing each other, shrieking and screaming.

"Can they do nothing without creating so much noise?" asked Edmond with a grimace.

"Very little," laughed Cécile. "You must accustom yourself to it or go mad."

He slowly removed his moccasins, leggings and shirt, then stood before her in only his breechcloth, waiting for her reaction. For once his poised manner seemed to falter a bit. The very white skin of his chest and arms was covered with a fine pattern of tattoos, delicate lines and triangles, done almost certainly when he was among the Mohawks. They are all three marked in some way, Cécile thought suddenly. She looked down at her palm, at the faint thin scar from the cut Lesharo had made. Even I am marked. How odd.

"You are not disgusted," he said, for he had expected another reaction — surprise at the least, revulsion at the worst — but she was only regarding him with those cool eyes of hers. "You do not cease to amaze me, Cécile."

"Why would I be? They are very good tattoos," she said lightly. "And you wear them well. I came quite close to having a tattoo myself the first year we were out among the indiens. I only wanted a tiny one." She smiled at the memory. "Papa caught us — me and several other girls — at it. He was so cross! I had to content myself with drawing on marks with a burned stick. Perhaps I will have one yet."

No tattoo should ever mar your skin, Edmond thought. He prudently left the words unspoken, knowing they would be out of place. Instead, he joined the others in the water, walking out and then diving in.

"Come in, Cécile!" shouted Jacques. "It is not cold at all."

"Swim with us, Cécile!" called Toine. "We will not splash you so very much."

"I will just wade," she called back. She would have to swim clothed otherwise, since she knew her father would not permit her to seek out a secluded spot alone.

Lesharo popped up from under the surface of the river, water streaming from him in silvery sheets. He swam until he could walk back ashore.

"I will take Cécile beyond the trees, there," he called to Robert, who was floating on his back, "so she may swim in privacy."

"Take your weapons," Robert called back lazily.

Lesharo retied his belt around his waist, picked up his medicine bag and armed himself. They left the beach and walked into the trees, Toine's and Jacques's insistence that they must also have tattoos echoing behind them. It was quiet in the narrow band of forest, damp and close. Clouds of gnats instantly set upon them. A cicada began to buzz, the sound rising up and pulsing in the still air before it drifted away to nothing.

Lesharo held back a low branch, and Cécile stepped out onto the beach. The water was very still near the shore, with only tiny wavelets reaching up to wet the sand. Farther out, a stiff breeze ruffled the water and the current swirled, but here the giant ashes and elms blocked the wind entirely.

Lesharo dropped down onto the sand, facing away from the river. With anyone but her, he was ill at ease about his back and, until today, hesitant to show it if whites were present. That had been shame rather than modesty, the second not being a practical quality in his opinion. There was often little privacy in the longhouses here and the lodges of the Pawnee. One observed people in all states of dress and undress. It meant little.

"I will keep my back turned," he promised Cécile, in deference to her ways. "Swim as long as you like."

"This will be wonderful," Cécile said.

Lesharo heard the whisper of her clothing dropping to the sand. "Do not go out too far," he said when she splashed into the water. "The currents are strong; you can easily be swept away."

"I can swim well, Lesharo."

"You will obey me, Cécile."

"I think I will swim to the shore," she said thoughtfully. "I like the look of it there."

Lesharo was on his feet in an instant, sand spraying everywhere. "Do not dare or I will —"

"You will what?"

There was the sound of her stroking through the water. I care nothing for her modesty! he thought wildly and turned around. Cécile, standing in water that was well above her knees, quite properly covered by the long linen blouse that floated around her legs, began to laugh helplessly.

"Your face! You should see your face!"

Lesharo slowly took the tomahawk from his belt and dropped it to the sand next to his bow, quiver and medicine bag. He undid the belt and dropped it as well. When he sprinted into the water, Cécile whirled and tried to run, but he easily caught her. Down they both went with a tremendous splash; when they came back up Lesharo was growling and Cécile screaming wildly through her laughter.

"I am sorry!" she cried. "I could not help it. No! Do not even think to tickle me! I hate that!"

"Then I will surely do so. And I should make you beg for mercy."

"I *am* begging."

Cécile lay back in the water and closed her eyes. The sunshine was warm on her face and the cool water delicious against her skin. "I should have remembered soap," she murmured. Her voice sounded very odd with her ears under water. All the noises — the gulls crying overhead, the boys' shouts, the shrill calls of jays and cardinals from the forest — were muffled. She listened to her heartbeat slowing, to the sound of the river as it rushed past.

"Do you wish me to get it for you? Tell me where it is." Though he was standing close to her, his words seemed to come from far away.

She undid her braid and let her hair float all around her head. "This will be good enough for now," Cécile said, scrubbing at her scalp. "You do too much for me."

"I would do anything for you, Cécile. Surely you know that."

Lesharo was standing, looking down at the red cloud of her hair floating around her head and shoulders. Her eyes were the color of river water, the dark red lashes wet and spiky. Cécile held out her hands and he pulled her to her feet. For an instant she saw him as others did: tall and well-muscled, with a wiry strength and an air of cool detachment. He had none of Edmond Saint-Germain's brilliance, his golden handsomeness. He has something different, though, thought Cécile. It is all inside him, where no one can see it but me. She put her hands on his shoulders and Lesharo set his on her waist. He leaned his face close to hers.

Cécile shut her eyes. I have never been kissed before, she thought. Not like this. How perfect that he will be the first.

I hope I do it properly, thought Lesharo, and that it pleases her as it surely will me. She is my first.

"Is she drowning?" screeched Jacques, who was standing on the beach with his brother, and Lesharo and Cécile leaped apart. "Have we come in time?" he called through his cupped hands. "Can we help you, Lesharo?"

"He has already saved her. We missed it," Toine complained with a petulant stomp of his bare foot. "We miss all the best things."

"Is everything quite right?" asked Robert quietly. He was leaning against the trunk of a tree, his arms crossed, his face expressionless. "Is anything amiss?"

"Nothing is wrong, Robert, except that your daughter is cruel beyond belief," Lesharo called out evenly. "She torments me." How long had Robert been standing there in the shadows? He searched the older man's face for a sign of disapproval.

"Is that all?" said Robert, his eyes moving from his daughter to Lesharo and back again. He saw Lesharo step forward so that he was slightly ahead of Cécile. There was nothing proprietary in the act; rather it was very clear that Lesharo meant to take the full brunt of his anger when it came. Somehow it moved Robert, and the corners of his mouth lifted in the smile he could no longer control. "Now you know what I have suffered all these years," was all he said.

They came out of the water, Cécile blushing furiously, Lesharo glowering at the boys, and picked up their clothing and his weapons and medicine bag. Cécile plucked up her scapular and simply carried it, not wanting to get it wet lest the dye run. On the other side of the trees a camp had been set up, a small tent had been pitched and Edmond was crouched by a fire, feeding sticks into it. He stood slowly, narrowing his eyes at Cécile.

"I trust the water was refreshing?" he asked quietly, looking away at last.

"Yes," Cécile answered, suddenly very conscious of her wet linen. It was heavy and covered her quite decently, but it was sticking to her skin here and there. "I must get this out in the sun to dry," she mumbled, pulling it away from herself.

"Your packs are in the tent," said her father. "The boys had some odd notion that they would be having it for themselves. You alone may use it, if you wish."

"If I am eaten by bears, Maman will not like it at all," Jacques warned. "It will put her in a mood."

"It would be interesting to watch, though," Toine said sincerely. "You would yell loudly, I suspect."

"They would spit you out or be sick from the taste of you," called Lesharo, from inside the shirt he was pulling over his head. His face emerged and he said, "And if you do not stop your rudeness to each other, I will give you both reasons to scream. Come with me. We will find more wood and chase off all the bears. We are warriors, are we not?"

Cécile entered the tent and let the flaps fall. She stripped off her wet clothing, found a dry blouse, and slipped it and then her scapular over her head. There was no need for a fresh skirt; this one would do. The scene at the river pushed firmly from her mind, she took a deep breath. Then, with her wet blouse and a comb in her hand, she came out again.

Later she would look back on the rest of this day and recall that it was one of the most perfect of her life. She declared there would be no lessons, so the boys played and swam until they were thoroughly worn out. She dried her hair in the hot sunshine, combing it until it crackled, and let it hang loose, while Lesharo and Robert fished and Edmond gathered freshwater mussels. They would make the evening meal, they told her; why did she not sleep in the shade? She accepted the invitation. When Cécile woke the sun was a red ball low in the sky. She could smell fish cooking.

"I could stay here forever," Cécile said much later. The boys were finally asleep, their screaming at an end, their bellies full, their bodies worn out from the day's activities.

"Perhaps we shall," said Robert, picking his teeth with a fish bone. "Tomorrow we will explore the island to see if it has all we need. If not, there is the mainland." He stood, his knees popping. "A walk before bed to loosen my muscles, I think. Come and keep me company, Cécile."

Lesharo and Edmond remained seated, the fire separating them. Neither said anything for a while. Lesharo was poking at the logs with a stick, causing sparks to rise up and consume themselves when Edmond said abruptly, "She seems happier out here."

Lesharo tossed a woodchip into the fire. "Of course she is happier. Cécile is not suited to Détroit. What does she need with the sort of life they live there?"

"The company of people of her own kind, for one thing, I suppose. The Church."

"Her own kind? She is not like them, and as for the Church ..." Lesharo spat. "The lies they tell and the fear they put into those who listen sickens me. Cécile does not need any of that either."

"You think you know her mind well, I suppose."

"I know her very well. We are bound in friendship and in blood."

"Ah, yes. The scar on her palm. The one that was not there when she arrived." Edmond leaned back on his hands and studied the river. "She will marry some day, you know. It is only a matter of time."

Lesharo felt himself go quite cold. Of course she would marry; Cécile must have a husband and children of her own, but where would his place be in all of that?

"She will wed in the Church, just as Marguerite and Pierre will." Lesharo just stared and Edmond went on. "She is a Catholic, you understand, and so she will only wed another Catholic. Do you think for one minute that Robert would permit her to marry in the indien way as I did? And even if he could accept it, do you think she would abandon her faith?" He shook his head. "The shame of it would be unspeakable for her. She would never again be accepted by her own people. For they are her people, no matter how she bridles against it, Lesharo; make no mistake about that. No. I suspect that Cécile, in time, will have a husband who shares her love of the wilderness, but one to whom she can be properly married in the eyes of the Church."

"Why are you telling me this?" asked Lesharo, knowing exactly why Edmond was doing it.

"So that you understand," Edmond answered, and although his voice was not hurtful, despair as bitter as gall washed over Lesharo. "So that you do not make the mistake of deceiving yourself. You do want her to be happy, do you not?"

"Of course!"

"Then remember my words."

• • •

I thought that Papa asked me to walk alone with him so that he could perhaps say something about what he saw today. He did not. It was the same between us as it always is. Only when we paused for a moment, just before we returned to the camp with the sound of Lesharo's and

Edmond's voices drifting up into the night with the smoke from our fire, did he say anything. "Do you know your own heart, Cécile?" he asked me, and I said that yes, I did. He nodded and looked at me with something near to sadness. Then he smiled. "Take care, Cécile," he said. "It is a fragile thing, a person's heart," he said. "I would not care to see it broken."

I will not let myself think of whose heart he was speaking.

• • •

The island was more than suitable. It was heavily wooded with small natural canals running through it. Kingfishers called from where they perched on low branches, tiny button eyes eagerly studying the water. Dragonflies — small flashes of iridescent green or blue — streaked through the warm air. The fishing would be good; pickerel and plump catfish were visible in the green depths. Beneath the long grass on shore, the soil was rich and dark; it was perfect for a garden, and there were endless places where a house could be built. It smelled fresh and clean here, with none of the rank odors common to Détroit or the villages. Cécile drew the damp air deeply into her lungs, enjoying the scent and taste.

"It is far enough from the fort so that we are not bothered, and yet close enough so that we may bother them if we choose to do so," her father said with a chuckle. "How do you feel about it, Cécile? Can you be contented here?"

"It is so very beautiful," she admitted. "There is small game and there are ducks and pigeons. There will be geese later on. I have seen hickories and oaks, so there will be nuts in the fall, and I found patches of wild asparagus and onions just back there." She bent over, picked leaves from a plant and rubbed them between her hands. "Bergamot," she said, breathing in the sweet scent of the crushed leaves.

"I saw signs of deer, but the island is so small that it would not take long to hunt them out," said Edmond. "Would it not be wiser to settle on the mainland?"

"The game there is already hard to find, as you well know," said Lesharo. "It will only get worse." They had seen a dozen canoes come out of Lake St. Clair that morning; other tribes were coming to join the thousands of indiens already living around the fort.

"What do you think, Lesharo? Do you think it is possible to make a good life here?" Cécile asked. They were standing in a small clearing. Beyond it was a scattering of wild apple trees. Toine and Jacques had climbed into two of them and were pelting each other with the hard, unripened fruit.

"We can, yes," said Lesharo, and he could not help himself. His gaze went to Edmond who was shaking his head in what seemed like pity.

By the next day, her father had decided to build a longhouse first; a proper house would take much longer. They paced out a spot near the apple trees for the structure and set stones where holes would be dug for the poles. Robert found a grove of young birch saplings, tall thin trees that they would bend to make the outer frame, and a stand of whip-slender ashes that would be perfect for the rafters.

It was grueling work. Removing the bark would keep insects from damaging the wood, so Cécile and the boys peeled each of the saplings after they were carried to the clearing. Jacques and Toine were not permitted to touch the tomahawks, but only worked with small knives, since Cécile wished to return them to their mother with all of their fingers still attached. The men dug the holes for the outer frames and strained and sweated to bend the saplings and fix them into place. Then the rafters were lashed on with strips of leather.

"We can trade with the Wendat for bark for the covering," said Robert. "In spring we will harvest our own. And you will have a proper hearth, Cécile. I think that I may be able to build a chimney with those stones that are in the canal."

"There will be four sleeping cubicles," Cécile explained to the boys. They stood inside the longhouse's frame, sunlight and shadow slanting in between the branches to stripe their faces. "One for each of us and another for guests. That will be where you will sleep when you come to visit."

There were still lessons some afternoons, but they were short ones and increasingly infrequent. Jacques and Toine could not focus, and besides, Cécile decided they were learning more important things from working beside the men. The boys still fought like small animals and, when they thought they could not be heard, used the foul language of the soldiers, but they had shown themselves to be willing workers.

Cécile had never felt so at peace. A letter from Soeur Adele, relayed from the fort by a party of Miamis, had set her at ease. Grandmère was in fine good health now, due surely to her devotion to the Blessed Mother and the scapular she herself wore. She trusted that Robert was well, that Cécile's devotions were fervent and that she was not slouching. She continued to pray for the conversion of the pani, wherever he was.

The days were warm and sunny, the food good and the evenings filled with pleasantly aimless conversation. Life was not without small problems, almost always brought upon them by the boys. Both Jacques and Toine had managed to wander into a patch of poison ivy. Their legs coated with a paste of jewelweed that Cécile had made, they had at least stopped scratching.

"She will be so cross when she sees them," wailed Cécile in pretended hopelessness. In truth, the boys looked very fit. Tanned all over from spending their days clad only in the breechcloths, their arms and legs were sleek with youthful muscle; their teeth were white in their brown faces.

"They are only blisters. They will heal and fade. It is the tattoos of which I despair," Lesharo laughed. The boys had scratched themselves with pins and rubbed ashes into the wounds. "May she never see them. Given where they decided to mark themselves, I doubt that she will." He winced. "How could they have done that?"

Cécile's months among the Wendat had been happy ones, but always the fort and its intrigues had loomed in the distance. Life here was different. Her hair was often tangled, she was doing laundry in a stream, but she was contented.

Only one odd thing marred it in the end.

They were to leave the island in the morning for Pierre's and Marguerite's wedding. Now, the boys were asleep after one last late swim, and Edmond was playing chess with her father. She and Lesharo walked on the beach in blessed solitude, with only the melancholy sound of crickets and the soft wash of waves on the beach for company.

At the water, Lesharo stopped and faced downriver to where Détroit lay unseen in the distance. "Will it please you to return to the church?" he asked suddenly. He picked up a stone and flung it out into the water as hard as he could.

"Do you mean to mass? Yes, I suppose it will. It is too far to travel for just the one day and we are Catholic, after all." She lifted her shoulders. "Living here is more important to me, though. I suppose I should not feel that way, but I do."

"Could you live where there was no church?"

She laughed. "Of course. We did so for all those years. Now and again, we would come upon a priest and be able to confess and attend mass. The rest of the time we could not."

"What did you do then?"

Why was he asking this? He had nothing but dislike for the priests and the Church. "I prayed, as I do now."

"Are your prayers answered, Cécile? Does your god hear you?"

"Oh yes. I prayed for Papa to return. I prayed that we might be able to live somewhere without interference, and I prayed for happiness. Perhaps it is selfish, but le bon Dieu answered me. I have it all now." She rubbed her arms briskly and shivered a little. "It is becoming chilly and it would be warmer at the fire. Let us turn around and walk back."

As they meandered back to the camp, they talked a little more of tomorrow's journey and of how fine it would be to see Marguerite and Pierre once more. Lesharo heard himself speaking. He felt his lips stretching in a smile and heard his own laughter when she made a joke. Cécile had felt cold and so they were returning to camp, but Lesharo's coldness was deep within himself.

Chapter 12

We have returned to the fort and are now more or less settled in once again at Pierre's house. Marie-Thérèse's pregnancy goes no easier, but she is determined not to lose this child, and so she remains in bed a good deal of the time. Marguerite is helping to maintain the Cadillac household with another Miami woman. There is no question of the boys being there all the time, since it would disturb their mother's rest. They will remain with me on the days that Marie-Thérèse feels weak or unwell.

Cadillac and Tonti are not speaking, and Marie-Anne is considering a return to Montréal, having had quite enough of Fort Détroit and the wilderness. Not a bit of it is my affair. Only the wedding of Marguerite and Pierre is important.

• • •

A splendid feast was to be held in Marguerite's honor. It did not seem to matter to her people or to the Wendat that she had accepted the god of the whites; she was still one of them, after all. Miami warriors had hunted; they had been gone for days out into the forests to the north in search of game. Their successful return was met by an eager crowd outside the village, with excited children getting in the way of the women who took charge of the carcasses they would skin and cut up for the pots or spits. The meat — venison, raccoon, braces of turkeys and even a plump young wapiti — would feed everyone.

Cécile worked with the other women to prepare the food. She husked corn and picked early squash and wild onions. With Lesharo, she took the boys out into the forest and meadows on a damp morning to search for mushrooms, strawberries and the tender heads of ferns. One evening they fished in the river by torchlight, Jacques and Toine using the small bows that Lesharo had fashioned for them. They hit nothing at all, and spent all of their time retrieving the arrows tied with thin cord, but Lesharo brought in a large basket of salmon and pickerel.

There should have been lessons. Surrounded by other children, though, the boys found it difficult to concentrate. Even if Cécile took them away from the village, the voices of the Miami and Wendat boys echoing through the woods and across the fields as they played distracted Jacques and Toine horribly. Cécile knew that she should not, but in the end she let them run off to join the other boys.

"They are becoming like indien children, and it is your fault," Lesharo teased. "I think their mother must not be pleased with that. Their darkened skin? The breechcloths?"

"They are growing boys who have darkened because they have been playing in the sunshine," Cécile answered, refusing to rise to his bait. "They are far more strong and healthy than when we first met them. How could she disapprove? Marie-Thérèse really did not seem to mind so much when she saw them in their breechcloths. Many of the soldiers and all the voyageurs wear them, after all. Besides, with this child coming, she has more important things to concern her now than fashion."

The morning of the feast was a Sunday, and so Cécile attended mass with Marguerite as she had most days since their return. Marie-Thérèse, feeling well enough to leave her home, sat with Cadillac and their sons, the boys uncomfortable in breeches, wool coats and stockings.

Cécile was equally uncomfortable. She wore one of her old bodices and a skirt for church, the sort of clothing she had not put on since the night of Marie-Thérèse's supper, and it was all rather tight. I am growing fat! she had thought when she dressed herself that morning, but she quickly realized that she was mistaken. She had simply taken on a more womanly shape since then. Her indien garments, loose and shapeless, had kept that fact hidden. This clothing drew the eyes of the soldiers to her. The glances were admiring and carefully timed so that

Lieutenant Saint-Germain would not scowl at them, but Cécile did not care for it at all.

After mass, she exited the church, her eyes on the wooden floor so that she would not have to see their gawking, if there was any. In the crowd, her father jostled her a little, and when she looked up it was to see Lesharo at the back of the church near the door.

"What are you doing in here?" she whispered to him in surprise when he joined her.

"Was it … was it wrong for me to come inside?" he asked. Discomfort stiffened his face and made him stumble a bit over his words.

"Of course not!" Cécile said warmly. "Anyone is welcome. You should know that very well." She waved to Edmond who had come out ahead of them, and who was now working his way back.

"You are not entirely correct in that."

Cécile groaned inwardly. It was that wretched Tonti. They had managed to avoid him since they had returned, but it had been inevitable.

"The church is for Catholics," he continued. "Les sauvages have no business defiling it."

"I did not mean any disrespect," Lesharo repeated, flushing.

"What is this? What is this? Lesharo, my son! How wonderful that you joined us. Is it not a wondrous thing when a soul approaches le bon Dieu, Capitaine?" Père Nicholas pinned Tonti with his fierce look and waited. "Can you not hear me? Shall I shout? Not to show kindness and a welcoming heart in this church — this house of God, the very first building constructed here, as it should have been — would be a sin of enormous seriousness. A huge sin! A sin that would require the most severe penance. More severe than the one I gave you yesterday. A sin, I believe, that would also necessitate an offering to the Church in the form of many livres and —"

"It is a wondrous thing!" Tonti hissed, his thin lips white with anger. There was something else, too, Cécile realized, something there under his rage. He is afraid of Père Nicholas. Why would he fear such a sweet man, she wondered? "You will excuse me, Père Nicholas. I plan to be gone most of the day. Come, Marie-Anne."

"Not hunting on Sunday again, Capitaine?" The priest clucked his tongue in disapproval. "I suppose it is necessary work, and I do know that you will share with me what you bring in."

Tonti muttered something and dragged off his wife. Marie-Anne's complaints could be heard as she struggled to keep up with him in her stylish shoes.

"You are always welcome in Ste. Anne's, my son." He sighed deeply and mournfully and beat his breast. "*Mea culpa, mea culpa, mea maxima culpa.* I fear I am far too enthusiastic in my giving of penances. It is a sad thing. I must pray about it and I believe I may do so as I walk by the river this lovely morning. A nap under the birches may clear my mind and bring peace to my soul, although I sadly doubt it may affect my horrible penances. I will also pray that the day is sunny and fine for your wedding, my children." He winked at Pierre and Marguerite and strolled away to his home next to the church, humming a hymn as he went.

"What is all this about penances?" asked Robert.

"It appears that certain truths emerged while you were on the island," said Pierre.

"I would take care with what you say," cautioned Edmond, who had joined their group and was now at Cécile's side. He glanced cautiously at Cadillac, who was slowly escorting his wife down the street.

"It is common knowledge," said Pierre, noting the direction of Edmond's gaze. "Cadillac is fully aware that Tonti has been corresponding with the Jesuits at Michilimackinac. It seems there has been discussion about creating another trading post, one that would rival this one."

"Will it happen?" asked Cécile. "This fort has just been built!"

"No," said Pierre. "Cadillac would never permit such a thing; he hates the Jesuits, and they return his sentiment. Neither would the Company. Monsieurs Radisson and Arnault were furious when they learned of the plan, but Cadillac forgave Tonti, much to the relief of their wives, who have no one else with whom to socialize. Cadillac's and Tonti's friendship is an old one, and besides, it seems Tonti swears that the idea was the Jesuits', not his. Père

Nicholas, however, took a different view. Deceit-fulness was involved, you see."

"And so the penance," said Cécile.

"And so the penance for Tonti's deceitfulness and the very idea of taking anything away from the trade here," Pierre confirmed. "Père Nicholas is a Recollect, not a Jesuit, as you know. There is rivalry between the two orders."

"For furs?" asked Lesharo incredulously.

"No," answered Robert. "Not furs, but for the souls of men."

"The souls of men!" said Lesharo with a short laugh. "The priests want our souls. Is it not enough that Tonti and Cadillac take the land and that the people work for them?"

Cécile said nothing, but felt cold unease creeping over her as a passing soldier said something under his breath to another who was with him.

"Perhaps it would be best to continue this con-versation at the house," said Robert, noting the direction of his daughter's glance. "Tonti's men support him. Père Nicholas is very powerful, but there is only so much even he can do."

"I have no fear of Tonti," Lesharo insisted. "What I say is the truth."

"You would think to stand up to him armed only with a bow and arrow, or perhaps a knife?" Edmond scoffed. "He is an expert marksman and quite deadly with a sword. Do not confuse bravery with foolishness, and do not underestimate what he is capable of if angered, or if his authority is even slightly threatened."

"No more arguing," coaxed Cécile, trying for a cheerfulness she did not really feel. "I, for one, intend to forget Tonti, Lesharo; his rudeness is not worth even a second more of our time. Come. Walk back with us to Pierre's house, Edmond. It is Sunday. We will all do something enjoyable."

"Nothing would please me more, but I am afraid that I have letters to write and reports to make. Unfortunately, even on Sunday my duties call me." Edmond reluctantly stepped back from her.

"Will you join us at the feast?" Pierre asked. "You are more than welcome."

"Merci. If I can, I certainly will," said Edmond. "It has been a while since I have attended an indien feast, and of course," he let his eyes slide to Lesharo and then to Cécile, where they remained, "there would be the pleasure of your company."

Her father, Pierre and Marguerite began to walk away from the church then, but Lesharo remained with Cécile, his stance rigid. He watched Edmond as he strode away, his hands behind his back, entirely at ease.

"What he said means nothing," she tried to explain. "It is an expression only — the pleasure of your company — it is something the French say."

"Nothing?" he said. "Like the kissing of hands and the bowing, like the endless offers of service?

Nothing? Then why say it? I do not understand your customs."

"It is but a gesture, and it is meaningless. People say it all the time." She laid a hand lightly on his arm. "He was speaking to you as well, Lesharo."

I think not, Lesharo said to himself as they followed along behind the others. There is only one whose company Edmond seeks. But he kept this to himself, as though to say it aloud would give it life and make it worse.

Back at Pierre's house, Cécile disappeared into the bedroom. She unlaced the bodice and shrugged out of it, then removed her skirt and chemise quickly as though she loathed the feel of them, as though they chafed her spirit as well as her skin. She pulled the tie from her hair, then ran her fingers through the braid, letting it fall loose and cool upon her bare skin.

Beyond the closed door she could hear their voices, Marguerite chattering about the evening, her father and Pierre answering now and again. Only Lesharo was silent. He had said nothing more to her as they had walked back from the church, Tonti's remarks and Edmond's words hanging in the air between them.

The pleasure of your company. She turned the phrase over in her mind as she dressed herself in indien garments and folded her other clothing. It was only a token phrase, something people uttered in what Grandmère had been fond of calling "society." What harm was there in friendship and company? I enjoy Edmond's as well, but there is no friendship between him and Lesharo. The thought, finally admitted, drained her. She rubbed her temples with her fingertips and shut her eyes. Why must it be this way? Surely she could bring them together somehow? But for now the answer eluded her.

Troubled, she combed and rebraided her hair and then came out of the bedroom. As she knew he would be, Lesharo was watching her closely, trying to read her expression. She smiled at him in reassurance, and he smiled back. He is my dearest friend, she thought. No matter what else happens, I must make certain he knows that.

"You are certain you wish to make your home here, Pierre? There is room on the island for two houses," her father was saying. "This place is nothing but trouble. The plotting and lying alone would be enough to drive me away, but Cadillac's greed! He is worse than he ever was."

"For now Détroit is only a funnel for the furs that go back to Québec," Pierre admitted. "It is all the Company cares about. They are not at all interested in seeing families clearing the land and farming, no matter what Cadillac tells people. But it will happen. Mark my words."

"I will mark them from a safe distance," Robert said wryly. "How shall we spend the day, my friend? Perhaps fishing out on the river? Père Nicholas will welcome some fat trout for his table." Then he looked down at Cécile's bare legs. "No stockings or leggings?"

"Why? It is too warm for leggings." Seeing where her father was taking this, she added. "This skirt comes nearly to the middle of my shins, Papa. It is perfectly proper."

There were polite knocks at the door.

"What fine manners you have!" exclaimed Pierre when he opened it and stepped back.

Toine entered, followed by his brother. They each made a quick bow, which looked odd since beneath their shirts they were now wearing breechcloths that revealed their knobby scabbed knees. "Merci," Toine said. "Maman says we are to spend the day with you. If you will have us, that is."

"May we swim, Cécile? It is so hot." Jacques's face was shiny with perspiration. "The Miami boys will be swimming. They know how to keep cool, and it is not far from the fort, so Maman will not mind."

"I can think of nothing better," Cécile said. "We will go over to the village. The beach there is best," she added.

"Cécile," said Robert as they were walking out the door.

"Yes, Papa?"

"We will meet you at the village later, then, for Marguerite's feast. And remember; this is not the island. This is Détroit." His eyes met Lesharo's, and the other gave a slight nod. "Keep that in mind."

They walked to the west gate and out of the fort, the boys running on ahead, stripping off their shirts as they called to the laughing children who were already in the river.

"It is such a happy sound, their laughter," Cécile said.

"Are you happy, Cécile?" Lesharo asked suddenly.

"Yes," she answered, but he could hear something in her voice, a small catch of hesitancy.

"What would make you happier?" He studied her face; she would speak the truth to him. She always did.

"I will be far happier when we are back at the island," she said firmly. "Détroit seems to cause only difficulty for us."

"But here you have your church. Is that not a comfort? It gives you happiness to hear the priest say his prayers, to be a part of his mass, does it not?"

"Yes, I suppose it does. It is the one thing about this fort that makes me feel peaceful." She looked sideways at him. "I have always thought that you disliked the Church and anything to do with it. Why *were* you at mass this morning?" Before he could answer, Cécile shouted, "Wait for us! Do not go in alone!" The boys had splashed through the creek and were racing madly toward the beach.

"Then hurry!" called Jacques, kicking off his sodden moccasins. "We are dying of this heat."

"Come in with us," Toine shouted to her. He had done the same and was standing in the river, waves washing around his ankles. "It feels so good. Hurry!"

There were other children swimming in front of the Wendat village. Warriors leaned on their muskets watching them; this was their place, theirs and the Miamis', and only they swam here. Cécile began to undo her skirt. Lesharo and the boys were already in the water calling for her. She stopped.

Three voyageurs and two soldiers had come up behind her. They strolled over to the warriors, who seemed to know them, and their quiet talking began. There was low laughter, a slippery unpleasant sound that she did not like. Cécile retied her skirt, took off her moccasins and walked in.

"What is wrong?" called Lesharo, wading out of the water to where Cécile was standing, holding up her skirt only a very little above her knees.

"Nothing," she said evenly. "I will just wade, I think."

Lesharo looked past her to where the men were plainly watching her. He frowned. "Let us find another spot."

"Then the boys will have no one with whom they may play. I am fine."

"You are hot and will remain hot if you do not come into the river. It is because of them."

She scooped up water and splashed her face, leaning back her head to let it run down her neck. "I can swim another time."

The day was spoiled for him, somehow. The men wandered off in time, but no amount of begging from Toine and Jacques could get Cécile into the water. Finally, they tired of pleading with her and swam with the other boys, Lesharo having left the river to sit with Cécile in the shade of a weeping willow despite her protests.

"There is no satisfaction in it for me," he said. "I do not like seeing you sit here alone."

"Then swim with your eyes shut," she teased. He did not smile at that, so she said, "Marie-Thérèse and Marie-Anne would never swim in the presence of men. I cannot either. This is not the island, as Papa said."

"And yet you swam there with me, but not with Edmond."

"Yes. That is different, though."

"How? Am I not a man, Cécile?"

"What a thing to say. Of course you are, but Edmond is a French officer," she tried to explain. "His view of — well, things — is different, and what he expects of me is different, even after his years with the Mohawks."

"What does Edmond see that I do not? What right has he to expect anything of you?" he snapped. "Is it because he is a Christian, as you are?"

Not once had he ever spoken to her like that. It stung horribly, and so she drew back a little. "What is wrong?" she whispered. "What has he said to you?"

"Forgive me. I am trying to understand your ways, that is all," he fumbled, deeply ashamed that he had lashed out at her in his frustration. "All this time

I have lived among whites, but there is still so much I do not understand — your customs, your Church — I must understand them, Cécile."

She had never seen this side of him. He had no real interest in the customs of whites; it was his own Pawnee ways that he held precious. And as for the Church! The priests had beaten him and shown him nothing but contempt. No. Something was wrong, and he would not tell her in spite of their closeness. He was not lying to her, but he felt he could not tell her what was behind this.

"When we return to the island you are going to become thoroughly weary of my customs," she said, again trying to make him smile a little. It worked. "I will have my own house, you see, and I intend to be a perfect tyrant. Enjoy any leisure moments while you still have them. Now, let us take Toine and Jacques home." She called to the boys.

Their lips were blue and the tips of their fingers as wrinkled as raisins, but still they whined all the way back to the fort. I will find a quiet place and we will talk further, Cécile thought. But there would be no time for talking. From the sounds of drumming that just then began to come from the Wendat village, the feast had already begun.

• • •

What would a celebration be without good food and a full belly, after all? Roasted venison and raccoon, meats of all sorts, smoked over fires, and stews bubbled in large cooking pots. The smells made Cécile's mouth water. Cold water and cider were offered, but no brandy. Marguerite did not want drunkenness and fighting at the feast.

The children and young people ran races outside the palisade. Some warriors wrestled, their lithe bodies slick with bear grease and sweat. Other men gambled, and women gossiped, giggling behind their hands. When darkness came, torches were lit, and a Miami elder brought out a large drum for the dancing. Six strong drummers sat down on the ground around it.

"This is the Stomp Dance," Marguerite explained. She was tying garters around her legs just beneath her knees. "This dance is for when another tribe is among us." She stomped her feet, and Cécile heard the jingle of the small brass bells that were sewn on the garters.

The dancers — men, women and children from both of the tribes — formed a circle around a large fire. Cécile stood in line between Lesharo and her father as the drummers began to beat. The Miami elder danced around the innermost part of the circle, singing loudly as the dancers moved forward. Other singers joined in. The women pounded their feet as they went, and their garters — hung with bells, the hooves of deer or small turtle shells filled with pebbles — made a rhythmic rattling noise. There were no special steps, people moved to the music as they wished, leaving the circle to drink from gourds or to stretch out on the ground to rest and talk.

The drumming stopped; the dancers dispersed and then formed up again. Now they would dance the Two Step, the only dance in which men and women ever touched. A double line formed behind Pierre and Marguerite as the drumming and singing began again.

"We danced something like it, as I recall," whispered a voice close to Cécile's ear.

"You are here," she said to Edmond with undisguised delight. He was out of his uniform tonight. He took her hand firmly in his and pulled her away from Lesharo and into the line.

It is only a dance, Lesharo told himself. It means nothing. I could ask any unmarried woman to dance with me, and perhaps I shall. But he stepped back into the shadow of a longhouse. Cécile was looking all around her, searching for him. She stumbled a bit over her own feet and Edmond caught her, his face growing serious as he pretended to scold her for her awkwardness. She laughed.

There were other whites here — Robert and Pierre and a few voyageurs — but none were as noticeable as Cécile and Edmond. Even by torchlight they stood out, her hair as bright as new copper, his as golden as the cup Père Nicholas had used in his mass. They made a fine couple. With a great wrenching pain in his heart, Lesharo saw how right they must seem together to anyone who watched them. He swallowed hard and thought, it is clear to me that there is only one thing I may do or all will be lost to me. In the morning, I will speak with him.

Cécile was laughing, pulling away from Edmond and shaking her head. Lesharo stepped out from the shadows and forced a smile onto his face.

"Where have you been?" Cécile called out to him.

"Only watching," Lesharo said carelessly. There were stoppered gourds in a pile; he reached down and handed Cécile one of them. She uncorked it and drank, then passed it back to him. Lesharo put it to his lips, took a long swallow and, knowing he must for the sake of her high regard, held it out to Edmond.

"Thank you, but I have no thirst for water," he said.

Lesharo shrugged and drank again. "There is only water here in these gourds. No brandy. That is for Cadillac's table; for an officer's table."

"Those men have brandy," said Cécile. She was watching a group of voyageurs passing a bottle around their circle, each of them taking long swallows. "There will probably be fighting; there is always fighting when such men drink brandy in the way they are doing. How unpleasant for Marguerite." She called out to the men, "Take your bottle and yourselves from here. There is to be no drinking at this feast."

"If you are wise you will keep your tongue in your mouth, L'Indienne Blanche," one of the men shouted back. "What we do is none of your concern."

"Perhaps she will set her chien on us," slurred another. "I tremble in great fear. Take care!"

Cécile stiffened at their words and grabbed at Lesharo's arm to hold him back. "Ignore them. They are drunken fools."

"You will apologize to Mademoiselle Chesne for that," said Edmond, walking slowly forward, his moccasins soundless. "Now."

"You have no authority over us here in this village, Lieutenant," said one of the men. He took another drink from the bottle. He sniggered and then belched. "These are the Wendat, not the Mohawk."

"That may be so, but if I see you in the fort again I will have you thrown from it. You will not trade there any more."

"We work for Tonti and we trade with Tonti," called the drunkest of them, as he fell to his knees. "Better prices." His companions growled at him to be quiet, but he cursed foully and brushed them away. "Take it to Tonti, as though he cares what we call her." He fell forward on his face.

"Lieutenant Saint-Germain may have no authority here, but I do." Pierre was holding his musket, as were Robert and the Miami warriors who stood around him. Others held knives or tomahawks, running their fingers over the weapons' sharp edges. "If you apologize to Mademoiselle Chesne and leave here immediately, it is possible that you may do so without a problem. If not, I cannot be accountable for what these men may do. She is well thought of here — one of them, in some ways — and to give offense to her is to do the same to them."

There were mumbled apologies and then the men withdrew, dragging their companion, who was now vomiting copiously.

"I am so sorry, Marguerite," Cécile whispered, hugging her. "It is my fault."

"It is the fault of the men themselves," assured Marguerite. "Do not let this spoil the night for you. I myself intend to ignore it."

Her father patted her shoulder. "Cécile, you will do the same. Those men are pigs. Animals. Trading with Tonti, indeed. What do you know of that, Edmond?"

"Nothing." Edmond shrugged his shoulders. "There are rumors, but there are always rumors."

"And you will not repeat them, I suppose?" Cécile asked him. "Are you so loyal to him? I would not be surprised if those names they call us came from him."

"He is my superior. And he is a gentleman, Cécile."

"As you are?" Lesharo snapped. "I spit on all such gentlemen and their women."

"But then you know no better, do you Lesharo?" Edmond said smoothly. "I would expect little more from you."

"Edmond! Lesharo!" warned Robert. "Think of what you are saying, each of you. You have been friends up until now."

"Friends? How can you say that, Papa? No. Let them fight," said Cécile. "With knives or pistols or with their bare fists. I am sick of this! Sick of it!" She was trembling now. "Fight and put an end to what is rotting between both of you, but leave me out of it."

"Enough, Cécile!" shouted Robert.

"No! It is not enough!" she shot back at him. "The end of their pointless bickering would be enough. Always I must be in the middle, waiting to see who will snap at the other. Leave me out of it, I say!" Sobbing now, she ran past them to the Miami longhouse, Marguerite following.

"You will do as she said," Robert ordered them angrily. "Your continued goodwill means a great deal to Cécile. I will settle for the pretence of it, since neither of you seems to be able to manage anything better."

Lesharo and Edmond were each breathing hard, but whatever anger they had felt was gone, swept away in the storm of Cécile's emotion and Robert's frank words.

"I spoke harshly," said Lesharo.

"As did I," said Edmond.

"Good enough," said Robert. "Leave Cécile alone for the rest of the night. Perhaps cooling your hot heads in the river might be best."

"What do you know of this business with Tonti, Pierre?" asked Robert, watching Edmond and Lesharo. They had set out together, but now they were separating, each going off in a different direction. So much for their apologies.

"There is talk that the thievery is because of him, that he spirits goods away for sale elsewhere."

Robert sighed. "If it is so, I suppose it means little to us, but someone besides Tonti will take the blame for it, and it will almost certainly be someone who is not white. I am convinced of that."

"Cécile has no idea of why they argue, has she?" asked Pierre suddenly.

"I think in her heart she does," Robert slowly answered. He rubbed his forehead as though the thought of all this pained him. "But she cannot admit that it is she they argue over. She cares deeply for Lesharo, but in her own fashion she cares for Edmond as well."

"They will both ask for her in time, I think, Robert."

"That is what I am afraid of, my friend," said Robert wearily. "That is what I am afraid of."

Chapter 13

It rained before dawn the next morning, a soft gentle pattering upon the roof, and at first Cécile feared that the wedding day would be spoiled by muddy streets. But the sun came out at last. The morning smelled of high summer, of the corn that was slowly ripening in the fields beyond the palisade and of sweet grass, newly bruised under the feet of the grazing oxen. Robins hopped about searching for worms, terns wheeled and cried over the river and the fort had a freshly washed look.

The fort. How she despised it. Each time she came here something unpleasant happened. She longed for the island, to be away from this place, for it was nothing but trouble.

"I look dreadful," she said hopelessly to Marguerite in the bedroom. She was staring at her face in the looking glass. "My eyes are red and swollen, and my hair is standing on end."

"Wash your face once more with cold water and the swelling will go down. I will comb out your hair for you. You could wear what Cadillac's wife gave you over your blouse," teased Marguerite. "Sit, so I can do this." She began to run a comb through Cécile's thick hair, gently loosening the snarls. "I could lace you very tightly into the corset."

Cécile gave a loud groan and said with heavy sarcasm, "You are such a good friend, Marguerite." Then, gently, "I would not ruin these beautiful things you made for me by putting on that ugly corset." She smoothed her hand over the rose-colored fabric all edged with green ribbon the shade of new leaves, then burst out, "I should burn it! I am so tired of all their concern over what I wear! Perhaps I shall go to church in nothing at all."

"That would give them something to talk about," laughed Marguerite. "And if you burn the corset, burn it outside. It will stink. Now come, we are ready." She also was in new clothing she had sewn for her wedding day, a blouse, skirt and leggings of fine white cloth with blue ribbons trimming them. Her hair, like Cécile's, was unbound and hanging down her back.

When they came out of the bedroom only Lesharo, whom she had not seen since the night before, was in the kitchen. The front door was open and Cécile's father was waiting outside, enjoying the brilliant sunshine. Marguerite breezed out to join him and wait for Pierre.

"Have you breakfasted?" Cécile asked awkwardly, trying for something that sounded normal. Of course he would have.

"I did not." He made a small gesture with his hand. "Your father did not eat, and so I thought it best to wait."

"But we will receive communion," Cécile reminded him. "There is no need for you to fast." We will argue. I can feel it coming! Why is this happening? she thought wildly. "Please. Let us have a happy day, Lesharo. I want nothing to spoil it for us."

He had expected coolness. She had been so upset last night, and so her warmth sent a rush of relief through him. "Nothing will spoil it, Cécile. I promise that."

Outside the house, Pierre had arrived, and a small procession was forming. One soldier with a fife and another man with a fiddle were to lead it. Robert would escort Marguerite, since her own father was not there to do so. Cécile, Lesharo and Pierre walked behind them.

Other people followed as they made their way to Ste. Anne's; someone was ringing the church's bell as though to call them. A wedding was a special occasion, a reason to celebrate, and the fact that there was to be a baptism first made it even more important. Cécile saw the Tontis and the Cadillacs waiting near the door of the church with Edmond. Jacques and Toine waved frantically to her and made grotesque faces until their father caught them at it. At a single sharp word from Cadillac, the mischievous boys settled into silence, proudly holding the ribbons they held stretched across the open door.

"It is an old French custom. You must cut the ribbon," Marie-Thérèse explained to Marguerite.

"Why?" she asked, when Cécile handed Marguerite her scissors.

"So that you will be able to get in," suggested Lesharo. Marie-Anne's shriek of laughter rang out.

"It is only a symbol of the obstacles that will meet you in life," Cécile explained. "Just snip it." She raised her voice and finished pointedly, "You cannot get in otherwise, can you?" The ribbon was cut, she pocketed her scissors and the wedding party began to move into the church.

"Marie-Anne has no manners," said Cécile brusquely to Lesharo, dropping behind the others.

"That is true, but she understands the ways of your god. I do not."

"It is an old country tradition — a silly thing, if the truth be told — but it is something people have done for a long time. It has nothing to do with God. Now," she said, "it will be a long service with the baptism and the wedding and the mass. It is going to be another hot day. You had best find a shady spot in which to wait."

"I am coming in with you," he told her, to her surprise. "If I may, that is."

She hesitated only a little, baffled by why he would want to set foot in the church again, and then said cheerily, "Good. It will truly please Marguerite to see you are here."

But did it please Cécile? Lesharo asked himself.

Inside, he sat next to Cécile, keeping his face carefully expressionless, meeting no one's eyes, but very conscious of the soldiers who were staring at him. He saw Edmond, his head bent in prayer. Lesharo stood and knelt when Cécile did. He could make no sense of what the priest was saying, or of the prayers that everyone else knew. He had risen at dawn to pray to the Morning Star, to ask for forgiveness for what he planned to do. Heavy clouds had covered the sky, and rain had been pouring down as though the heavens wept for him. Still he had prayed, but somehow he had known his prayers and entreaties had gone unheard.

Now he was here inside a hot building filled with sweating people while the priest spoke on and on. Then it appeared to be over. Pierre was kissing Marguerite, and there were pleased murmurs. Cécile smiled, her happiness for them making her face glow.

Outside the church, minutes later, men slapped Pierre's back. Cécile kissed Marguerite and then Pierre. "I am so happy for you," she said.

"May you have many children," said Robert. "May they fill your lives with joy."

"Children just like us! Correct, Cécile?" Jacques shouted, grinning up at her.

Pierre was barely able to conceal his look of horror, but Cécile laughed and said, "Yes, children just like you. You are good boys."

"I offer my congratulations as well," said Marie-Thérèse. She was now very pale and leaning heavily on Cadillac's arm, one hand held protectively over her belly. "You will take the boys for the day, Cécile? I rest more easily if the house is quiet."

"With pleasure. I certainly can for today, but we are returning to the island tomorrow. I have no idea how long we will remain there this time."

"We do not care," Jacques said quickly. "We want another adventure, Maman."

"We were good in church and we deserve one. Were we not good in church, Père Nicholas?" Toine called to the priest.

"Yes, for once. There was scarcely any wiggling. What is this? What is this?" asked Père Nicholas. "You are returning to the island, Cécile? How will I instruct Lesharo if he goes with you, as he surely will?"

"Instruct him?" asked Cécile. Scarcely able to believe what she had just heard, she looked back and forth from Lesharo to the priest. Père Nicholas was beaming, although clearly confused, but Lesharo was a picture of uneasiness.

"Ah. I see it was to be a surprise. Lesharo came to me very early this morning, my daughter, and we spoke at length. He wishes to be baptized and brought into the Church." He stroked his chin thoughtfully. "You could instruct him. When he is ready, I will simply question him to make certain that he knows his prayers and understands his responsibilities to God and the Church."

"I cannot do that," sputtered Cécile.

"Nonsense, my daughter," laughed the priest. "You teach Cadillac's children, do you not? I think it is your duty to do this, as a matter of fact. You are his friend, he tells me. What better thing might one friend do for another than to lead his soul to le bon Dieu?" And raising his hand to bless them, Père Nicholas gave Cécile a meaningful stare that had penance engraved upon it.

"Why are you doing this?" she asked Lesharo incredulously. She had him gripped by the arm and was pulling him away from the crowd that surrounded Pierre and Marguerite.

"I thought you would be pleased," he confessed in complete puzzlement. He had watched her reaction, the distress that she had been unable to hide racing across her features. "You were happy for Marguerite."

"You cannot do this just to please me, Lesharo!" She ran a hand through her hair, trying to think of how to explain. "You would be giving up your own beliefs, denying your gods and all the things that have been so important to you. Would you sacrifice all that?"

"Yes. I would make such a sacrifice. If you will not tell me what I need to know, Cécile, I must remain here at the fort so that the priest can do so. I must have the answers to my questions. I need to understand what you believe so that I may believe it as well." This had all gone very badly. He had been certain that it would make her happy, but it had turned sour. And he could tell by the way she was holding herself, by the way her eyes flashed, that it would not take much for her temper to rise. He wanted no repetition of last night, but suddenly he felt a bubble of irritation growing within himself, and his expression darkened a little. "All this time I have shared my stories with you. I have told you about my beliefs and my gods. Now you will not do the same for me when I ask it of you."

She put her hands over her face and then took them away. It is not the same thing, she wanted to shout. But soldiers were now regarding their heated discussion curiously, and her father had turned, his eyebrows lifted in surprise at the tone with which she was speaking. Edmond was there next to him. Something she could not decipher, but did not quite like, was in his eyes.

"I am thoughtless," she said quietly to Lesharo. "You have always been open with me, and I have no right to deny you this. Very well. I will teach you all I know and understand, but you must swear to me that this is what you want for yourself."

"I swear it."

She searched his face for even the hint of uncertainty, but Lesharo, long accustomed to concealing his feelings and thoughts, hid it from her.

Cécile sighed. "Then it does make me happy."

It should have made him happy as well. Instead, a strange hollowness settled around his heart.

• • •

There was yet another celebration that night. The food was much the same, and there was dancing and music, but there the similarities ended, for this celebration was purely French. Marie-Thérèse remained at home in bed, but Cadillac arrived to leave his sons with Cécile for a few hours. He also left several bottles of brandy; cider and wine were already there for those who had a taste for it. There was no room for dancing inside Pierre's small house, so the man who brought out his fiddle stood in the street to play. Candles in lanterns burned on tables that had been set out, and above the fort an almost full moon rode high in the sky, shedding pale light down upon the gathering.

Cécile and Marguerite were the only females there among Pierre's friends who had come to the house. The lack of partners did not trouble the men. They danced with each other. It looked odd to Cécile, who had politely declined the invitations extended to her, but the men were enjoying themselves. Toine and Jacques danced together, although they did not know the steps, giggling and falling as they mimicked the dancers. Back in Québec, the priest would have frowned upon such things, but this was not Québec, and Père Nicholas favored tolerance. Even he took a cup of cider and tapped his foot to the music.

"I would ask you, Cécile, but it has been years since I have done these dances," said Robert in apology.

"And I have never danced them," Cécile replied. "They are so much more complicated than indien dances." As is everything else here, she thought, as the truth of that became quite evident to her.

"*Bonsoir*, Cécile. Robert," It was Edmond in his finest uniform, his hair brushed to a smooth golden gloss. Toine and Jacques, seeing him, left the dancing and ran over.

"Bonsoir, Edmond," said Cécile.

Robert cleared his throat with great emphasis.

"Have you swallowed a moth, Monsieur Chesne?" Jacques asked.

"We would be pleased to hit you on the back with big sticks if you have," said Toine, "though once when I was small and I ate a cricket, Papa picked me up by my feet, held me upside down and shook me. You are too large for that I am afraid."

Robert did not answer; he only waited, regarding Lesharo and Edmond speculatively. Cécile's hands grew damp and her mouth dry.

Lesharo did not want to offer a greeting, not when it was clear that the officer had no intention of speaking first. He saw how Cécile had paled and how Robert was becoming angry; he did not want to be the one responsible for either of those things.

"Bonsoir, Edmond," he said, forcing out the words.

Edmond saw the approval in Robert's eyes and silently cursed himself, wishing he had been the first to speak. "Bonsoir, Lesharo."

"Dance with Lieutenant Saint-Germain," Toine suggested to Cécile. "He knows the steps."

"No, I cannot do that," Cécile said quickly. "It is not the same sort of dancing. I have no wish to be passed from partner to partner." She put her hands behind her back, just as she had the first time she and Edmond had met. The excuse was ridiculous, but last night's argument had begun after the dancing, and she would not have a repetition of anything so upsetting.

"Well, if she will not dance with you, then dance with me," said Toine. "I will hold tightly to your hand and let no one else come near." Even Cécile had to smile at that.

"This is a celebration, and so you should dance with Edmond," Lesharo said suddenly. How it cost him! "And then you will dance with me. I do not know the steps either, but we can make up our own."

"An excellent idea, Lesharo," said Robert. "In that case, even I will dance with my daughter. I know she will be happy to step on all our feet. Enjoy yourself, Cécile; it is only dancing after all."

For the second time that night, Edmond cursed himself for not seeing what would content Robert. And I consider myself the strategist, he thought ruefully. "Touché, Lesharo," he said under his breath and then took Cécile's hand and led her out.

"They make a lovely couple, Robert, even though Cécile persists with her sauvage finery," said Marie-Anne who was strolling over with her husband. "It is unfortunate. Somehow we must make her understand how important appearances are, especially here." She held her hand up, refusing the cup of cider Pierre was offering her. "We will only stay a few minutes. Marie-Thérèse is having an uncomfortable night, and I will be sitting with her until she sleeps." She heaved a great sigh of martyrdom. "Only another woman can give comfort at a time such as this; it will be a long night for us both, but I am certainly happy I chanced upon such a lovely sight as Cécile and Edmond together."

"They are simply dancing, Madame," said Robert. "Nothing more."

"Dancing is a beginning, is it not?" She looked at Lesharo, then back to Robert. "Edmond is a wealthy man. Did you know that, Robert? The woman he finally marries will be well provided for and will live in comfort. Not like peasants as we do here."

"He has been married," said Lesharo. Unable to stop himself, he went on, "As for appearances, Cécile knows very well that it does not matter what one looks like on the outside."

"What a quaint notion! Of course it matters for her. And that marriage of which you spoke just now? It was not truly a marriage at all, you see," corrected Marie-Anne. "For one who is taking instruction, surely you had best learn to understand the difference." She dismissed Lesharo then, with a small wave of her hand. "Let us go, my dear. I promised Marie-Thérèse that I would not be gone long."

Tonti was gesturing to Edmond, calling him over, but Cécile had already left the dancing and was walking quickly to where Lesharo stood, his jaw clenched so that he would say nothing more.

"There is trouble outside the fort, Lieutenant Saint-Germain," said Tonti. "Nothing much, only the sauvages fighting amongst themselves — Miamis and the Ottawas, I believe — but I have posted extra guards at the bastions. I regret depriving you of Mademoiselle Chesne's companionship, but you will take a detachment of men who are not on duty and make your presence known. It matters not if they slaughter each other. However, I want no fighting anywhere near the palisade."

Cécile reached out and took hold of Lesharo's arm, digging in her fingers. She could feel how the muscle was tensed and trembling. Tonti had been watching him, not Edmond, the entire time he had spoken, baiting him and daring him to say something for which he could be punished or thrown out of the fort. *He will have you beaten!* She tried to send her words through her very fingertips and perhaps it worked, for Lesharo remained soundless.

"Very well, Capitaine," said Edmond with resignation.

"You understand these sauvages, Lieutenant," Tonti finished. "You will not fail me. Our congratulations, by the way, Pierre."

"Papa, let us leave for the island now," said Cécile.

"It is night," cautioned Edmond. "And there is trouble. That would be inadvisable. I will complete my assignment and then return, once I am assured of the fort's safety. We will all continue this celebration."

"That would be wonderful, Edmond, but I disagree," said Cécile. "We are all but ready, Papa. I will load the canoe myself." She begged her father with her eyes and mouthed the word "Please."

"Robert, I must insist you do not do this," said Edmond, but Tonti lifted a hand and he reluctantly restrained himself.

"I have given you an assignment, Lieutenant. If Mademoiselle Chesne wishes to leave us, perhaps it is best that she do so. I give my permission, since Cadillac is not here to give his."

"How generous of you," Robert said dryly. "Very well, Cécile. Night travel does not trouble me at all. What of you, Lesharo?"

"I am ready," he answered.

Hastily saying good-bye to Marguerite and Pierre, who generously offered them the use of their own canoe, Cécile ran to the house with Jacques and Toine, who insisted that they must help her. The canoes were loaded in less than an hour, with all of them carrying the gear and supplies.

Inside the fort, the wedding celebrations continued, fiddle music rising into the warm night air. Thunder rumbled in the distance. Sweat ran down Cécile's sides and face as she worked. Her skirt tucked into her sash, she packed blankets and sacks while Lesharo and Robert held the canoes. She looked up when she heard the sound of someone coming down the embankment.

"You boys are to return with me and get into your bed at your mother's orders," Edmond said briskly. Then in a gentler tone he added, "We did not say farewell properly, Cécile."

"No, you have not. You kissed Pierre and Marguerite good-bye," called Jacques to Cécile. He yawned enormously. "Move over, Toine; you are crowding me and I shall fall into the river. I have no room. Why do you not kiss Edmond good-bye, Cécile?"

"You have all the room, Jacques." Toine drove an elbow into his brother's ribs.

"Stop fighting this instant," Cécile said, her cheeks flaming. "The one thing has nothing to do with the other."

"But when you were swimming with Lesharo," Toine insisted, "we saw you —"

Robert coughed very loudly. "You two will be silent, or I may push you into the river myself." He turned his attention to Edmond, who now seemed sorely tempted to do the same thing. "What of the indiens? What has happened?"

"It was nothing, really, just two young men arguing over a musket lost while gambling. It was finished before we arrived." He looked back to where the Odawa village stood in the darkness. "It is only a matter of time before something serious occurs, though."

"Which is all the more reason for us to leave," Cécile said shortly, pushing her hair back from her face.

"May I call on you if I can get away, Cécile?" asked Edmond.

"I am surprised that Toine's and Jacques's mother did not order you to go with us, even though they are to remain behind," Lesharo said in a casual manner. He had been broodingly mute since they had left the fort, waiting for Edmond to arrive, as he knew he would.

"She did, in fact, but it is more important that I remain here, and besides, Cadillac refused her," Edmond replied, matching Lesharo's tone precisely. "May I call on your daughter, Robert?"

"So courtly, Edmond?" Cécile said quickly. "I am not accustomed to such ceremony, as you very well know. Yes. Call on *us*." She said the last word with great emphasis.

Edmond gave a short laugh. "Very well, I shall call on all of you, then."

Once in the canoe with Lesharo, Cécile waved to the boys and then turned her face to the river. She could almost feel Edmond's eyes upon her back as they paddled away. There was no more conversation from anyone for a long while. Side by side, their canoes passed the Odawa village, quiet and tranquil. It is not really tranquil at all, though, thought Cécile, any more than is my own life. Thunder rumbled and lightning lit the undersides of clouds. It is all waiting to happen, just like that storm, and there seems to be nothing I can do to stop it. Perhaps it would have been better if we had not left Québec. She sighed and sat straighter, dipping her paddle to match Lesharo's rhythm. They had left the city, and they were here; she must make the best of it.

It was nearly dawn by the time they reached the island and the cove, and the storm that had been threatening them all night was coming closer. Cécile, bleary with lack of sleep, began to help carry up several heavy sacks.

"No," said Robert. "Lesharo and I will do this. Take the canvas sheet and drag the tent up on it. You can shelter under it if the storm breaks before we can put up the tent."

Now he will say something, thought Lesharo; all night he has been thinking about what the boys said. But to Lesharo's surprise, Robert only worked in silence. They tied the canoes to the fallen log and unloaded all the supplies, carrying them up to the longhouse where Cécile was spreading the tent. Once they had covered everything with the canvas and weighted it down with stones, Robert and Lesharo went back for the canoes.

"Cécile will be contented here," said Robert. "It suits her."

"Yes," said Lesharo, braced for the scathing words that would surely come.

"Her happiness is more important to me than anything else in the world."

"It is to me as well, Robert."

The older man searched Lesharo's face. "I believe it is. I would not look kindly upon any man who hurt her. Her feelings are easily wounded; she is quite like her mother in that way." He looked back at Cécile. "Quarreling and conflict upset her greatly. She values friendship. We left everything behind in Québec, and although she does not place great value upon possessions or money, she treasures her friends and the people she is close to. The boys, Pierre, Marguerite." He paused and then said, "Edmond. And, of course, you. You — all of you — are everything she has, and I think it is really all she needs to be happy."

"I understand, Robert," said Lesharo.

"Do you? For years since her mother has been gone, Cécile has made her own decisions and chosen her own companions. She has always been wise in her choices, and it is seldom that I have had to interfere, but if there were something or someone that might hurt her, I would not hesitate to step in."

"As you should. You are her father."

"Your interest in the Church, your desire to have her instruct you. It is sincere?"

"It is. I want to understand your god as Cécile does, and as you do."

"You want what is best for her, do you not? No matter how hard that would be?"

"You know that I do." He swallowed and said suddenly. "Speak plainly to me, Robert."

"I thought I had been." He squeezed Lesharo's shoulder. "Let us get this canoe to shelter and help her before the tent blows away."

The tent was up before the storm broke, but only just. It took them a long while to settle down; they watched the lightning and marveled at the power of the violent wind. Slowly, the thunder receded into the west and only heavy rain fell.

"It is so good to be back here, Papa," Cécile whispered.

"I could not agree more," said her father quietly.

"What do you think?" she asked Lesharo, but he lay on his back, his eyes closed. He is asleep, thought Cécile, turning onto her side away from him.

Lesharo lay awake for a long while, fighting the weariness of mind and spirit that wanted to drag him into darkness. He prayed, but his prayers were empty, like hollow shells upon a beach. He sat up, meaning to go out, to walk and think.

"It will all settle out, Lesharo," said Robert. He had remained awake, watching the young man. "Try to sleep. You need to be rested, my friend, for what lies ahead."

Lesharo lifted a questioning brow.

"We have a longhouse to finish," whispered Robert. "And then there is swimming with my daughter and such. Perhaps she may need to be saved from drowning again. Sleep well." Then he grinned and turned over.

• • •

For the next weeks, they worked on the small longhouse. Robert had traded with the Wendat for elm bark. This they lashed onto the frames, and a second layer of framework was added to hold down the bark. Four sleeping platforms were constructed, and Robert began to gather rocks for the hearth he would build.

The days were warm and fine; from working in the brilliant sunshine, Cécile's fair skin grew tinged with color, and streaks of reddish gold ran through her hair. She walked along the marshy areas gathering cattails that were ready to explode into seed, so that she could stuff the mattresses she planned to make. They scooped up kettles of thick clay with which they began to chink the cracks in the longhouse walls. Each afternoon they swam, reveling in the cool water and play of sunlight upon the rippled sand beneath their feet.

In the evenings, there was her journal. She wrote of her day, of what she had seen, or perhaps how the work had gone; facts only, for there were no more stories from Lesharo.

"You have heard all my stories," he said when coaxed.

Strangely disappointed at his reluctance to do something he had once so enjoyed, she tried telling them tales about the Church, and the saints and sacraments. Hearing those things would help Lesharo with what he needed to know. But somehow it did not seem right with her father listening, so she saved anything about the Church for Lesharo when they were alone together. Lesharo would listen patiently, repeating what she told him, trying to understand what she had said.

"You will be baptized. You will confess your sins and then you may receive communion as we do," she explained to him one time. "When the priest blesses the bread and wine, you see, they become the body and blood of Jesus."

"How can such a thing be?" he had asked.

"Well, it just is. I cannot really put it into plain words. Think of all the things in which you have believed up to now: that the moon and the sun wedded and through them people came into being."

"But that is true. That is a simple thing in which to believe."

"No. It is faith, Lesharo. You must pray for faith."

Prayer did not help him. Her religion held no meaning at all, but still he listened and asked endless questions in hopes of puzzling it out. There was no comfort in it, in the thoughts of bread and wine, of blood, of the incense-scented church that awaited him like a cage in which his spirit and prayers could not rise to the heavens. Rather, it left him empty. His heart was as cold as the pitiless stars that shone down upon him at night.

Edmond did not come, but they saw many other canoes traveling into the river from Lake St. Clair and the north. More indiens were moving their villages to Détroit, joining the thousands that already crowded around the fort in uneasy company. Then one afternoon three canoes stopped at the island; in them were Wendat warriors who were taking their families away from the fort. That night, Cécile, Lesharo and Robert walked through the forest to the clearing where the Wendat had made their camp.

"What word is there of Détroit?" asked Robert. He had his pipe and passed a bag of tobacco around the circle of men.

"There is fighting. They hide it from Cadillac, but the young warriors cannot be controlled," one man told them as he filled his pipe. "Cadillac's prices are too high, and the game grows scarcer. Then there is the spirit."

"What spirit?" asked Lesharo. Until now he had been quietly listening, half lost in thought, locked within himself as he so often was these days. At the man's words he straightened and Cécile saw his face fill with keen interest.

"There is a great wolf that has been seen," said the man uneasily. "It is very bold. The sachems say it is a spirit wolf that may come and go as it will. It seeks something it has lost, so it is very dangerous. Such a thing should not be interfered with. Everyone knows that, but Tonti has encouraged men to hunt for it. He blames the spirit wolf for the lack of game. Tonti is a fool."

In time, Cécile and the others returned to their longhouse and their own fire. Lesharo was silent all the rest of that evening, finally disappearing into the darkness to return very late that night. Cécile heard him creep in, but she did not call to him; earlier, each time she had tried to speak to him about the wolf, he had turned away from her. She drifted back to sleep, wishing she could help him and knowing she could not.

Cécile woke before dawn. Lesharo's bed was empty. A heavy dew had fallen, soaking the grass, and his footprints led in the direction of the beach. He has run away! she thought frantically. He has taken one of the canoes and left. She hurried through the woods, through the low fog that misted the ground and spangled spider webs with droplets, expecting to see nothing. But there was Lesharo kneeling in the damp sand, his arms outstretched, facing the eastern sky. He was praying in Pawnee, his voice hoarse with emotion.

Perhaps she should have left him. She could not. They had been together too long, sharing nearly everything, and she wanted to share this with him as well. Cécile crossed the beach and stopped just behind him. When she put a gentle hand upon his shoulder, he lowered his arms and his head dropped.

"It is my fault that they hunt the wolf."

"Lesharo, how can you possibly think such a thing? It is not your fault at all. If anyone is to blame, it is Tonti."

"I have betrayed my gods and myself. I am worthless in the eyes of my people." He stood and faced her. "I cannot do it, Cécile. I cannot be baptized. It is wrong."

"That does not matter to me. It never has. What I do not understand is why you even considered such a thing. It was right for Marguerite. She loves Pierre and would do anything for him, even give up her gods." Lesharo looked away from her and back again. "You were doing it for me," she finished in confusion. "Why?"

"I thought that perhaps if I accepted your god, if I was baptized as Edmond is, perhaps one day I might be as worthy as he."

"Worthy of what? You are the finest person I know."

"I hoped that perhaps someday, if you were willing, if your feelings for me were ever to go beyond friendship, that I would speak to your father and we two might —" He shook himself, as though by doing so he could shed the burden of what he carried. "There is no chance for that now."

Cécile felt herself go very cold, and then a sweet warmth surged through her, filling her face with color. Of course. This was what it had always been, and deep inside herself she had always known it. She put her fingertips over his mouth. "My feelings go far beyond friendship, Lesharo. How could you have thought that anything would change you in my eyes? It is I who am not worthy of you, and yes, yes, you *will* speak to Papa in time. We have nothing but time here."

He took her hand away from his face and squeezed it. "No. It is too late, Cécile; there is no time left at all. I must leave here before there is nothing of me that remains."

"No! You cannot leave!"

The canoe was already down at the water's edge. In it were a single blanket, his bow and his quiver of arrows. He had taken no food, but a water gourd lay upon his folded capot. "Tell your father that I would not be taking the canoe, but there is no other way for me to get to the mainland. I will leave the canoe in the bushes just near the large beech tree there on the other side. I am not a thief."

He had begun walking, Cécile at his side, speechless now. She grabbed at his arm and pulled him to a stop.

"Please do not go! Lesharo, it may not even be the same wolf."

"You know it is the same wolf that followed us here. There was a reason it did so, Cécile. I could not see that reason until now. I am Skidi. I am Pawnee, and I cannot turn my back on what I am. They hunt the wolf. I cannot stop them from doing so, but I can keep them from killing it."

"How?" she cried. "How can you possibly do that?"

"You spoke to me of faith. I have faith that it will follow me where I go. I will travel far from here, and the wolf will remain alive." He pulled her into his arms then, in a close embrace. For many minutes, he simply held her, knowing that it would be the only time in his life that he would do so. He kissed her mouth with infinite tenderness and then held her away from himself, studying her face so that he would always remember it. He let her go. "You have said to me that your god sacrificed his son for all people. There is sacrifice among the Pawnee. I have not told you that, have I? Each spring, a young woman who has been taken as a prisoner is sacrificed to the Morning Star. Then the lands will be fertile. Life will remain good."

"Why are you telling me this now?" cried Cécile. "What has this to do with us?"

"What I feel for you is my sacrifice to the Morning Star, Cécile. I offer it in hope of finding my way." He stepped back from her.

"Not like this," begged Cécile. "I have nothing of you if you leave like this."

He reached into his shirt, took out his medicine bag and pulled it over his head. Then he slipped it over Cécile's head and let it fall upon her chest. "For remembrance," he said.

Her hands shaking, Cécile removed her scapular and put it over his head. "For remembrance," she said.

"Tell your father I will never forget his goodness. Nor yours." He paused and then whispered, "Do not harden your heart to Edmond when he offers his friendship to you, Cécile. We did not like each other — we could not — but I know that he is a good man."

She watched him push the canoe out and then climb in. He did not call farewell, or wave, or even look back, and she was as still as though she had been carved from stone. There was just the sound of his paddle dipping into the water and the soft plopping of water droplets on the glassy river. The canoe disappeared into the mist, the sounds faded and she was alone.

Cécile let herself sink down onto the wet sand. The sun came up and the mist disappeared; gulls called to each other as they fought over fish. Still, she sat there, her mind numb, until she heard someone approaching. It was her father.

"He is gone?" Robert squatted down next to her. "It does not surprise me at all."

"I could have tried harder to stop him." Cécile's breath was suddenly coming as quickly as though she had been running. Her chest ached and her heart was pounding.

"You could not have held him here. It was right to let him go. Now come back to the longhouse."

Cécile shook her head. She drew up her legs and leaned her head down upon her knees. "Leave me alone for a while, please, Papa," came her muffled words. "Just a little while. I promise I will come soon."

Robert hugged her hard, and then climbed to his feet and brushed the sand from himself.

"Could we try to find him, Papa?" she asked faintly.

"I think, if you love him, you will not consider such a thing. Lesharo must seek his own path, Cécile." His moccasins crunched in the sand, and then there was only the soft wash of waves upon the beach and the morning calls of robins.

If I love him? thought Cécile, clutching his medicine bag tightly with both of her hands. What have I done?

• • •

We went across for the canoe today, Papa saying that there was no need to hurry. It was there, hidden just as Lesharo had said it would be. There is so much thievery at the fort, and yet a canoe may lie safely hidden in the bushes for so many days. Strange.

Papa misses him very much. For myself, I can no longer feel anything at all.

Chapter 14

Lesharo reached out his hand and traced a circle around the print with his forefinger. He was on one knee, thoughtfully chewing his lip, his brows drawn down in complete concentration as he stared at the wolf's large paw print. For more than two weeks he had lived like the wolf itself, emptying his mind of everything but the search. He had stayed away from the places of men, keeping to the deepest parts of the forest. Still he heard them and, hidden in the cool shadows, watched them passing as a wary animal watches the hunter. They defiled the forest with their noise and their endless threat of death. Even this morning he had heard muskets firing, the sound angering him, for he was certain they hunted the wolf.

"The Wendat said you were seen near the fort, but that is because you were searching for me," he whispered. He stood and turned slowly around, letting his eyes drift carefully over the trees. He drew in a deep breath, but there was only the smell of dead leaves and damp loam. "Why will you not come to me?"

He had seen the wolf at a distance a number of times, watching him in perfect calmness, ears cocked forward, yellow eyes curious, there one moment and gone the next. He could feel when it was near him; it seemed as though the air would tremble the way it did before lightning struck. Once, drinking at a stream, the cold water cupped in his hands, he had looked up to see the wolf sitting on the other side. It had yawned, stretched languidly and then trotted away with its tail waving.

He sighed, annoyed at himself for the restlessness he now felt. He must pray for patience and let the wolf do as it would. Squinting into the sky, he decided to end his search for today. Sunset came earlier now, and he should think about food. Picking up his bow, he set out.

There had been a time when he had wanted to own a musket badly, so that he could hunt as Robert did. He had hoped to trade for one at the fort some day. Now he was grateful for his bow. Gunfire would have drawn people to him and that he did not want. Still, it would have been good to hunt with Robert, both of them armed in the same way. He gave himself a hard jerk. The musket would have changed him no more than baptism would have. It was done with, and he would not think of Robert or muskets or Cécile. He had made his sacrifice.

But she was always there, like some elusive thing floating just beneath the surface of his thoughts when he was awake. In his dreams he saw her green-blue eyes and the flame of her hair. He could not rid himself of her memory, any more than he could stop breathing or stop the flow of blood through his veins. Likely it was the blood, for some of hers flowed within his veins and was both a comfort and a torment to him. I will pray harder, he thought. Tomorrow I will fast again, and it will be easier not to think of what I must forget.

The ground sloped here; above him on the rise was a tangle of dead ash trees, old ones that had come down in a storm, each knocking the other over like the bowling pins the whites played at. Lesharo looked down, careful of his footing. Here were more of the wolf's prints. He stooped and touched one, then licked his finger, cringing at the taste of blood. There were droplets everywhere but no sign of heavy gouts, and so perhaps the animal was not wounded badly. He looked up and saw where its claws had skidded down the slope, leaving the muddy earth bare of leaves. There were no more tracks; the trail ended at this place. Iciness gripped him when he found the wolf in the bushes where its body had slammed against an outcropping of rock. Leaves and mud were matted into the silvery-red coat of the huge beast. And blood. There was a thin groove across its muzzle and another across its shoulder. It was not dead, though; there was a very shallow rising and falling as breath entered and left its chest.

Rage as hot as the branding iron that had been set upon his arm burned into him. He fought it. If he were to do anything to help the wolf, he must remain calm. If it woke and its injuries were small ones, it would rouse itself and bolt away. But there might be wounds he could not yet be sure of, bones broken, or bleeding deep within from the fall.

He ran his hand over its coat and stroked its head gently. "I will release you if I have to," he whispered, pulling his knife from its sheath. He tested it on his thumb. Blood welled up, bright and red. "You will not suffer. I will be quick, my brother."

Men shouted. Someone fired a musket. Lesharo whirled and stood over the body of the wolf, just as an Odawa warrior raced down the slope, screaming war cries.

"Step away from it!" the Odawa shouted in French. He raised his musket and aimed. "Step away, I tell you."

"Be gone from here," said Lesharo, his eyes drawn to more men who were coming down the slope. There were six. He was one. "The wolf is mine."

"I have wounded it!" the warrior bellowed. "Step away or I will shoot through you."

"No. I found this wolf and it is mine."

"Well, well," said another of the Odawas, staring hard at Lesharo. "This is the chien who thought he was above the laws of Détroit. The one who stayed with L'Indienne Blanche and then with the Miami." He pushed through the loose circle of men that had formed around Lesharo and the wolf. "Tonti may pay us for this wolf. I wonder if he would pay a bounty for you, chien? I have heard he hates you. Shall we see? Move away from the wolf. We need only the head and pelt as proof that it is dead."

"It is not dead. It is but wounded."

"Do not kill it!" shouted a warrior excitedly. "Let us bring it back alive. Think of what he will pay then."

"You should not have meddled, chien." The man made a small motion with his chin and two warriors struck Lesharo from behind; a musket came down across his wrist with sickening pain, and his knife flew into the leaves. They dragged him up. "Tie him securely and take his weapons." They bound Lesharo's wrists together and hobbled his ankles so that he would not be able to run.

Lesharo wanted to turn his face away. He could not bear what they were doing to the wolf. They tied its muzzle tightly closed and bound together all four feet with strips of leather. Now they were pulling its head down to lash it to the leather that bound its legs. The indien leaning over the animal suddenly screamed and leaped back. The wolf's eyes had opened. Growling and making horrible noises, it struggled to free itself. Its head lashed wildly and its body jerked, but it could not escape.

They dragged the creature through the forest. It struggled at first, shrieking and twitching. Lesharo stumbled on behind it, calling to the wolf in Pawnee. It closed its eyes and grew quiet, its sides heaving. Some of the Odawas muttered at that, looking sideways at Lesharo so that the whites of their eyes showed their fear.

"It is exhausted, you fools. He has no power over it," said their leader. "Take care where you drag it. Tonti will not want the fur damaged. It will not be hurt, chien. Not yet, anyway. That I promise you."

It was sunset when they reached the fort. The gates were just being closed for the night.

"We must see Tonti. We have something for him." The warrior gestured to the wolf, its eyes now open. A deep growl rumbled in its chest.

"Are you crazy, bringing that here?" asked the guard incredulously.

"Let me see Tonti. Let us speak with Cadillac," the warrior demanded.

"You will see no one." It was Edmond, bristling with irritation. His eyes widened when he saw what lay on the ground.

"He will want to see the wolf," said the warrior. "He will want to see this as well." Lesharo was pulled from the group of warriors and shoved forward to trip and fall at Edmond's feet. Edmond helped him up. Pulling out a knife, he cut the ropes from Lesharo's wrists, to angry shouts from the Odawas.

"See to your ankles," said Edmond, handing him the knife. "Who has his weapons?" There was no answer, only more angry muttering. "No one, of course. Very well; keep the knife, Lesharo."

"The wolf, Edmond," said Lesharo. He slipped the knife into the sheath that hung inside his shirt.

"Let them have it, Lesharo. It is against my better judgment, but come inside and tell me what it is you are doing here. *Caporal*, shut and bar the gate."

"No. I will not leave the wolf," Lesharo said.

"It is ours, chien. We will return with it tomorrow," said the Odawa.

"Edmond." Lesharo swallowed hard. "I beg you. It will die if tied like that all night."

"It is only a wolf. I will not start an incident over a wolf. Not for you. Not for anyone."

"Not even for Cécile?" he begged. "She is sister to the wolf. She has Pawnee blood in her veins."

"The scar on her palm," Edmond whispered. There was silence, his soldiers waiting, ready for his command, the Odawas tense. "Look up," said Edmond with a slow smile. The Odawas did. There were armed men in the bastions; their muskets aimed and ready. "As you know, we are many and you are but a brave few. A wise man would leave the wolf here and return tomorrow. I will take you to Tonti myself then."

"You give your word?" asked the warrior, glaring at Lesharo.

"You have my word."

The Odawa is only saving face, thought Lesharo. He would not dare to order his warriors to fire. Still, he felt relief wash over him when the warrior muttered something in his own tongue and the men followed him away.

"Delisle and Leroy; drag this thing in and do not be foolish. It cannot bite, as you see." The gate was closed and barred, as Edmond set his hands on his hips. "What do you suggest we do now, Lesharo?"

"Free it, once we are certain the Odawas are gone. I will cut the bonds, and then I will leave. It will follow me."

"It is a wild animal," laughed Edmond. "It will run into the woods and be shot or caught again. There are snares all around the fort."

Lesharo shook his head. "It is more than a wolf, Edmond. It is part of me, and so it is part of my spirit."

"I do think it could be far more than a wolf. Do you not agree, Antoine?" asked Tonti. He smiled at Edmond and then at Lesharo as he stepped forward. "Who gave you permission to bring this beast in here, Lieutenant?"

"I thought it best, Capitaine," Edmond answered. "There might have been trouble otherwise with the Odawas."

"Get rid of it," snapped Cadillac. "Marie-Thérèse is terrified of wolves."

"Not so quickly, Antoine." Tonti was walking slowly around the wolf, stroking his mustache. He poked it with the toe of his shoe, and its low growling rose to a roar.

"Do not touch it!" Lesharo shouted. He lunged toward Tonti, his fists clenched, his eyes hot and angry.

Tonti had his sword from its scabbard in a flash and the tip of it pressed under Lesharo's chin. "Stand still like a good chien. Do it, or I will order that this beast be shot and its body dumped in the river, which would be a waste." Lesharo stood in mute defiance, a line of blood snaking down his throat. "You all saw him attack me. We still have those two crates in which we transported the calves? Yes. They are in the small barn next to the church, I believe. Put this creature in one of them and the wolf in the other. Make certain to move any of our fowl from the barn first so they are not distressed."

"Listen to me, Antoine," said Tonti. He sheathed his sword as Lesharo and the wolf were dragged away. "We shall send the beast to Québec to the Company. Such a unique offering made in friendship? It cannot hurt our relationship with them."

"*My* relationship, Alphonse. *I* have a relationship with the Company. You have a relationship with me, may I remind you?" Cadillac answered wryly. "Although, I will admit that it is a brilliant idea, if unorthodox."

"What is to be done with the indien?" Edmond asked Tonti quietly. "Lesharo is a friend of Robert Chesne and his daughter, Cécile, as you know, Capitaine."

"Oh, I am fully aware of that, Lieutenant, though it does not matter to me in the least. Chesne and his daughter may have their sauvage back in time, though he will be somewhat the worse for wear. I intend to have him lashed thoroughly in the morning. The humiliation and pain will do him good, and perhaps our mademoiselle may learn a lesson herself."

"Capitaine," said Edmond in disbelief. "This has nothing to do with Cécile."

"There you are wrong, Lieutenant Saint-Germain. She must learn to understand her place in the scheme of things here. I am certain you will be able to change the thinking in that pretty head of hers in time. Until then, the flogging of her pani will make a good beginning for you." He nodded to Cadillac and sauntered away, his hands behind his back, glowing with satisfaction and the perfection of his plan.

"Sieur Cadillac, will you not reconsider? There was no attack," said Edmond when Tonti was gone. "Lesharo is no friend of mine, but this is vengeance only. His loyalties lie only with himself."

"I trust you are speaking about the sauvage and not your superior, Lieutenant. As for this Lesharo, yes, he is Robert's friend, but he did openly threaten an officer. I cannot have that sort of behavior. I think it would be best for you to reconsider something as well, Lieutenant. Where do your own loyalties lie? Now, if you will excuse me, I have things to which I must see."

• • •

"Robert! Cécile!"

Pierre's voice woke her. He was there at the door of the longhouse, silhouetted against the rising sun's rosy light. Her father was out of his bed immediately. "What is wrong? Has there been an attack?"

"Dress quickly and arm yourself. It could scarcely be worse."

He told them about Lesharo and the wolf. Edmond had come to him in the night, several hours ago. Pierre had then gone to the Miami longhouse for men who would help him.

"If I know Tonti, he will have Lesharo beaten until his pride is broken."

"He will never be able to do that. Lesharo will die before he bends to Tonti," said Cécile, her voice quivering. "We must get there quickly, Papa."

"You will stay here on the island, Cécile," her father said shortly. He slung his powder horn and hunting bag over his shoulder and picked up his musket. "I will bring Lesharo home."

"I will bring him home," she said. "I should never have let him leave."

"You will obey me!" shouted Robert. "I will not have you involved in this!"

"I have been involved since I bought him. I will not be left behind," said Cécile. "If I have to swim to shore and walk to Détroit, I will go."

Her father stared at her, his face set and angry. "Do not do this. Not now. You will obey me, Cécile," he whispered.

"I have obeyed you. You told me not long ago that a person's heart is a fragile thing. That you would not care to see anyone's heart broken, and I have thought about that every day since, Papa. A broken heart may be mended, given time. But the wrong choice made when I know my own heart very well — that would never heal within me. I *will* go with you, Papa."

A moment passed, and then Robert cleared his throat. "Come, then," he said, his voice as steady as he could make it.

"We can be there in a few hours," said Pierre, as they ran to the canoes that were already floating in the water, tethered to the log.

A few hours! she cried within herself, fighting the fear that was blossoming there like a dark flower. And she began to pray.

• • •

The barn had been dark. Once the soldiers were gone, a heavy silence had descended upon the two stout oak crates that stood next to each other. In time, the feet of mice began once again to patter about, as the little animals searched for spilled corn or grain. Lesharo had listened to the wolf's labored breathing for a long while.

"Be still," he said in Pawnee. "I will free you, but I must have light to do so."

He talked to the wolf, telling it stories, keeping his voice low and even. Then when the sun came up and tiny lines of dusty pink light filtered into the barn, Lesharo took Edmond's knife from his sheath.

"First your muzzle. I will not hurt you, and you must not bite me, no matter how badly you might want to."

He reached his left hand into the crate and reached toward the massive head. The wolf was very still; as his hand touched it, a low growl began deep in its chest. Then slowly he extended his right hand, the knife in it. He slid the knife tip under the binding and partially slit it. The wolf did not move. Lesharo sawed at the leather with which its feet were tied together. His forehead was against one of the crate's slats, sweat running down his face. The knife slipped and nicked one of the wolf's front legs. It roared and arched its spine, and in an instant, the leather parted. It was on its feet clawing at its face, falling, its legs out of control until the leather was off. It stood unsteadily, head lowered, an angry growl rumbling in its throat. Then it sank down as far from Lesharo as it could.

The door of the barn opened and Edmond strode in. He had two canteens slung over his shoulder. "Are you mad?" he asked, staring at the wolf, which was licking its cut leg. It rose to its feet at his approach, lips drawn back in a snarl, poised for attack. "He means to have you whipped as an example. Tonti will be furious when he sees that you have not only freed this thing, but that you have injured it. You may end up with worse than a beating."

"It does not matter," Lesharo said wearily. He had slept only a little, and his dreams had been of the island and Cécile, vivid and disturbing. "It might have died had I not."

"You may be dead when he is done with you. You will wish you were. Here." He crouched and held out one of the canteens.

"What is in it?"

"Brandy. Drink it all quickly and the pain will be less for you."

Lesharo shook his head. "I will bear the pain."

"I thought as much." Edmond passed the other canteen through the slats. "It is water only." The wolf threw itself at the side of its crate, snapping and snarling, and Edmond jumped to his feet and stepped back.

Lesharo uncorked the canteen. He sipped, then reached into the wolf's crate and poured water onto the floor, the wolf backing into a corner as he did so. It lowered its head and sniffed, then cautiously stretched out its neck and lapped at the water, its yellow eyes sliding from Lesharo to Edmond. Then it backed into the corner of the crate, still growling softly.

"I have not seen such a thing in all my days," whispered Edmond.

"Open your eyes, Edmond," said Lesharo. "You see with the eyes of a white man. Oh, you are white, but you once saw differently. Open your eyes and see what is happening in this place, what they are doing to the land and the people." He rubbed his hands over his face. "The wolf? It would bite me if it could.

Perhaps it would kill me. It is a wolf, after all, but it is more than that to me. Those are the ways of the Pawnee and the wolf. Loyalty. Family." He lowered his voice and asked, "What are the ways of Edmond Saint-Germain?"

"What is this? What is this?" Père Nicholas rushed into the barn. He was in his vestments, dressed to say mass. "They said a prisoner was in here. What have you done, my son?"

"This is not Church business, Père Nicholas!" said Tonti brusquely, following close behind. He had a party of armed men with him. Two of them had coils of rope. Another large strong fellow who was already in his shirtsleeves carried a whip. Tonti stopped dead, his face white and rigid. "Who freed the wolf?"

"I did," said Lesharo. He could not stand in the crate, and so he sat as tall as he could. "With my knife."

"Toss it out." Lesharo stared at Tonti insolently. "Shoot the wolf, Parent. Aim for, say, the leg. Do not kill it." The man aimed. Lesharo pulled out the knife and tossed it onto the barn's dirt floor. Tonti picked it up and turned it over in his hands. "This is a very fine weapon. You have one much like it, do you not, Lieutenant?"

"I stole it from him long ago," said Lesharo. "It was easy since he is so careless."

"The knife is mine. I gave it to him last night because he has never had a decent weapon of his own."

"Now, now, Lieutenant. Enough of this banter. You know, I rather think I believe you, sauvage. I rather think you are our thief. I have long suspected it. Open the crate and get him out. If he resists, shoot the wolf."

"There will be no whippings today," Père Nicholas commanded. "In fact, all of you who are not necessary to the safety of the fort will attend mass! It is a holy day, I remind you."

"It is October fifth. There is no holy day," scoffed Tonti.

"It is the feast of St. Jerome, the patron of scholars. As an indifferent and struggling scholar, I had a special devotion to St. Jerome and often prayed to him in my years at the seminary. To miss mass today would be a sin of proportions I can barely describe." He was rocking on his heels, staring at the rafters of the barn. "The penance! It makes my thoughts spin to think of the penance; and then, of course, there would be the offering to the Church."

"To mass! All of you!" shouted Tonti. He began to swear under his breath and then thought better of it, considering the penance that could easily result. "This will wait until midnight when St. Jerome's feast is over. I trust there are no saints waiting to be honored tomorrow, Père Nicholas. The patron of canoe makers or the patron of milkmaids?" He stormed out after his men.

"Not particularly," mused Père Nicholas. "Oddly enough, yesterday, the fourth, was the feast of St. Francis of Assisi, the founder of my Recollect order."

The priest smiled gently at Lesharo. "He is the saint who looks after all animals, my son. Tell me; are you ready for baptism? Has Cécile prepared you well?"

Lesharo forced himself to meet the man's kind eyes. "She tried hard, but no. I will not be baptized."

"I see. Perhaps in time."

"No. I will not have the water poured over my head as Marguerite did."

"There are other sorts of baptism, my son. There is baptism of desire, where one comes to le bon Dieu simply by the force of faith and longing. There is also baptism by fire, where one dies for one's belief and then the soul passes on to its eternal rest. Surely that will not be your fate; but I believe that you will be baptized yet. You are closer to God than you suspect, for he watches over you always."

"I have my own faith and my own god. I pray to the Morning Star."

"How delightful! You are unaware, then, that the Church calls Mary, the mother of Jesus, the Morning Star? It is quite possible Cécile does not know of that, I suppose. A strange coincidence, is it not? But then life is full of such things." He blessed Lesharo and then he blessed the wolf. "I will pray for you, my son." At the door of the barn he paused. "Will they get here in time, do you think, Lieutenant? I give you dispensation from mass, naturally, so that you may watch for them."

"They will come," Edmond answered, his voice grim, as the priest walked out.

Lesharo stared at Edmond, a look of horror on his face. "What did you do? Tell me you have not sent word to her." He gripped the slats of the crate, and the wolf began to growl once more.

Edmond lifted his head. A sound was coming from the distance, low and steady. It was the beating of indien drums, something not often heard during the day without good reason. Without even glancing at Lesharo, he walked to the barn's door and leaned against the frame.

"There will be trouble. I can feel it in the very sound of those drums," he said thoughtfully.

"Answer me!" cried Lesharo. "Have you sent for her?"

"Yes!" Edmond shouted, turning on him. "What else could I do? She would never forgive me had I not!"

"They beat their war drums, and you are bringing her here!" Lesharo shook the slats yet again, and then let his head hang limply between his upraised arms, not hearing the sound of Edmond's shoes on the hard-packed dirt as he walked away. The drums went on, heavy and ominous, beating a message at which Lesharo could only guess. He buried his face in his hands. The drums beat on, and the wolf threw back its head and howled.

Chapter 15

"No one enters the fort for the time being unless they reside here or work for Sieur Cadillac," the sentry repeated slowly and clearly, as though speaking to the simpleminded. A nervous man, his pale face was shiny with sweat and his eyes darted everywhere. Cécile could smell his fear as she stepped aside for the group of angry Odawas who had just been turned away. They brushed by her, casting threatening looks back at the soldiers. "You, Pierre, may enter. Do so quickly, though."

"What is this foolishness?" asked Pierre. "Has all the trading been stopped?"

"It has not, but we are taking care who enters the fort. There is yet another problem with les sauvages, you see." He leaned out and looked uneasily toward the Odawa village. "They and the Hurons have been beating their cursed drums for hours. Come in so that we may close and secure the gate. I for one have no wish to lose my scalp."

Cécile struggled with her temper, her meager patience gone. All the way down the river she had planned what she would say to Lesharo, changing her words a hundred times. Fear for him had knotted her stomach and caused her palms to sweat and slip upon her paddle. Now they were here, and the fact that she could not go to him made her furious.

"Where is Lieutenant Saint-Germain?" said Cécile, pushing past her father. She stood with her fists on her hips, leaning forward, her face very close to the soldier's. "Find him for me at once!"

"Silence, Cécile!" shouted her father. "I will deal with this."

"Is that an order your daughter is giving me, Monsieur? What a pity. I cannot leave my post," said the soldier with exaggerated courtesy. Someone snickered and the soldier added, "At any rate, you have one chien already, Mademoiselle, do you not? Or is there the necessity of a military version?" There was uproarious laughter at this.

"It is to my great regret that you no longer work for me, Robert, and so cannot rightly seek shelter here in the fort," called Cadillac from the southeast bastion. When the guards had reported that canoes were coming down the river, canoes in which Robert, his daughter and Pierre Roy were riding, he had climbed up to watch their progress. Now he descended once more. "Come inside, Roy, if that is your intention. How thoughtful of you to have returned him to us, Robert. I suggest, though, that you make haste and flee to your island, if that is your plan, or go to the Huron village and shelter there. As you have heard, there may be trouble today."

"There will be trouble if you do not let us in," said Robert bleakly, stepping close to Cadillac. "Where is Lesharo? He had best not be hurt. Release him to me and we will trouble you no longer."

Cécile took a deep breath, ready to defy her father and risk his anger, but Cadillac held up a silencing finger close to her face.

"I recall that I once thought your daughter to be docile, Robert," he said. He crossed his arms and looked down at her. "It was quite obviously a grave mistake in judgment. Mademoiselle, you would be wise to close your mouth and show what few manners you actually do possess. I might have made an exception and let you and your father in, you know. It is out of the question now, since you clearly would interfere with the proceedings."

"You will not speak to my daughter in such a way." Robert's voice was soft and menacing. "You would be wise to close your own mouth, and wiser still to release Lesharo. It was a mistake for us ever to have come here, or for me to have trusted you, but nothing compared to the mistake you are making at this moment. Our friendship has clearly reached its end."

There were gasps from the soldiers standing behind their commander, but Cadillac only laughed uneasily and said, "That saddens me, but you are still one to speak your mind no matter the consequences,

Robert." Then to Cécile, with elaborate, oozing courtesy, "Very well, Mademoiselle. You come by your temperament quite honestly, I suppose, being Robert's daughter. Still, I beg your pardon for my ill-chosen words.

"Unfortunately, Robert, I fear that I am unable to release your sauvage. Not yet, at least. There is a punishment to be meted out to him." Cadillac smoothed his mustache and wiped the corners of his mouth with his fingertips. "He will be turned over to you after midnight tonight. I cannot have insubordination here. He defied Tonti yet again, and he made a threatening gesture to him — my second in command! He might as well have done it to me for what may come of it if he goes unpunished. No, I cannot have it! Everything hangs upon order and control with the sauvages. You know that, Robert. Listen to their drums! It was only the Ottawas at first, but now it is the Hurons as well."

"What will be done to him?" asked Cécile faintly. "Tell me that, at least."

"He will be lashed. It is far less than he deserves, and perhaps it will cool his hot blood. Now, are you coming in or not, Roy?"

"Marguerite is at the village. Take Cécile to her there," whispered Pierre as he passed Robert. "I am so sorry, my friend. I will bring word to you as soon as I can."

The gate closed. There was a solid wooden thump inside as the heavy bar dropped into place. "We cannot just leave him here, Papa," said Cécile miserably. "We must do something."

"What can we do? They will not let us in."

"The Miamis will help us. They are back at the village, but they will help."

"Help in what way? Storm the fort? Begin a war? Think, Cécile. Do you believe that Lesharo would want to be the cause of something so horrible? There is nothing to be done," he said very gently. "There is nothing to be done but wait."

• • •

They went to the Wendat village, the drums growing louder and louder as they made their way through the maze. No one interfered with them when they emerged; instead, a great murmuring like the wind in the trees began when Cécile and her father appeared. Gradually, the voices quieted and the drumming stopped. The crowd parted; Marguerite came forward and embraced Cécile.

"They have him, Marguerite," she whispered, her voice breaking. "They have him, and he will be whipped, and I do not know what I can do."

"Do as I would do — as any of us here would do. Ask for guidance. Seek wisdom." She held Cécile at arm's length. "It is what Lesharo would do."

"How?"

"Speak to the elders. The oldest of the women are in the longhouse, and they are both shamans of great power. Will you speak with them?" She smiled a little at the astonishment that Cécile could not hide. "I am a Christian, yes, but I am an indien still. Do you think that believing in God has changed that? It is still there, whether one believes it or not. You cannot see the wind, but you can feel its power and see how it moves the world." Now her face was filled with sympathy. "Let the unseen power move you, Cécile, as it moves Lesharo. I think that is the only way you will be helped."

Cécile hesitated and looked to her father, whose expression was guarded. "This is for you to decide. You are a child no longer." He reached out and stroked his daughter's cheek. "No matter how you wish to live your life, no matter what you do or believe, I will stand by you."

"Then I will ask them for guidance," she said simply.

Inside the Miami longhouse, the two old women sat by one of the fires. No one else was there. In spite of her resignation, tiny wisps of discomfort brushed up Cécile's back and her scalp prickled.

"We have been waiting for you," said one of the women in French. "You have taken long enough to arrive." She was the Miami elder; Cécile, now accustomed to the longhouse's dim light, recognized her seamed face.

"You silly old woman. We have nothing but time," laughed the old Wendat shaman. "Years and years behind us, though who can say how many lie ahead." She patted an empty mat which lay between them. "Come and sit with us, child. We do not bite."

"And if we do it will not hurt much."

"We have no teeth, you see!" cackled the other.

Cécile hesitated, glancing at her father.

"Go to them," he said. "I will be here."

She sat between them, cross-legged as they were. "Lesharo is in the hands of the French, Grandmère," she told the Miami elder respectfully. "You have wisdom, all the wisdom of your years. How can I help him?"

"By listening. We must remind you of something. We are of the same clan, you see," she answered.

"I have no clan, Grandmère," said Cécile in confusion. What was this craziness? She wanted to run screaming from the longhouse, back to the fort. It was Lesharo who needed her; she was wasting her time with these half-mad old women.

"Different tribes, Wendat and Miami, but the same clan," explained the Wendat woman relentlessly. "It would be meaningless, except that we are of the wolf clan."

"I am not indien. I have no clan." Cécile said each word loudly and clearly. "I want only to help Lesharo. Will you help me to do that?"

"We are old, but we can still hear, so you need not shout. Besides, it is rude. Many tribes hold the wolf to be sacred, but none so much as the Pawnee, they say," the Miami shaman went on. She took Cécile's hand in hers. "Life holds many difficult choices."

The old Wendat woman picked up her other hand; she stroked the scar on Cécile's palm. "The choice will be yours to make, Cécile. Your brother or his life. If you choose as your heart bids you, his spirit will die. Use his medicine."

Cécile's brows drew together as she thought hard. Someone had said those very words to her once, but she could not recall who or when. What did it matter, with Lesharo about to be beaten until his back was raw and bloody? He might escape with his life, but what would the beating do to his spirit? She pulled her hands away from the old women and folded them in her lap. "I have no brother. I do not understand." Her voice was wavering, and tears were coming into her eyes. "I want to, but I am not indien and these are not my customs."

"All ways are the same, child, if you will open your heart and see that," said the Miami elder kindly.

"Some say that the path of the whites and that of the indiens are like two rivers flowing side by side. The canoes in them will travel along next to each other, but their courses will never meet," the Wendat shaman said.

"There is only one river, though," said the Miami woman with great conviction. "What you wear beneath your blouse should tell you that."

Her eyes wide with astonishment, Cécile clapped a hand to her chest. Beneath the linen she could feel Lesharo's medicine bag.

"You are frightening my daughter," Robert broke in. "Come, Cécile." She stood and went to her father.

The old women laughed until the tears ran down their faces, their toothless mouths open, their gums shiny and pink. "There is no fear in that one," the Miami finally managed to gasp. She fanned her face with her hand as a fresh burst of laughter came from her.

"She is like a female wolf whose pack is threatened. There is nothing fiercer," the Wendat added, wiping away tears from her wrinkled cheeks. "It is good to laugh like that. Thank you."

People were starting to return to the longhouse, calling to each other; some of the women carried pots of food. Two young girls helped the old Wendat to her feet. She motioned that they were to stop. "Eat something, child," she said to Cécile. "It will help."

"I am not hungry. How could it possibly help me? I do not understand any of this," said Cécile, struggling to keep her tone respectful.

"You are as thin as a stick. Good food will help put meat on your bones. Your choices will not be easy ones, but it will be better to make them on a full belly," said the woman, her tiny eyes twinkling within their folds of skin. "Now, you lazy girls who do nothing all day but sigh over the unmarried warriors, take me to my own fire. The Miami are good company, but their cooking gives me wind."

. . .

By midday, she had given up arguing with her father that they must return to the fort. Instead, she sat inside the longhouse or paced the village with Marguerite, walking only to the end of the maze to stand staring at the fort. There was no drumming from the Odawa village now; all was quiet. Cécile tried to put the old women and their strange words from her mind. She was unable to. She could make no sense of what they had told her, and yet somehow she knew that in their words was a truth that for now was entirely beyond her reach, as was Lesharo. Was he in pain? Did he thirst or was he hungry? And what of the wolf? How it would hurt Lesharo if the animal was suffering.

Pierre came just before sunset.

"They have him in the church's barn. He is not comfortable, but he is unharmed for the time being," he said, his eyes flicking to Cécile and away again.

She drew herself up and took a deep breath to keep her voice even. "I want to hear it. I will not leave so you can tell only my father, Pierre."

He sighed. "Very well, if you are certain, but it is not pleasant news. He is in one of the crates in which they brought the calves when Cadillac and his men first came out. Lesharo cannot stand; he can only sit. He has water — Edmond has seen to that — but he has not been given food. Lesharo is young and strong; missing a meal or two will not hurt him."

"But the punishment. The beating!" cried Cécile.

"He can bear that as well, Cécile, but you must be strong for him," said Marguerite. "He will feel your strength even though you are not with him."

"The punishment will be carried out at midnight, and he will then be thrown from the fort," Pierre finished. "Edmond said you should come to the water gate to meet him. Lesharo will be brought there."

"We have no timepiece," Cécile said. "How will we know?"

"Moonrise was near midnight last night."

"Why is Edmond not stopping it? He could free Lesharo," Cécile said angrily. "I will never forgive him for this!" Neither man answered her. At that, Cécile ran to the opposite end of the longhouse and lay in her cubicle as close to the wall as she could, her back to the passageway.

"It will go very badly for him, Robert," said Pierre. "It is all about the wolf, I think, though some of the Odawas have not been at peace since they came here. Young warriors thought that they would be paid for the wolf by Tonti, it seems. They are hot-blooded troublemakers, and where they ever got such an idea, I cannot imagine. There is unrest inside the fort as well as out. Cadillac and Tonti have quarreled again, I have heard. Tonti is in a temper." He lifted his shoulders. "I would stop this flogging if I could, Robert. So would Edmond."

"I know that, Pierre, but Cécile would never believe it now." He sighed deeply. "She will heal him. When he comes out we will return to the island and she will heal him."

Cécile lay there in silence. Later, when her father came with food, she only said, "I cannot eat. Come for me when it is time."

The village grew quiet, yet there was a restlessness that had infected many. People who usually would long ago have gone to their beds talked and wandered about from fire to fire. Dogs barked and children ran between the longhouses, stopping now and again to listen to the wind that was rising. It will storm, someone shouted, but no one went inside, even when lightning forked across the sky like the silvery tongue of a snake.

Cécile lay there in the darkness, trying not to think, trying to calm herself and quiet the storm that was raging inside her. I will go to him, she said to herself. I will get inside somehow. She prayed, her lips moving, but the words she had learned as a small child held no meaning tonight.

Cécile sat up and crept from the cubicle. Unchallenged, she walked through the longhouse and paused at the door. She scanned the groups of men, but her father and Pierre were nowhere to be seen. If he notices me I will run, and if he catches me I will try again, she thought.

But it was not her father whom she met in the darkness.

"I knew you would do this," said Marguerite. Cécile was certain that she could hear happiness in her voice. "You could no more be stopped than the river could be stopped from flowing."

"You would do the same for Pierre," whispered Cécile, her hand on the other's arm.

"That and more." She put her palm on Cécile's cheek. "Shall I come with you?"

Cécile shook her head. "No. It is for me to do alone."

Marguerite laughed softly. "It is our fate to do the hardest things alone — to wait while our men are gone to war, to bear a child, to mourn a fallen warrior — we do it all alone. Tell me, Cécile. Did the elders help you? Did they give you what you needed to know?"

"I did not understand them, Marguerite," she answered, wanting to leave, wanting to get to the fort. "They said that —"

"No! Tell me nothing; just keep it inside you. They are wise women, and even if you cannot see the way now, you will in time."

"Please do not tell my father or Pierre that I am gone," she pleaded. "I am not asking you to lie for me, but unless Papa asks you, say nothing."

"I will say nothing. Take great care, my dear friend."

No one else challenged her. Cécile walked through the village, staying close to the shadowy palisade until she was at the door to the maze. Then she darted in. No one was inside it, only she. At the end, she hesitated. A few women were crossing the field, coming back from the river. Cécile walked out as casually as they. Once at the riverbank, she broke into a run, splashing through the creek, and did not stop until she was close to the fort.

No one was outside. Her heart was pounding in her chest, so hard that she was certain the sentries in the bastions would hear it. She crouched in the grass, trying to slow her labored breathing. There were no drums now and all was quiet. *Perhaps someone will open the gate and come out. Perhaps I can run in somehow.* She put her head into her hands. *Perhaps wings will sprout from my back and I will fly over the walls,* she thought hopelessly.

Cécile looked up into a sky that was spangled with stars as bright as tiny chips of ice on a sheet of black silk. *They were only stars; anyone could see that. It is what I have always believed,* she thought, *but what am I to believe now?* She searched for the North Star, small and motionless, around which all other stars wheeled through the night. He-Who-Does-Not-Walk, Lesharo had called it. Reaching into the neck of her blouse, she pulled out the medicine bag and squeezed it.

"You are his god," she whispered uncertainly. "Soeur Adele and Père Nicholas would surely say that it is a sin for me to pray to you, but I do not care. Watch over Lesharo and give him strength. Help him bear this. If you can hear me, and Lesharo believes that you can, know that he never turned his back on you, nor on the Morning Star. Not in his heart."

She turned her face from the star then, and reached into her pocket to finger her rosary. Late crickets chirped in the grass and the wind blew harder. Cécile thought about the path her life had now taken and waited alone for the rising of the moon.

• • •

Lesharo stood with his arms above his head. Soldiers had come some time ago. One of them had held a musket pointed at the wolf, and the others had pulled him from the crate and pushed it against the south wall. His muscles had been stiff and aching from the confinement, but they had not given him time to recover. Flinging a rope up over a rafter, they bound his wrists to it so that he faced the back wall. They tied his ankles together and then, realizing that they had neglected to have him remove his shirt, they cut it from him.

The soldier who was to beat him had given a low whistle. "You are no stranger to it, I see." He had tapped Lesharo's back with the handle of his whip. "That is good, sauvage, since in a short time you are about to be reacquainted with the touch of the whip."

"He wears a scapular," scoffed another soldier. "Do you think it will protect you, sauvage? Do you think the Holy Mother will see your suffering and give you comfort? She will turn her eyes from you as she does from all your kind."

"Nothing will protect you from the whip, sauvage. I will leave both the lantern and it here so that you may admire it."

Lesharo had held his head high as the soldier set the whip down on the floor in front of him, well out of his reach, the lantern near it. When they were gone, he had let out his breath. Slowly, slowly in the quiet barn, despair began to seep into him until it filled him like water in a gourd. He tried to pray for strength. No prayers would come to his mind. He squeezed his eyes shut, and in that moment he was back in Québec, tied to the wall, waiting for the searing pain of the brand. His very spirit had cringed from it.

Then he had seen Cécile.

I will think of her hair, Lesharo told himself. I will let myself wonder whether it is as warm as copper, or as cool as chilled wine. He laughed a little. I still do not know the answer to that, he thought, smiling absently. The smile left his lips when he heard the sound of feet approaching through the doorway behind him.

"Wait outside until I call you in," Edmond shouted angrily over his shoulder.

"Is it time? Is it your midnight?" asked Lesharo. "Have you come to tell me that?"

"No," Edmond answered. He cleared his throat. "Tonti is occupied. I know that he would dearly love to see your punishment carried out, but he is with Cadillac. There has been another theft from the magasin, you see, a significant amount of gunpowder this time."

"Why are you here then?"

"I am to make certain your punishment is carried out to the letter." Edmond uttered the last few words as though they tasted very foul in his mouth. "I am sorry. You are to have fifty lashes."

Lesharo said nothing, but his throat moved as he swallowed. Worse than the despair, fear was beginning to creep into his heart, and the shame of that stung worse than the lash ever had. He fought it back, fought it with a memory all red and warm and perfect. The fear evaporated like mist touched by sunlight in the warmth of that memory.

"Do what you must, Edmond," he said calmly.

"There are canoes coming, Lieutenant Saint-Germain!" a soldier shouted. "It may be an attack."

"Go to the water gate! I will follow!" shouted Edmond. "Do as I must? I am cursed by duty! I am sick of it! Drink the brandy, Lesharo. You will feel the pain less. Drink it, I say!" He uncorked the canteen and held it to Lesharo's lips, but Lesharo turned his face away. Edmond flung the canteen into a corner with an angry oath and ran out.

Cécile, now close to the fort, lay on her belly in the shadows, her eyes upon the closed gate. She heard the shouting inside, and a musket went off from one of the bastions, fire shooting from its barrel. There was more shouting and cursing. Then a woman screamed, and what she screamed turned Cécile's blood to ice.

"Fire! God help us! Fire!"

Chapter 16

The gate was flung open, and soldiers carrying wooden buckets streaked toward the river. Smoke was now rising in greasy clouds from the fort. Cécile stood and sprinted to the gate, her hair streaming out behind her. No one stopped her; no one was on guard now. She ran through the men, pushing them out of her way. Once she fell and was kicked hard in the side when a soldier tripped over her. Smoke, acrid and stinking, met her nostrils. It was coming from the east side of the fort; sparks carried by the strong wind were flying everywhere, landing on the sides and roofs of the houses and on the palisade. Tonti was shouting, ordering men to wet the roofs, to stop the fires before they could begin in earnest. The church was in flames, as were Cadillac's and Tonti's houses; black smoke was pouring from the open windows and doors. Fire shot up high into the air, twisting in the wind, licking at the palisade.

"Save it! We must save the church! Bring water!" cried Père Nicholas.

Marie-Thérèse and Marie-Anne were weeping, clinging to each other as they stood in the street in their nightdresses. "The houses! The church! In the name of God, Antoine, let the men put out the fires!" sobbed Marie-Thérèse, clutching at her belly. "We will lose everything!"

"Get the ammunition out of the magasin before the entire fort is blown to pieces!" Cadillac shouted. "Save the powder and the lead. Get the muskets. More water! See to the roof! Curse the Ottawas for what they have done!"

Cécile ran down the street against the flow of the soldiers, screaming that they must let her pass; they must let her get to the barn. The wind swooped up, lifting her unbound hair, clearing the smoke.

The barn was afire. The wind, fickle even now, roared across its roof, partially smothering the flames, then fanning them to life once more. The south wall was an inferno; burning bits of wood sailed into the sky. Hens and a goose, some of them with their feathers singed, flew out the door followed by two soldiers who were coughing and scrubbing at their eyes.

"That is the last of them. Stupid things to go back in," one of them gasped.

"Lesharo! The indien! Is he still inside?" Cécile screamed, grabbing at him.

"Yes!"

She ran past him. The other soldier seized her arm and said, "I tried, Mademoiselle, but the wolf is nearly out. It bit me and I will not go back again."

MAXINE TROTTIER

"Let him burn! It was the sauvages who started this! They would have roasted us in our beds!" called the other soldier.

Cécile wrenched away and ran into the barn through the smoke and the crackling of the fire. The ropes had been cut from Lesharo's ankles; his arms were still tied above his head. He had kicked at the wolf's crate, trying to free it, and he had broken one of the slats. The wolf, insane with fear, had its head through the opening, but there was not enough room for it to get out. It pulled back and ran in tight circles, then thrust its head through once more. The broken slats tore the skin of its muzzle, and blood dripped from the wound as it struggled madly to escape.

Lesharo was straining at the rope, his head thrown back, the cords in his neck standing out, his eyes shut. He was struggling to breathe, and through his coughing he was singing in Pawnee.

"I am here!" she cried, and his eyes flew open.

"Cécile!"

Already she had her knife in her hand. She stood on her toes, reaching, straining, but she could not even touch his wrists. What could she stand upon? The crate in which he had been imprisoned was on fire; the wolf's crate in which the terrified animal howled was too far away. There was nothing.

Lesharo had grown very still. "Free the wolf, Cécile." He coughed heavily and gasped. "Free it first and then free me!"

"No!"

324

"Do it, Cécile," he pleaded. "Free it first. Then me."

"I cannot! I will not!" She was reaching up past him, trying to pull herself up, but she was not strong enough and he would die.

"Please, Cécile, for the sake of what is between us," he gasped. "Open the crate and free your brother the wolf."

"Do not ask me to choose it over you!" she screamed, and the old woman's words rang in her mind, an echo of what the wolf had once said to her in a dream long ago. *Your brother or his life. If you choose as your heart bids you, his spirit will die. Use his medicine.*

"You must do this," he whispered.

She ran to the cage and pulled at the wooden latch. The wolf snapped at her, its saliva spraying onto her fingers. She fell back. "I cannot, Lesharo!"

"You can! Pull harder." He roared out in pain as bits of flaming wood showered down upon his shoulders and head. Cécile leaped to her feet and slapped at his burning hair, tears running down her soot-smeared face. "Free the wolf, Cécile!" he shouted. "Then get out! Get out!"

"I will not leave you here!" she sobbed. *Use his medicine,* came a voice from inside her. She whipped off the medicine bag from around her neck, shrieking in frustration when it tangled in her hair. Looping its cord around the latch, she twisted it around her hands and pulled as hard as she could, ignoring the pain when it cut into her flesh. Lesharo sang to the wolf in Pawnee, trying to soothe it, to calm it, but the smoke and fire had maddened the creature beyond all sense. He sang, and it rammed its head through the broken slat, just as Cécile's bleeding hands wrenched the latch from its fitting, just as Edmond raced into the barn. The wolf burst open the crate's door, knocked Cécile to the floor and was gone, ears flat upon its head.

"Edmond! Help him!" she screamed, and then the rope was cut and they were dragging her from the barn, through the smoke, into the street, where she and Lesharo fell to their hands and knees, coughing and retching.

"Get up," shouted Edmond. "Get her out of here now while you can. There is her father!"

"The medicine bag! I dropped it!" she cried, but then there was no more talking. They ran down the street and out the west gate, Cécile between Lesharo and Edmond. She tripped. They tried to hold her, but she went down into the grass, retching once more.

"Get her to the village," said Edmond. "Her arms are burned."

Cécile struggled up. "The children. What of them?"

"They are unhurt and with their mother," said Edmond. "Go now!"

Lesharo reached out to Edmond. "You saved my life," he began hoarsely. "For that I thank you, but I thank you more for Cécile. She could not reach the rope. She would not have left until it was too late, and she would surely have been —"

"I saw. Get her to the village," Edmond said harshly. She would have died rather than leave him, he thought. It was then that he realized that he had entirely misjudged the depth of feeling that ran between Cécile and Lesharo. She would have risked being burned alive rather than abandon him to die alone. Shaken and profoundly moved, Edmond turned and ran back to the burning fort.

• • •

Cécile woke and for a terrified heartbeat had no idea where she was. Then the dark clinging tide of panic slowly receded; she drew a deep breath and let it out. She lay in a cubicle in the Miami longhouse where there was no fire and where it was safe.

They had talked until nearly dawn, making plans. Once in bed, she had not slept well; horrible dreams of howling death all edged with the stench of burning flesh had tormented her. When she moaned and cried out in her sleep, her father had gently shaken her awake. Each time, Lesharo had reached out across him to pat her shoulder or squeeze her hand to reassure her that, yes, he was there next to Robert. She must not worry any longer. He would not leave her again. Finally, she had slept, long past the time when most people had risen for the day.

Cécile cleared her throat and tasted smoke; with a grimace, she picked up the gourd of cider that had been left for her and drank deeply. Her mouth freshened, she stretched her arms above her head. The clothing she wore was not hers; she had no idea where her own garments were, since they had been taken from her last night when the Miami women had insisted she bathe in the cold water of the river. She had heard Lesharo and her father some distance away, doing the same thing, their splashing and quiet voices carrying over the water.

Cécile had not seen them, for it was dark, and she had not paid much attention to what was a private conversation until she had heard her own name come from Lesharo. He had asked her father a question. In spite of the cold water that was raising tiny bumps upon her bare skin, she was filled with warmth at her father's answer.

"It is her life to live, Lesharo, as is yours. I have confidence that the two of you will make peace with all this in time; so yes, you have my blessing."

Later, their wounds had been dressed. Cécile studied her arms and then her hands. She had only a few burns; the worst was a blistered spot over the scar on her palm. The cuts from the medicine bag's cord were shallow and already crusted over.

Lesharo's shoulders and his right cheek had been covered with painful blisters. There was a small spot on his scalp that had been burned badly; it was unlikely that any hair would grow there again. That would remain with him, but the rest of his injuries were not serious, the women had assured them. They would heal and leave no scars.

"Miami ointment will work best. I have been making it since I was a girl."

"Miami ointment is too strong. She has such fine smooth skin. She needs Wendat ointment."

"I think I need both, Grandmères," called Cécile, and the blanket was pulled back by the two old shaman women.

"Lazy girl, lying there when there is so much work to do," scolded the Miami elder. "Up all night, running about like a wild young she-wolf."

"Lazy, lazy, lazy, and of no use at all. She will just spend her day making big eyes at the warriors," said the Wendat elder mournfully. "Oh. I ask your pardon. *Warrior.*"

Cécile crawled out of her bedding. "I feel fortunate to have eyes at all after last night," she said.

"As do I," called Lesharo. He was easing a shirt over his body, grimacing a little, mindful of his shoulders. "You are well, Cécile?"

"I am well enough, Lesharo," she said with a brilliant smile. It faltered a bit. "Your burns? Your cheek. Do they give you pain?"

"The ointment has helped. They are nothing," Lesharo assured her. Then with worry in his voice, he asked, "What of you?"

She held out her hands so that he could examine them for himself.

"When you are finished staring at each other like owls, there is food for you in that basket and in the pot," said the Wendat elder. "I suppose you will eat it all and leave none for us. The young are greedy." She shook her head in disgust, her ancient eyes twinkling.

"We must go now and deprive you of our pleasant company. There is a council, you see, and some of us talk of leaving. This is a bad place." The old Miami studied Cécile critically, then said to Lesharo, "This one needs to be fattened up. She would be more pleasing to the eye."

"I can tell her many things, Grandmère, but not whether she should be fat or thin," Lesharo said doubtfully. "Besides, I find her pleasing as she is."

"Perhaps you do. Who can understand the ways of the young these days," the Miami shaman answered.

"Do not even try," counseled the other old woman. "It will give you a terrible headache." Then to Cécile, "Get some flesh on those bones of yours. I dreamed last night of your journey. We both did. You wish to be at your best, strong and fit and plump when his Pawnee people see you for the first time, do you not?" She did not wait for a response; she and the other old woman made their way slowly out, leaning on each other and cackling.

Cécile stared after them. We have told no one of our plans, she thought. She exchanged a look with Lesharo, but he only smiled. Before last night she would have questioned the woman's words and surely prayed for forgiveness that she had even listened. Now she only laughed a little and said, "Perhaps I will eat, after all."

"So that my people find you acceptable? They will like you fat, or thin, as I do."

"No," she answered archly, her nose in the air. "Because I am hungry," and at that they both laughed, suddenly aware of how very good it was to be alive and in this place together.

Cécile and Lesharo sat down by the low flames of a fire. They were nearly alone in the quiet longhouse, the good weather having drawn most people outside. The sound of voices drifted in, but neither of them really listened; they only sat there, nibbling at food that for some reason was very good. Had beans ever been so tender and sweet before; had corn soup ever tasted so wonderful? Lesharo reached for more bread, and Cécile winced when she saw his sleeve draw back.

All her joy disappeared. His wrist was worn raw, as was the other, from desperately fighting to free himself last night.

"Why did they leave you there? You would have died. The wolf would have died. Why did no one help us?" She covered her face with her hands and began to cry as the horror of the fire swept over her once more.

He pulled her hands away, squeezed them gently and let them go. "I have told you. Your father has told you. It was only a little while. Only a few minutes, as you say. The soldiers did try to free me, but it was my fate to have cowards as rescuers."

She laughed a bit at that and sniffled. "It seemed as though it went on forever."

"I vow to you that it was only a few minutes. Edmond came as soon as he saw you enter the barn, when the men he sent ran off." He knew her. He knew what was forming in her mind. "Edmond would have come had you not been inside, Cécile. He would have come had it only been me. I know that. So do you. Tell me that you do not doubt it. As I said, he is a good man."

"Yes." She wiped her face and nose with her sleeve. "He is a good man. I know that."

"What is this? You have the manners of Jacques and Toine," he scolded in mock disgust.

At that she truly laughed. "I will miss them, really miss them, and we cannot even say farewell." They would leave the village tonight. No one was searching for them; Tonti and Cadillac had more important things to attend to, but that would end in time.

"Some friendships do not need farewells. They will be with you, I think."

"What of the wolf? Will we see it again?"

Lesharo lightly touched her cheek. "I believe that we will in time." He put his hand on his chest and added, "Until then, carry him in your heart as I do."

Cécile put her fingers to her own chest and moaned softly. "Your medicine bag. I am so sorry."

"It was not mine anymore; it was yours, Cécile. In the end it became a sacrifice, did it not? You used it well." He pulled the scapular out so that she could see it. "Your gift protected me and kept me from dying in the fire. It truly is strong medicine, as your grandmother said back in Québec when she gave it to you. Perhaps she is a shaman."

Grandmère a shaman with a turtle-shell rattle? Cécile thought of how to explain, to say that no, the scapular had never been meant for that purpose; it is the fires of hell against which the scapular will protect you. But then she stopped. It had been a hell through which they had passed last night, a hell of hatred as hot as the flames that had nearly consumed them. And although she was not a shaman, Soeur Adele had her own sort of wisdom. Instead, she tucked it back inside his shirt and said, "Yes. It is strong medicine."

Cécile and Lesharo looked up at the sound of voices.

"You would be safe here. After what happened last night with the Odawas, Tonti would not dare send anyone after Lesharo," Pierre was saying to Robert. "The indiens in this village say that they will give up their own stores to help Cadillac. He will be in their debt, and he will not let Tonti do anything to threaten the goodwill that exists for now."

"Perhaps you are correct," answered her father "We may stay here, certainly; we could even stay on the island." He settled himself next to Cécile and hugged her. "You slept soundly? No more dreams? And you, Lesharo? Good." He went on to Pierre: "No. We made our decision last night. We will leave."

"Is the fire out?" asked Cécile. "Was anyone injured?" Edmond, she thought. Is he hurt?

"The church is gone and so are Père Nicholas's house and all the church records," said Pierre. "Cadillac's and Tonti's houses are badly damaged. Cadillac's letters and papers? Gone. All burned to ashes. It started in the big barn outside, it seems, and then spread to the palisade and houses. Most of the small barn is in ruins, but they can salvage some wood." He crossed himself. "That the entire fort did not burn to the ground is a miracle. I thank le bon Dieu that my own house was spared."

"What of the magasin?" Cécile asked bitterly. "They worked hard to save that."

"It is undamaged. All the ammunition and goods were removed. Cadillac's hand was burned — it is but a trifling thing, although he goes on about it — and he says he lost nearly forty-four hundred livres, which burns him more, I think." Pierre made a rude sound and said in disgust, "They shot an Odawa they seemed to think started the fire. How can they know that?"

She will not ask about Edmond, thought Lesharo. Part of him wanted to dwell upon that, to puzzle it out, to worry it like a jealous animal with a bone. No, he thought. She has made her choice, but we three are bound together by what happened last night.

"What of Edmond?" Lesharo asked for her, and the grateful look she gave him told him he was correct.

"He is quite well."

"He sent no word?"

"No word at all," said Pierre. He paused and then added with a shrug of his shoulders, "But then his duties occupy him, as you can well imagine. Marguerite sends a message, though. You will leave at moonrise, you say, Robert? She wishes to say good-bye to you, and so I will bring her to the river in front of the fort. Now, I must leave." He rolled his eyes dramatically and gave a mournful sigh. "Père Nicholas is keen to rebuild the church, and there is much work to do. Horrible unending penances are promised for those who do not help."

They stayed inside the village all that day, talking and going over their plans. They would go west, of course, first to the Miami for the winter, where they would find an open welcome from Marguerite's village and her brother Le Pied Froid, then farther west to Lesharo's people in the spring. If that did not suit them, there were other directions, and even a return to Québec was possible in time. She was excited and hopeful, but the events of last night had taken a great deal from her.

"Come sit with me in the cubicle for a while. If we are to paddle all night, then I must sleep, I am afraid," she said to Lesharo, yawning behind her hand. "I can barely keep my eyes open."

"If you snore I will leave," he teased, watching her arrange blankets over herself as he sat next to her.

"Then I must never snore," she said lightly. She lay on her side, her head pillowed on her arm. "And you will have to stay."

"Cécile."

"Yes." He said nothing and so she raised herself up on her elbow. "What is it?"

"Before the fire, the priest Père Nicholas told me things," he said slowly. "I have been thinking about them."

"What sorts of things?"

"I cannot forget his words. No priest has ever said such things to me. He talked of baptism of desire and of baptism of fire." He shuddered, thinking of how close he had come to being burned alive. No matter what he said to her, he had thought himself dead last night. It had been his death song he had been singing for himself and for the wolf. And for Cécile. "He talked about the Morning Star, the mother of your god. Might we speak of those things in time? There are priests at Marguerite's village — good men, your father said — perhaps I may speak with them and seek their wisdom."

"Yes. We two will talk about those things, and we will speak with the priests once we are there, but only if you swear to me that you will tell me your stories again. The shamans told me things as well, before the fire. Promise you will help me understand them. How will I be able to manage otherwise when we find your people?" She took a deep breath and then went on. "I had a dream long ago before we met. I dreamed of a wolf. It told me —"

"Not now. In time you will tell me and perhaps together we will understand it all. If not, there is faith." She smiled at that, and happiness filled him. "You will manage. I swear it." He reached out and ran his hand over her hair. It was quite cool and silky, but beneath the coolness he felt her warmth. Lesharo took her hand and twined his fingers through hers. "Now sleep, Cécile. I will be here."

She lay back down and closed her eyes. *I knew that,* she thought.

Chapter 17

A silvery bow of moon shone down upon the ripples, down upon the canoe and the perfect spreading vee of the wake it left behind as it moved up the river. The craft rode high in the water, for only Cécile, Robert and Lesharo were in it. They would stop at the island for a few days to gather their possessions and then quickly journey west. Then the canoe would be low indeed.

Marguerite and Pierre were waiting on the beach in front of the fort when they arrived. Détroit was quiet, but unseen guards watched as they landed the canoe. Cécile was certain of it.

They would stay only a little while, since voyaging upriver never got easier, her father insisted. He was correct, of course, and yet still they lingered, whispering in the darkness, Marguerite and Cécile standing with their arms around each other's waists.

"We have company," said Robert, as two small figures in only their linen shirts and moccasins hurtled down the embankment. A taller figure followed. It was Edmond.

"I had to say farewell," cried Jacques, clinging to Cécile. His thumb moved toward his mouth, but he did not put it in. "I will miss you so much until I see you once more."

"I will miss you." Cécile's throat tightened. There probably will not be a once more, she thought, but I can say nothing, lest Cadillac somehow learn of it and stop us from leaving. "And I will miss you, Toine. Tell Maman that your book of stories is at the longhouse on the island. I will leave it — that is, I mean to say, she must have someone come to get it."

Toine was standing straight, his hands behind his back, trying to look brave. He threw himself into her arms. "Papa said we could come out with Edmond. Papa is inside. He said it would not be appropriate for him to be here, and Maman is in bed." He could not keep his voice from wavering.

Cécile looked up to the open gate. She could not be certain, but it seemed as though someone stood in the shadows. The person began to raise an arm, apparently thought better of it, and then withdrew into the fort. She kissed the boys and whispered to them, her chest tight as she watched them walk back, hand in hand.

"I wish you all the best of luck," said Edmond stepping forward. "You are going to the island, of course?"

"Of course," answered Robert evenly.

"Cadillac will want to know where you are," Edmond went on. "He wants to know where everyone travels, you understand."

"I recall that," said Robert. "He and the Company will never change."

"Since you have told me of your destination, what more can I ask?" said Edmond briskly. "The island it is." He reached out for Cécile's hand, hesitated, and then let his arm drop to his side. "No. I think perhaps that would no longer do, would it?" He inclined his head to Lesharo who was watching, relaxed and confident, then held out his open palm to Cécile. "This was in the street, just outside the barn. I believe it is yours."

It was the medicine bag.

Cécile touched it with one finger and then she looked to Lesharo, a question in her eyes. He nodded solemnly, and so with both her hands, she closed Edmond's fingers over the bag and squeezed them. "Now it is yours, Edmond. Keep it in remembrance."

They climbed into the canoe and Pierre gave it a shove. Cécile called, "I thank you for everything." She faltered, wanting to say more but knowing it would be best not to. "*Adieu*, Edmond."

"Adieu," he answered. He put the medicine bag over his head and tucked it inside his shirt. "I hope our paths will cross again in time."

"That is my hope as well, Edmond."

"I am in your debt for many things. I wish only happiness for you," called Lesharo sincerely.

"Well! You are a lucky man, so I shall surely have it," Edmond called back, filling his voice with cheer. "I can live with that." I shall have to, he thought wistfully, as the canoe pulled away.

● ● ●

Janvier 1704. How strange the New Year always looks when I write it down. Few pages remain in this journal. Some I have set aside to use for letters to Grandmère. As for other entries, I believe I will not write again unless there is something important to record. I wish that I had been able to ask Marie-Thérèse for just one more of her ledgers. There is nothing to be done now, since Détroit is far behind us and we are wintering with the Miami. That is a relief to me, and yet I cannot help but wonder what is happening back there. Are Jacques and Toine studying and reading their book? Do they have a sister or brother now? I pray for them all.

Epilogue

On a bitterly cold afternoon that February, a hunting party of Wendats walked across the ice to the small island at the mouth of the Détroit River. The week had been an exciting one at the fort. Word had come that The Yellow Hair must no longer wear the white coat of the soldiers. He had feasted with the Wendat and the Miami and then, the next day, was gone — some said to the Mohawks and some strongly suspected to the west — although no one knew for certain.

Cadillac's wife had borne him a healthy daughter, the first child to have the water poured upon its head in the church that had been rebuilt after the fire. The infant thrived. Why should it not grow fat on the milk of the nursing mother Cadillac had sent for from Québec, so that his wife would not have to feed the child herself? The ways of the French were very strange.

They poked about the longhouse, looking for anything of value, but there was little. It was a good longhouse, though, small but well made, and it would serve to shelter them for the night. They made a fire, starting it with pages from a book much like the one in which they had sometimes seen Lesharo's woman making her marks. It was the color of a robin's egg. They untied the ribbon that bound it and tore out pages, wondering at the markings, laughing at the drawings, feeding the paper into the fire. One by one Lesharo's stories drifted into the sky.

The wolf that stood in the trees lifted its enormous head and sniffed the air. It did not care for the smell of men, and as for smoke, that odor now caused its scarred muzzle to wrinkle and the red-gray hair to rise upon its hackles. But it did not growl. It was too wise for that. This smoke, though, stirred some deep memory in it and moved its untamable heart. It sniffed the air again, searching for what it knew it could no longer find here. Turning away, the wolf faced the setting sun and began to journey west.

Notes for
Sister to the Wolf

The story of Fort Détroit is also the story of two branches of my maternal family tree, the Roys and the LaButes, both numbered among the founding families of the fort. This book is a work of fiction, but it is based around the lives and experiences of people who were there. True to the period, I have used French spellings and constructions of that time.

My ancestor Pierre Roy remains a figure of some controversy. Cadillac claims that he and his party of fifty soldiers and civilian men in twenty-five canoes were the first whites to settle at Fort Détroit. However, there are sources that support the fact that Pierre and another man, Joseph Parent, were living there when Cadillac arrived. It is possible that Pierre's claim was discounted, since he would have been living among the Natives.

Pierre and Marguerite would likely have been a part of the remarkable events that took place during

1703. They were married there at Ste. Anne's Church that summer — no precise date is known — and it is also likely that they were at the fort during the fire. The fact that all the records burned has allowed me the luxury of fictionalizing their story.

Both Marie-Thérèse and Marie-Anne did lose children, although there is no record of the causes of death. A woman of Marie-Thérèse's social position simply did not breast-feed her own baby. There is the suggestion that those infants may have starved to death, although there is no proof.

There is the fact, though, that before Marie-Thérèse's next child was born at the fort, a contract was drawn up between her and a woman named Anne Pastourel in Montréal. Anne would serve for two years as a wet nurse for the child Marie-Thérèse was due to bear in February. She agreed to go to Détroit with the next party traveling there. Her pay would be 450 livres a year, beginning at the time of the child's birth. She was also to be given a dressing gown. To be fair, the Cadillacs promised to pay her half of the fee if the child was stillborn or if it died within its first six months. Anne set out with her two small children that July. She acted as wet nurse for Marie-Thérèse — the Cadillac infant — until she, Madame Cadillac and all three children returned to Montréal in 1704 with Cadillac's party.

Alphonse de Tonti was caught in an embezzlement plot that same year. Unbelievably, it was he who remained in charge while Cadillac was in Québec until his return in 1706. It is uncertain as to whether Marie-Anne remained with her husband at the fort or whether she returned to Montréal.

Between 1707 and 1710, Cadillac granted sixty-eight individual lots of lands to the private citizens at Détroit. Pierre Roy was granted lot fifty-one on Ste. Anne's Street. Not far to the west was lot 1, which had been granted to a man named Pierre Chesne dit LaButte (the original spelling). In time, LaButte's son Pierre would wed the Roy's daughter Marie Magdeleine. It is from that family line that I am descended; the LaButes remain in the Detroit/Windsor area to this day.

There was continual trouble with the Native people and with tribal rivalries. In 1706, a quarrel broke out among a number of Miamis and Odawas. Père Nicholas del Halle, who was outside the fort at the time, was taken captive. He was released but then shot and killed as he was entering the gate.

Criticism of the fort and Cadillac remained high. In time, he successfully managed to alienate almost everyone essential to the success of Détroit. A host of letters and documents tell a tale of disagreements with the Crown, its representatives in New France, his officers, the merchants and the Jesuits. In 1710, Cadillac was ordered to assume the position of Royal Governor of the Louisiana colony. When he and his family left Détroit, a complete inventory was done of their possessions, which were numerous and lavish by Détroit standards. Those goods and his buildings were disposed of by one Dubuisson, who had become the temporary commander. The Cadillacs were never reimbursed for those losses, although in 1722 Cadillac was granted 2000 livres by the king as compensation. Cadillac returned to France, where he died in 1730.

Lieutenant Edmond Saint-Germain and Robert and Cécile Chesne are fictional. They lived only in these pages. The characters of Cécile and Robert, though, are based on Lauren Jones and her father, Robert Jones. They, as well as I, are members of Le Detachement, a living-history unit that portrays the Canadian habitants of the 1750s serving with the militia.

Which leaves Lesharo.

Town rent was paid at Fort Détroit. The records for March 10, 1707, show that Pierre Roy, among others, "paid 3 livres 19 sols and 10 livres for other rights." His slave, a seven- or eight-year-old boy called Jacques Panis, did not, since he had no rights at all. There is no other mention of Jacques. He is simply a name on the page of a document, a child with no history, a boy whose past has been erased. It is he who was in my mind when I created Lesharo.

There will never be a way to be certain of the path Jacques's life took. I would like to think that Pierre bought him out of pity and kindness, and that

Jacques's existence with Pierre and Marguerite was a happy one. I will probably never know. He will remain a mystery, one of many children taken and forgotten.

It is my hope that, through Lesharo and this story, a memory of young Jacques Panis will live on.